The Fourth Circle of Hell

A Novel

GARY RAPPARD

All of the characters and events in this book are
fictitious, and any resemblance to actual persons, living
or dead, is purely coincidental.

DEDICATION

For Laura

ACKNOWLEDGMENTS

Writing a novel from scratch is as difficult as it sounds. I have to begin by thanking my amazing wife. She read my early drafts, giving me sage advice on turning my idea into a book. She encouraged me with love, patience and unending inspiration, instead of complaining about the amount of time it took me to complete the story.

I wish to thank my wonderful son and daughter, who provided crucial feedback on my drafts. My daughter's skill with photo manipulation and design proved invaluable in creating the book's beautiful cover. My son's computer skills were essential in overcoming the unique challenges of the digital age and my inevitable software issues.

I'm forever indebted to my father, who grew up during the Great Depression and whose stories and wisdom follow me every day of my life.

I am grateful to my mother, who encouraged me to follow my dreams, even when obstacles seemed insurmountable.

I would like to thank Erin Rivers for her excellent review and analysis of my book draft. Her superbly advanced literature skills and keen insight helped my story in numerous ways that made this a better book.

And last, I am eternally grateful to the wonderful teachers that helped me through my many years of education.

CHAPTER 1

I talian Ambassador Antonio Bocelli tapped the computer's hard-plastic keys in rapid fire motion in his Washington, D.C. Embassy office. His jaw muscles clenched.

If something happens to me this information must not die.

He leaned forward, squinting at the computer monitor on his mahogany desk, making his leather office chair's springs creak as if discontented. The screen showed a photo of him handing a small ceramic bust to a handsome gentleman in front of the Embassy's impressive ballroom stage. A seven-foot tall grandfather clock's brass pendulum chime broke the stillness with an echoed toll. He lifted his head to look in the sound's direction. The clock's round white face displayed two black hands pointed at the black serif roman numerals XII.

It was twelve-midnight.

A heavy thud and a heart-stopping crash resonated from the dark outer hall, interrupting his focus. The shatter of shards sliding across the hall's smooth tile floor, followed. The Ambassador stopped typing. His head jerked in the sound's direction as he swallowed hard.

Something's tipped over the antique Florentine vase on the console table outside.

He jumped up, his gaze focused laser-like toward the crash sound in the hall.

Did the night janitor knock it over?

He abandoned the idea seconds later when he remembered the maintenance staff had left an hour earlier after cleaning up for the evening. His hand shook as he reached underneath the center drawer, fingers fumbling in a frantic attempt to find the push button switch to call the security guard. He found the button, punching it hard with his index finger four times. The Embassy's security was excellent. Normally, pressing the button would result in the guard's prompt reply on the office intercom. But not tonight.

Where's the damn guard? Why the hell doesn't he answer?

A slow squeaking sound drifted across the room. The office's heavy door swung open. A tall trim man with hollow eyes and a two-inch scar across one cheek, stepped out of the doorway's shadow. His shoulder-length jet-black hair was slicked back with pomade. It framed a battle-lined face devoid of emotion. His husky monotone voice sounded like it came from the devil himself. "You shouldn't have stayed here tonight... it makes my job too easy."

The Ambassador froze. Both hands clenched as his own cold fingers dug into the palms. Right now, he wished he were anywhere in the world but in his office confronted by this demon. But the Ambassador still exercised authority, even alone and unarmed. "Who are you? You've no right to be here."

The intruder's tight-lipped mouth curled. "Never mind who I am. Where'd you hide it?"

He knows about my discovery! How could he?

The Ambassador coughed twice into one hand to stall for time while he considered how to respond. *I can't give it to him, even if it risks my life.* "I... I don't know what you're talking about."

The intruder scowled. His gloved hand gripped a 9mm handgun with silencer next to his right thigh. The firearm's color blended with the glove's gray calfskin leather as if they were meant to be a pair. He raised his straight arm, pointing the weapon at the Ambassador's forehead.

The Ambassador stared at the gun barrel. He realized all too well he stood in the presence of a killer. His eyebrows raised. "You've made a mistake."

"Your secret's worth a great deal to my Patron. I know how you found it."

How could he know? I told only one person what I'd found. I've been betrayed.

"I won't hesitate to kill you." The gunman edged closer, stopping short three feet from the Ambassador's face. His rock-steady hand held the gun as still as death.

"It's not here." The Ambassador's stomach turned as he shook his head from side to side. "It's at my residence, Villa Firenze."

"Then let's take a little trip there." The gunman gave a condescending sneer as he waved the pistol, motioning for the Ambassador to move toward the open door.

The Ambassador's fleeting hope for survival shrunk as he stepped across the room toward the doorway. The gunman followed two feet behind, and the Ambassador sensed the man's eyes boring a hole in his back.

They exited the office and had taken two steps into the shadow filled hall when the gunman gave a sudden unexpected yell, "Oh, Shi-i-i-it."

The Ambassador whipped around to face his assailant in time to see the gunman's hard-soled dress shoe heel slip on a slick glazed ceramic shard on the hall's smooth tile floor. The intruder tripped and fell. His shoulder slammed against the hall console table's sharp edge, the force knocking the gun out of his hand. It bounced once off the white tile, sliding across the floor and landing next to the biggest shard from the earlier crash.

The Ambassador was a brave man who had no choice. If he did nothing, the intruder would recover in a couple seconds and gun him down after obtaining the secret.

This is my only chance. It's now or never.

The Ambassador lunged to the floor for the liberated gun. The intruder scrambled across the tile, getting there first. His thick muscular hand vibrated with force as the Ambassador struggled with all his might to push the assailant's grip off the cold, hard gun barrel. The two grunted, wrestling for the firearm.

God, his grip's like a vise. I'll never get it from him.

They rolled over each other across the tile, their bodies crashing against a free-standing curio cabinet. The impact rocked it back and forth like a ship on the high seas. Italian bone china plates and cups tumbled as if bowling pins to the hard floor. The fragile items smashed into pieces that spread in all directions. The curio cabinet almost tipped over but somehow

3

righted itself at the very last moment.

The gun went off with a muffled pop followed by a human gasp. The frenzied struggle stopped. The Ambassador's body lay motionless. Blood trickled from a hole near his left shirt pocket onto the floor next to the cabinet. His open unblinking eyes stared at the ceiling. Above him, on the wall, hung a wood framed print. The image depicted a moon eclipsing a radiant yellow sun, followed by more stages of the eclipse until the sun fully emerged. He had bought it as a reminder the sun's disappearance was only temporary, like the truth's.

After a moment of silence, the gunman stumbled up off the floor, grasping his knees while his head bobbed for raspy huffs of breath. Sweat beads covered his forehead. *The Ambassador had been much stronger than he'd anticipated.* He wiped his forehead with a white linen handkerchief and brushed the ceramic fragments off his pants, while he regained his composure.

The gunman pressed two fingertips against the Ambassador's neck to check for a pulse. He found none. *He's of no use to me now. I'll have to find the secret on my own.*

He shoved one hand into the Ambassador's pants pocket to retrieve the man's wallet. Inside the delicate calf-skin leather he found a U.S. State Department issued foreign diplomat's driver's license. The Ambassador's residence address appeared underneath his photo. The gunman gave a knowing nod. *Villa Firenze would be easy enough to find.*

He put his hand in the Ambassador's suit-coat pocket, pulling out a folded embossed program from the Embassy event earlier that evening.

Italian Embassy
Join Us for a Night of Celebration
Machiavelli and da Vinci, The Collaboration of Geniuses
A Presentation by Joe Richmond, Smithsonian Institution

Tucked inside the brochure was a business card with Joe Richmond's name and business address at the Smithsonian Castle. The gunman held it up to the light to study it. Someone had scrawled the words 'meet this week' in ink across the card's face.

A visit to Villa Firenze was in order. He slipped the embossed program and Richmond's business card into his coat pocket. Armed with the information, he slipped out of the Embassy and sped off in his car toward the Ambassador's residence.

CHAPTER 2

Joe Richmond leaned back in a black ergonomic mesh chair at his Smithsonian Castle's Consortia Department office. Christmas greens adorned the walnut mantel clock on a nearby shelf showing the time, 5:30 a.m. Framed images of Plato, Aristotle and other great minds from Ancient Greece adorned the walls. A two-inch thick draft book manuscript entitled, Machiavelli and da Vinci, The Collaboration of Geniuses laid on his desk.

He glanced at the white desk calendar. His gaze landed on the entry for the long-awaited Machiavelli-da Vinci Exhibit scheduled to open the next day at the Smithsonian Arts and Exhibition Hall next door.

I've got to finish the interactive video display for the exhibit, this morning. We're running out of time.

The display featured Machiavelli and da Vinci's wartime project, diverting Renaissance Italy's Arno river to help Florence defeat its downstream enemy Pisa. Da Vinci designed the project in 1503. He painted his masterpiece, the *Mona Lisa*, the same year.

Joe switched his gaze to the high definition computer monitor mounted on the wall across from his desk. Highly-magnified sections of the *Mona Lisa's* background, the Arno River Valley, filled the screen. He clicked the mouse, interacting with the sections involving Machiavelli and da Vinci's collaboration. He had to be sure the exhibit's visitors would be able to experience the audio and written descriptions.

He rubbed his stiff neck and closed his eyes. His clammy fingers and hands felt like ice packs against his warm skin. A shiver went through his body as he realized he'd been sitting for half-an-hour without physical activity.

"Joe, you have a visitor."

He turned in his chair. The unexpected female voice behind him jarred him out of his concentration. He pushed on the desk, wheeling the chair around to face the speaker. Co-worker Barbara stood in the doorway, both arms folded across her chest. She also had come in early this morning to work on the exhibit. Next to her stood a slender woman he'd never seen before, with light olive skin and dark-brown hair pulled back in a short ponytail. Her black nylon glasses gave her an attractive intelligent look. Her determined eyes and confident air caught his attention.

"This is Ms. Gina Bocelli," Barbara said.

"You don't know me, but I believe you know my ex-husband Ambassador Bocelli." Gina stepped forward, offering her right hand to Joe with a warm handshake.

Joe stiffened. In his limited experience, ex-wives sometimes equated with drama. Especially ones showing up unexpected this early in the morning.

"I'll leave you two alone," Barbara said. She excused herself with a sly wink at Joe and disappeared out the door.

Thanks a lot Barb. And what was she insinuating with the wink? Joe frowned. She'd left him alone with this woman and now he had to figure a way to excuse himself to meet his deadline.

"Y-Y-Yes, I met him at the Embassy's Machiavelli-da Vinci Celebration last night," Joe said. He'd met the Ambassador only a few short hours ago, and now, here was his ex-wife at Joe's office interrupting his last-minute preparations. *What the hell?*

"I know this is unexpected, but I need to talk to you." Her voice had an urgent tone.

"Uh… this is a bad time." Joe's eyes narrowed at her insistence. "I'm right in the middle of some really important work."

"But I have to talk to you."

This woman doesn't take no for an answer. What do I have to do to get rid of her?

"I'm afraid I can't. Deadline's looming." He tried to tune her out, turning his chair away from her to refocus on the *Mona Lisa's* magnified section. "Barbara's probably finished, perhaps she can walk out with you. Now if you'll excuse me…"

He had started to touch the keyboard when the back of his chair jerked, and it spun back around until he faced her.

She gripped the chair arms, her flushed face less than one foot from his, eyes flaring. "I've been to hell and back tonight because I just lost the only man I ever loved. It sure wasn't easy tracking you down. I'm sorry to bother you, but you're damn well gonna make time for me."

To hell and back? Joe recoiled in his chair, gaping at her. She stood so close he could smell her subtle jasmine scent perfume.

"Turn on the cable. It's all over the news." She pointed her index finger at the oversize monitor attached to the opposite wall.

The news… what the devil's she talking about? Joe picked up a TV remote, switching the monitor's input to the local news channel. A perky female anchor appeared above the screen bottom's red scroll which read 'Breaking News.' The background displayed film of the Italian Embassy's exterior and emergency vehicles whose colored lights flashed.

"Italy's Ambassador to the U.S. was found dead after midnight from a fatal gunshot wound, in his office at the Italian Embassy," the Anchor said. "A second victim, an Embassy security guard, was discovered dead at the Embassy's front gate guard post. Police have no suspects in the case. They ask all persons who spoke with either victim last night to come forward and contact the tips hot-line."

"I'm so sorry Ms. Bocelli. I had no idea." He looked at her, noticing a tear in her eye. His gaze shifted down to the floor for a few moments while he tried to absorb it all. *I can't imagine what she must be going through.* His stomach rolled, remembering how after his Embassy presentation a few hours ago, he had shaken the now dead Ambassador's hand. Her persistence made much more sense now.

"He wanted to get back together." Gina looked away, her lip quivering when she spoke. "Now he's gone."

"I didn't know about his death. I left the Embassy before the celebration was over, to get some sleep before I came back here to work."

"I see." She hung her head for a moment before tilting her chin up. "Aren't you going to invite me to sit down and have something to drink?"

"Sure… absolutely. Make yourself comfortable." He took her coat and draped it over one arm. His shoulders relaxed. Maybe she only needed to talk with him about the Ambassador's final evening, to take her mind off her grief. He'd been too brusque with her earlier.

"Thanks for meeting me on such short notice." She plopped down in a contemporary style tan stuffed chair, exhaling with relief.

"I don't think you gave me much choice." Joe shook his head, hanging the coat on the oak coat tree near the door. He popped into the suite's kitchen and came back with a steaming cup of coffee. He handed the cup and saucer to her. *She's holding up better than most would in her situation.*

She accepted the drink, took a sip and looked up at him. "There's something I have to show you. It's important."

"It must be a doozy to bring you here this early in the morning."

"It is. Antonio sent me this email last night, shortly before he was killed." Gina pulled out her smartphone and handed it to Joe. "It must be a clue to what happened."

Joe stared at the bright screen containing the Ambassador's message. The email's body appeared blank. But the subject matter line read:

Joe Richmond and I at the Machiavelli Celebration

Why would he send a message to her with my name in the caption? And no explanation? It makes no sense.

A red icon appeared below the email's subject line, showing it contained an attachment. Joe touched the icon. The phone's screen displayed a photo showing Joe and the Ambassador shaking hands. *It's a snapshot of the Ambassador presenting me with a ten-inch high bronze bust of Machiavelli.* The image took Joe back to the celebration earlier the prior evening in the Italian Embassy's glass-domed ballroom, where the photo was taken.

The female moderator had flashed an assured smile while adjusting the microphone on the ballroom's stage podium. "Good evening, Ladies and Gentlemen. Tonight, we are fortunate to have our featured speaker Dr. Joe Richmond, Researcher at the Smithsonian Consortia and one of the world's foremost forensic linguists." She glanced over the top of her dark reading glasses at the audience, pausing for effect. "He's the author of the acclaimed best-seller *There's the Public Line, and Then There's the Real Story,* about exposing sometimes biased history. His soon to be released book, *Machiavelli and da Vinci, The Collaboration of Geniuses*, describes their amazing work together."

Her eyes twinkled when she read his bio's last line. "And, last-but-not-least, he's renowned for his ability to name almost any song's title after hearing only the first two or three notes."

The crowd chuckled at her description of his unusual talent. Joe groaned. *She could have talked all night and not brought that up.*

"And now, without further ado, let's welcome Dr. Joe Richmond." She extended her arm palm up toward Joe, waiving him onto the stage.

The audience burst into applause. Joe's face had a slight warm flush as he strode to the podium. The stage lights were hot and intense, beaming toward his eyes. He squinted, adjusting the microphone as he nodded toward the moderator.

"Thank you for that very kind introduction," he deadpanned. "My mother would have been proud because you read it exactly like she wrote it."

The audience laughed again and then grew quiet in anticipation.

Joe paused to take a sip from the crystal water glass on the podium. "History is written by the victors. They sometimes revise history to show themselves favorably and their opponents unfavorably. But, when we look at historical documents beyond the victors' control, we often find a different tale. There's the public line, and then there's the real story…."

Gina cleared her throat, snapping him out of his daydream about his prior presentation at the Embassy. She repeated her comment. "Antonio sent me this email last night. It refers to you but doesn't explain why."

"It's a photo taken of us last night by the Embassy staff." Joe stared at the photo, shaking his head from side to side. "Nothing special. I have no idea why he sent it."

"Where's the bust, now?" she asked. "I want to see it."

"Over here," Joe said, walking to the built-in maple shelves framing his office. He picked up the ten-inch high bust of Machiavelli's head, shoulders and chest, off the ledge. It portrayed a pleasant looking man with short hair, wearing a sleeveless mantle, or surcoat, over an undercoat. The chest contained a circular shiny silver medallion two inches in diameter, stamped with the raised words Niccolò Machiavelli - *The Prince*. Joe placed the bust into Gina's outstretched hands.

She turned it around, examining it from every angle, top to bottom, but finding no clues. She winced. Nothing about the bust seemed to shed any light on the Ambassador's secret. "Looks like a dead end."

He'd tried to tell her.

"It can't be." Gina shook her head from side to side. "My ex found something incredibly special, something men would kill for, something hidden. He sent this, so I'd contact you."

"I'm afraid I can't help you there."

"You must remember something he said." She clasped her wrist with her opposite hand. "Anything... Anything at all?"

Joe rolled his eyes. She wasn't going to give up until he summoned up every detail. "After my presentation, the female moderator led me to the VIP table in front of the ballroom. The Ambassador sat there talking to a lobbyist named Claude Zorak and Senator Benjamin Hogue. The moderator tapped the Ambassador on the shoulder and introduced me. He stood up and we shook hands."

"How did Zorak respond?"

How'd she know to ask that question? Joe's mouth dropped. He'd forgotten Zorak looked quite upset at the development. "He glared at the moderator. I think her introduction interrupted him while he was asking the Ambassador what seemed like a probing question."

"What about the bust?"

"It was a token of his appreciation for my presentation. The moderator photographed us holding it. The Ambassador told her to send him a copy right away. At the time, I didn't question why he wanted the image so soon."

"He wanted a copy to email to me," Gina said.

Apparently so, but why? "He invited me to sit next to him, saying he admired my new book. We talked about it for five minutes. Zorak and Hogue got bored and left to get fresh drinks."

"What happened after they left?"

"The Ambassador's eyes darted around like he was worried. He said he'd made a discovery but couldn't share it with me then. We agreed his assistant would call my office to set up lunch later this week to discuss it. I gave him my business card."

"That's it?" Her tone showed she was beginning to get his point.

"Yeah, pretty much. He excused himself and disappeared into the crowd. Then I left and headed back to the office."

Gina turned her attention back to the bust, now holding it a mere twelve inches in front of her face. She scowled. "I don't see anything on it that helps."

Joe stroked his chin. Since the answer wasn't obvious, it was time to think outside the box. Da Vinci and Machiavelli had practiced looking at objects from different perspectives to make new discoveries. Why not try the same thing here? "Maybe the clue's not *on the bust*."

"Like, maybe it's *inside*?"

His eyes focused on the shiny medallion in its chest. "Are you thinking what I'm thinking?"

Gina nodded. She pushed her red acrylic fingernails in the grooves at the medallion's edge, trying to pry it out. It didn't budge. She looked up at Joe. "No luck."

"Maybe the medallion doesn't pop out. Maybe it screws into the bust," Joe made a turning motion with his thumb, index and middle fingers, to illustrate.

She placed two fingertips and her thumb against the medallion's metal surface, slowly twisting clockwise. The medallion didn't budge. She pressed harder against the medallion until her fingertips turned white. Her hand twisted again. This time the medallion slowly turned a quarter turn.

They were on to something, here.

"It's moving." Gina's mouth gaped. She pressed again, turning the medallion until it broke free from the last thread of the grooves in the bust. The smooth metal fell out of the chest's hole and slid through her fingers. It made a clink sound when its alloy hit the bottom of the bronze bust. From there, it dropped to the floor, bouncing on the carpet to land face up.

In the chest's center appeared a three-inch diameter hole four inches deep. Gina pushed her thumb and index finger into the hole, pulling out a rolled-up slip of paper the size of an index card. She unrolled it on the desk, revealing a handwritten message on the page.

The scales of justice must be balanced.

"I'll be damned." Joe scratched his head. "It's kind of an odd thing to say. What do you think it means?"

"I have no idea. Scales of justice… a whole lot of help that is" She used both hands to set the bust back on the shelf and breathed a heavy sigh.

There must be some way to figure out what the Ambassador's trying to tell us. Joe jammed his hands into his pockets. "Think, concentrate, there must be something."

CHAPTER 3

The gunman, Tomas Lobo, fumed as he and his partner Axel sat in a black sedan parked outside the Smithsonian Castle on the street. The car dashboard's LED lights illuminated the cab's interior against the pre-dawn darkness. "I wasted half an hour last night searching the Ambassador's Villa Firenze estate for the secret, before the cops arrived. It was like finding a drop of sweat in the sea. Then I hid in the basement for four hours while they turned the place upside down. Finally, they left. While I was hiding, it dawned on me... maybe the Ambassador told Richmond the secret's location."

"So, you decided a visit to Mr. Richmond was in order," Axel said.

"Yeah. And you're going to handle him, while I figure out how to tell our Patron I haven't found the secret, yet."

Tomas gazed up at the Castle's towers, taking in the spectacular view. It was a mid-1800s tall red sandstone building in Gothic Revival style, with multiple towers of various heights, some round, some square. One of the towers had battlements, or crenels, a vestige through which guns might shoot in olden times. The Castle served as the Smithsonian's headquarters. Its staff oversaw several national museums and galleries from its offices.

A couple of second-floor arched windows revealed office lamps turned on in one of the office suites, for the employees working early that morning. The interior lights shone through those windows giving the red exterior an eerie glow.

Tomas checked his GPS online map in the dashboard against Joe's business card address. *This was the right place.* He read the phone number on the card while reaching into his coat pocket, pulling out a black burner phone making a call trace difficult. The lighted touchtone keys glowed in the dark, beeping as he dialed Joe's extension number.

Inside the Castle, Gina bit on her thumbnail as she paced back and forth across Joe's office on the Castle's second floor, trying to interpret the Ambassador's clue. The desk phone buzzed a couple of times. She stopped short, turning to scrutinize the intrusive noise.

Joe picked up the black receiver and held it against his ear. "Hello, Joe Richmond here." No one answered on the line's other end. He said, "Hello? Hello?" Ten seconds of silence passed before he slammed down the telephone receiver in disgust. "Wrong number," he muttered under his breath.

"Don't worry about the phone," Gina said. "We've got to focus."

In the black sedan, Tomas smirked and hung up without speaking. He had what he wanted, confirmation Joe was in his office working. He handed Axel the same nine-millimeter handgun with silencer Tomas used earlier to kill the Ambassador and Embassy security guard.

"I want you to plant the murder weapon in his office."

Axel listened to Tomas' final instructions, nodding to show he understood his mission. *This should be like shooting fish in a barrel.* He opened the sedan's driver side door, stepping away from the car onto the concrete sidewalk. His trim, muscular physique looked imposing as he strolled away toward the Castle. The dim moonlight shone on his body, casting a black shadow bobbing on the empty pavement.

Inside the Consortia suite, Joe and Gina resumed their speculation about the scales of justice clue. The office phone buzzed a second time, again interrupting them. They ignored it for half-a-minute, but the phone continued to buzz.

Not again. Joe groaned. "They're not giving up." He turned back toward his desk, putting the phone to his ear. His answer sounded terse. "Hello, Joe Richmond here. Hello."

At first, he couldn't hear anyone on the line. He covered the mouthpiece with his hand. "Must be the same idiot who called earlier," he hissed to Gina. He listened for a minute before his cheeks turned hot. His face took on a look of concern as he spoke into the mouthpiece. "I'm sorry Dave. I didn't mean to sound so abrupt. A wrong number called a few moments ago. I thought you were them again."

Joe paused to listen while Dave explained the reason for his call.

"Uh huh, does this really have to be done now?" Joe said. "I'm right in the middle of something… You're sure? Oh, alright I'll be there soon as I can."

It never rains but it pours. Joe rolled his eyes, hung up the phone and turned to Gina. "It's Dave the stager, from the Arts and Industries Building exhibit next door. He came in early because they ran into a snag on part of the Machiavelli-da Vinci exhibit. It has to be fixed before the final run-through tomorrow."

"There's no rest for the wicked," Gina nodded. "I'll come with you. We can brainstorm the clue on the way."

They grabbed their coats and headed out the Consortia department's suite door and out the building's side exit. The street light glowed brightly enough to guide them down the sidewalk in the dark outside the Castle. The concrete path led them across the ground's rose garden where bloomless stems resembled tentacles in the cool air. In less than a minute, they arrived at the Arts and Industries Building's double front door and walked inside.

Back on the street Axel's long dark overcoat and fedora hat helped him blend in with the night. His face appeared a mere hollow shadow under the hat's curved brim. *The chilly air feels good against my cheeks.* His gloved hands pulled up the coat collar tighter around his neck as he crept up the steps toward the Castle's side door. The facility had ultramodern security and it would take something special to hack it.

He popped the door's card reader cover off with a nail file, unscrewed the protective plate underneath and inserted a recently developed high-tech pirate chip into one of the reader's wires. The chip copied the card reader's recently received key codes and pin numbers, transmitting the info wirelessly to Axel's cellphone. That phone automatically sent a copy to Tomas, as well. Once he had the info, Axel re-attached the reader's cover and held his phone next to the reader, sending the copied code and pin as if he were an employee. A moment later the door unlocked. He grabbed the handle, pulled the door open, and headed straight for the building's stairwell.

All the building's second floor suite windows looked dark except one. Axel reached the Consortia Department's outer door with the word "Consortia" stenciled in black letters across the glass. *It won't be long now.* His black gloved right hand reached into his shoulder holster, pulling out the nine-millimeter handgun. His other gloved hand grabbed the department's door handle and turned it clockwise to enter the suite.

CHAPTER 4

The Castle was almost empty after Joe and Gina left for the Exhibit Hall early that morning. But in the Consortia department suite the remaining staff continued working on last minute items for the Exhibit's displays. Barbara, who had recruited Joe to the department, typed away on the keyboard in her office next to the reception area. While she worked, she talked with Jack, a co-worker, about tasks they needed to finish.

"Jack, would you put these files on Joe's desk for me?" Barbara asked. "He needs them right away and I've still got a pile of keyboarding to do."

"Sure, no problem." He scooped up the files and headed for Joe's office.

The suite's front door latch clicked open and closed, the sound filtering its way into Barbara's office behind the reception area. Her keyboarding paused. She got up from her chair and walked toward the front desk to investigate, forehead wrinkling at the sight of the dark coated stranger this time of morning.

She started to say, "May I help you," but only got to "May I....," before Axel raised his right arm, pointing the handgun at her head. Her mouth opened, but nothing came out, and both arms raised in surrender. The muffled sound of two shots sounded like corn kernels popping. She fell, hitting the carpet with a dull thud.

Axel walked over to where Barbara lay on the carpet and leered down at the body. Her eyes were open, but she didn't move. A stream of blood flowed down her blue blouse. It trickled-down like a meandering river on to the paperwork, still clutched in her hand. The rich red color smeared on the bright white paper. Axel snapped a photo of the victim with his phone.

So far, so good.

Axel took long-legged strides down the hall to Joe's office where he peered through the doorway. Jack stood next to Joe's desk. He stared fixated at the huge magnified inset photograph of the *Mona Lisa's* multi-arched stone bridge, still displayed on the video monitor.

That must be Richmond. Axel crept through the doorway toward Jack, raised the pistol, and shot him in the side of the head point blank. Jack's head hit the desk and his body crumpled to the floor. Axel grabbed one of Joe's business cards from the cardholder on the desk.

Richmond never knew what hit him.

Axel stepped over the body to get a closer look at the image that had so hypnotized his prey. His eyes narrowed. *What was so important about the Mona Lisa? And why was Richmond staring at it?*

Axel knew his Patron would very much want to see this image that had fascinated their target, so he snapped a photo of the screen with his phone. A moment later, he photographed the body.

Now, he had one more thing to do before leaving. Make it look like a murder/suicide.

His gloved hand pulled open Jack's fingers, folding them around the murder weapon's grip and trigger. Axel pointed the gun at the monitor, pressing Jack's finger against the trigger, firing a round. The monitor's glass shattered like ice falling from a roof. He left the gun clutched in Jack's hand where police would easily find it.

Axel's poker face never changed. It was mission accomplished, or so he thought. His cellphone rang less than a minute after he planted the murder weapon. He held the phone to his ear.

"Were you successful?" Tomas asked.

"Yeah, Richmond and a female employee."

"Text me his photo. We need it to get paid for the job."

Axel hung up. *Why does he always have to make everything so complicated? Isn't my word enough?* His finger tapped a button on his phone to snap the victim's photo. He attached the requested photo to a text, pushed the send button on his phone and plopped down in Joe's office chair to wait. His phone rang thirty seconds later.

"Idiot," Tomas hissed. "This isn't a photo of Richmond. You got the wrong guy."

Axel winced at the irritation in Tomas' voice. *Did I screw up big time? Who the hell else could it be?* "He was here a few minutes ago when you called his desk phone. I shot the guy standing in Richmond's office. There's no other male here."

"He must've slipped through your fingers. Check the other suites... see if their lights are on."

Crap. Why does this happen to me? Axel looked over at Jack's body on the floor and the gun curled in his hand. A worried look crossed his face. *I can't frame Richmond if the murder weapon's in somebody else's hand.*

Axel ran over to Jack's body, removed the gun from his hand, wiped off the fingerprints and shoved it into Joe's desk drawer. He bolted out the department's front door, leaving it ajar. He hurried down the hall, peering through the front door glass of the other suites, in a search for interior lights.

Meanwhile, in the Exhibition Hall, Joe had finished his interactive display repair. He and Gina crossed the Hall's tiny garden, making their way back to the Castle. The icy temperature caused Joe to shiver beneath his jacket. He hadn't finished buttoning it until they reached the Castle's side door. Entering the building this early in the morning felt surreal, the rhythmic slap of their footsteps on the tile being the only audible noise. They rounded the second floor's hall corner, approaching the entrance to the Consortia office suite.

The door's ajar. Joe's nose wrinkled. *That's odd. Barbara makes sure it's kept shut. She's a stickler about that.*

He pushed the door open wider, stepping into the department's reception area. Gina followed right behind him. His foot tripped on a blunt object on the floor beside the receptionist desk. He fell hard onto one knee against the rigid tile. "Ow... that smarts." His face grimaced as he rubbed the joint with both hands.

"Oh my god, it's a woman's leg?" Gina stifled a scream, pointing a couple feet to his right.

There on the floor in the direction she'd indicated, lay a bare female lower leg stuck out past the desk. He took a deep breath, peering behind the workstation. Barbara lay motionless in a bloody pool on the floor. He crawled over to place two fingers on her wrist, searching for a pulse, feeling none. Her arm already was a bit stiff and cool to the touch.

Who could have done this? He wobbled and put one hand on the desk to balance himself. His vision blurred as he backed away from Barbara's still body. He regretted his irritation at her earlier for leaving him alone with Gina.

"Where's Jack? He was working here when we left?"

Gina put her hand on his shoulder, waving one hand toward the inner offices. "We'd better check your office."

They crept out of the reception area, striding cautiously down the suite's inner hall, their every footstep planted with care to avoid making sound. Joe turned the corner to his office and stopped short in the doorway. He gritted his teeth and looked away. A male, with a bullet hole through his back, lay face down on the carpet ten feet away.

This can't be happening.

Joe walked over to the body, pulling on the shoulder to turn it over. Jack lay next to the desk with a bullet hole in his head near the temple. "No, God, not him too."

Gina checked his neck pulse, detecting a faint heartbeat. "He's still alive." She lifted Jack's head to help him breathe. "Who did this to you?" she asked.

Jack's mouth opened but the only sounds were a couple breathy unintelligible sighs. His hand shook, pointing an index finger toward the video monitor as his body heaved. He gave a faltering gasp and then lay still. Joe put his fingers to Jack's wrist to check his pulse, but he was gone. Lifeless eyes stared out from his face. Joe's stomach churned with nausea.

"He'd been here less than a year… one of the nicest guys I ever met." Joe stared at the scene, glassy eyed. "Damned awful luck." His lower lip started to quiver but he had no time to grieve.

Two co-workers killed in the last half-hour. Plus, the Ambassador and a guard at the Embassy.

Gina stared at the shattered monitor and the glass shards scattered across the floor. "If they didn't like the image, they could've changed it." She kicked two pieces of glass out of the way. "Whoever did this isn't here now. But they might still be in the building." Her eyes widened. "We could be in danger."

Joe glanced around the room, his heart going a million miles a minute.

"Let's get out of here, now. We'll call 911 when we're safely out of the building."

Joe and Gina rushed out of the suite's front door and down the Castle's empty second-floor hall. The gruesome images of his dead office mates flashed through his mind. It looked like assassination, pure and simple.

The police will ask me who'd want to kill them. Like I would know. How would anyone know?

They burst into the stairwell, rushing down the stairs two steps at a time until they reached the first-floor landing. Joe's hands quivered, pushing on the heavy stairwell door's metal latch. It made a loud clunk sound and the door opened.

They scurried out of the stairwell, entering the hall before skidding to a sudden stop. Axel stood twenty yards down the hall from them where he peered through a glass window into a first-floor office suite. They slid sideways into a nearby doorway, their bodies flattening up against the door. Its recessed frame supplied a temporary hiding spot.

"Damn, this has gone from bad to worse," Joe said. His heart beat faster with worry they'd be discovered. He rubbed both his clammy hands together. "The building's mostly empty this early in the morning. He's gotta be the killer."

"Can we make it to the exit?" She bit her thumbnail.

"He's between us and the door," Joe said. "We can't get out that way. He's too close."

Their options had narrowed. They couldn't go back to the stairwell because Axel would see them. He hadn't spotted them yet, but he was headed in their direction. It was only a matter of time.

We've got to find a place to hide until help arrives.

Joe peered around the corner of the doorway, spotting hope across the hall ten yards away. A white door with three hinges and a brass doorknob looked promising. A metal brass faceplate on the door frame's side sported two large black buttons. One button said "UP," and one said "DOWN." Another faceplate sat right above the door, with numbered floor level indicator lights. The lift lacked the traditional shiny steel sliding doors that open from the middle and retract to each side.

It's an elevator. It may buy us some time. Joe pointed toward it, whispering, "That's our best chance."

They bolted from the doorway's shelter, running full speed toward the elevator. Their moving bodies pushed the air out of the way, creating a noticeable breeze.

Axel heard the commotion and spun away from the glass window to face them. He stuck one hand inside his coat to reach for the handgun in his shoulder holster. "Halt or I shoot."

His hand came out empty. A look of irritated surprise crossed the assailant's hardened face. His lips pursed as he remembered the murder weapon placed in Joe's desk drawer upstairs. A split second later his body jerked back into action. He reached down with one hand, pulling up his right black pant leg and exposing a hairy pale right calf. Two leather straps held in place a leather sheath holding a six-inch long steel knife. He pulled the shiny blade out.

"Stop," he shouted as he raced toward them. "You'll only make this worse."

Gina stabbed the black plastic "UP" button twice with her index finger. The button wobbled, moving in and out of its hole in the faceplate.

Axel raced toward them with the determined look of a paid assassin.

Joe's face muscles tightened. *He's too close. There's no time to wait on this damn door.*

The elevator door opened, and they barged inside. Gina punched the button for the North Tower's top floor. The door closed. A second later they heard Axel's pounding on the other side. He cursed them, the elevator vibrating from the force of his blows.

Hurry up and move. The elevator floor push against his feet.as the electric motor kicked on with a whir. The numbered floor indicator lights flashed in succession, passing each consecutive story one by one.

"That was close." Gina leaned back against the wall and breathed a sigh of relief.

Joe looked around the small elevator compartment capable of holding three or four people at a time. The walls were painted deep blue with ornate brass trim. A brass light fixture hung on the ceiling. The elevator came to a stop on the top floor, interrupting his survey. The door didn't budge.

Come on, we don't have all day.

After a couple seconds, the door sprang open. They stepped out of the cab into a sparse high-ceilinged room of a bygone era closed off from the world. An old wooden ladder led from the floor upward to a galvanized roof access hatch in the ceiling.

"We're in the Castle's North Tower. We've got to find a place to hide." Joe approached the ladder, pushing sideways against its rails to test its strength. The gunman would be there soon. "We can't stop here." The ladder didn't budge, so he put one foot on the bottom rung. The vintage wood was rock solid and supported him with ease. He grabbed both rails and aggressively lifted his other foot onto the second rung. "Follow me."

He climbed to the ladder's top rung and looked down. Gina followed a few rungs behind. He pushed up hard on the ceiling's hinged metal hatch. To his surprise, it lifted open with ease on its compression springs. Cold fresh air rushed in through the hatch to displace the scent of yesteryear. Above him, the dark blue sky and twinkling stars just before sunrise appeared in the square opening.

"Whoa, that's brisk." Joe's eyes blinked. He climbed up through the open hatch until his upper body stuck out of the frame. With both hands firmly placed on the frame's sides, he hoisted himself onto the tower's octagonal shaped roof deck. A moment later, Gina reached the top ladder rung and her head popped up through the open hatch. Joe grabbed her hands, pulling her through the hatch opening onto the roof. A flip of his hand closed the hatch shut behind her with a click.

"How high is it?" Gina asked, standing up straight on the octagonal roof deck, gazing around in the dim starlight to get her bearings.

"It's the Castle's tallest tower, we're 145-feet up."

The tower roof measured 15 feet across, surrounded by a three-foot high perimeter stone wall. An enormous cast bronze bell sat in the roof's center beside a twenty-foot tall flag pole. A square metal, box big enough to walk across, capped the tower's elevator shaft. The box sat next to one side of the roof's stone border wall.

Gina stared in awe at the Castle's other towers looming nearby, framed by the city's skyline. "They're beautiful. What's that one?" she asked, pointing to a tall four-sided tower.

"The Campanile bell tower." Joe pointed to the opposite side of the National Mall across from the Castle. "See the shiny dome. That's the Smithsonian Museum of Natural History."

The wind gusts pushed against his body causing him to sway. *If it gets much stronger, it'll be hard to stand up.*

He leaned into the wind to keep his balance. Small careful steps carried him toward the low perimeter wall where he peered over the tower's edge.

He stared down at the ground and the scene began to spin like a kaleidoscope. He lunged back to grab the flag pole for support, clutching it for dear life. His eyes clenched eyes shut.

"Are you alright?" Gina frowned at him.

His pained expression said it all as he walked his hands hand over hand down the pole to lower his body until he sat down on the roof. The motion looked like a sandlot baseball player walking his hands up the bat to decide whose team went first, except Joe's hands moved downward. He exhaled fully, resting between the flagpole and the elevator shaft dome. After a minute he regained his balance. His shoulders relaxed.

"I'll be O.K. now."

"Heights bother you, don't they?" Gina crawled over to the pole and sat down on the roof next to him. She put her hands around his to keep them warm.

If she only knew how much. "It's a long story."

Meanwhile, in the first-floor hallway below, Axel had given up pounding on the elevator door. His eyes crinkled when he spied the elevator lights showing it's rise to the top floor. He raced up the stairs two at a time to the fourth level, rushing into the small room with the ladder. He looked around the empty room. His gaze landed on the ladder and followed it up to the hatch. A cruel smile spread across his face.

Axel clutched his knife in one hand while he climbed up the ladder rungs to the access hatch. Halfway up, the ladder's dust tickled his nose. "Ah-h-h-choo."

"Someone's coming," Gina hissed at Joe.

She crawled behind the elevator shaft box, with Joe right behind. The roof's gritty tar gravel surface scraped against his hands and pants, leaving tiny black indentations in his palms that hurt. He crouched down on the roof, gazing up at the pre-dawn sky filled with tiny dots of twinkling light. The view made his head spin again, so he closed his eyes. His heart pounded.

The access hatch squeaked, opening and flopping backwards on its hinge. It hit the roof with a hollow "plunk" sound. The glint of Axel's knife blade flashed its reflection in the bright moonlight. Joe caught a glimpse of it from behind the elevator shaft box. The only sounds were the wind and Axel's shoes scraping against the grit as he edged past the square box's corner. Axel stopped to stare at the flagpole. The wind blew his long

25

brown hair across his face. He brushed it back with one hand.

He's only a few feet away. He'll see us any time now. Joe clenched a fist, summoning all the courage he had left for the battle he knew was coming.

"BONG-G-G." An ear shattering peal shook the entire roof as the Castle clock struck 6:00 a.m., its mechanism triggering the massive bell to ring out the hour. The sudden boom startled Axel so much he jerked back. Stunned, he glared at the offending bell, turning away from Joe and Gina.

"We've got to climb over the box to get to the roof hatch," she whispered, grabbing Joe's arm and pointing to the elevator shaft box next to them. "Axel's blocked the only other route."

Joe nodded that he understood. The roof seemed to spin as his ancient fears overtook him. *Get ready. It's do or die.*

He jumped up on the box, with Gina close behind moving fast. His right foot slipped on an ice patch collecting its flat steel surface. His body struggled to stay upright. Gina grabbed his arm to steady him and released it after he regained his balance. Joe scrambled down the other side.

Axel heard the commotion and whirled around. "No, you don't."

He hopped onto the box as Gina scrambled to get down. "I've got you now." He grabbed her arm, pulling hard to stop her progress.

"Joe!!" Gina screamed.

Joe slammed his fist into Axel's grip, spraining it and allowing Gina to jerk free. Her escape removed the only opposing force counterbalancing Axel's pull. The assassin stumbled backward like a tug of war contestant whose opponent suddenly released the rope. His feet hit the ice patch causing him to slide on the metal box toward the roof's perimeter wall, both of equal height. He skidded off the box onto the wall's stone top. His upper body teetered in space beyond the top of the wall, his arms waving in a frantic circular motion trying to regain his balance.

Oh my God, he's gonna fall. Gina covered her mouth with one hand.

Axel's torso leaned further and further over the wall until it tipped sideways over the tower's side. He flipped over the edge head first, his feet flying up and following his body in free-fall. He screamed, plunging headfirst to the concrete below. A moment later, Joe and Gina heard what sounded like a large pumpkin smashing into pavement.

They inched their way on hands and knees over to the tower's edge, pulling themselves up to the low wall. Their eyes peeked over it to gaze at the ground. Axel's body lay motionless on the concrete sidewalk while his open blank eyes stared up at the stars.

"Couldn't happen to a nicer guy." Joe grimaced. He pulled himself back away from the tower's edge, legs wobbling as forced himself to stand up, still breathing heavily. The wind pushed against him hard. He leaned against the bell's sturdy frame to steady himself until the dizziness subsided.

Gina pulled out her smart phone and turned on flashlight mode to check Joe for injuries. The light also illuminated the helpful bell next to him, with its inscribed black plaque attached to the frame inscribed with the Smithsonian's mission.

This bell saved our lives. Joe's eyes sparkled as he leaned over it, brushing his fingers tenderly over the brass surface. He gave the bell a brief hug before stepping over to the open roof hatch and climbing back down the old ladder. Gina followed close behind.

Down on the street in the sedan, Tomas had nodded off in the firm leather driver's seat. His phone alarm buzzed, jerking him awake and reminding him to check in with Axel. He pressed speed dial to call his partner's number. Repeated ringing came from the speaker, but no answer.

Axel's always reliable. Something's very wrong.

He sprinted from the vehicle across the lawn toward the front steps and the building entrance. He winced, tripping over a large object in the dark on the concrete. A quick downward glance revealed Axel's body lying face up. Blood pooled next to his head. A shiny knife blade twinkled from where it lay two yards away from his outstretched hand.

Tomas nostrils flared. *The game is up.* Axel's death made this job much harder. Sirens wailed in the distance alerting him he would have to act fast. *I'll get the bastard that did this.* He peered up at the Castle, his eyes darting from window to window looking for a clue from which one Axel fell. But the panes were all dark and closed with no sign of life. He rushed to the side door and held his cellphone against the building's card reader. A moment later the door opened, and he rushed inside, gripping a gun in one hand.

Up in the tower, Joe and Gina staggered out of the small fourth floor room, heading toward the elevator. She extended her arm to press the down button to call the elevator. But, before she could reach the button, the sudden whir of the elevator's motor kicked in. Joe's body froze in mid-motion. His breathing stopped. A glance up at the yellow elevator indicator lights above the door, revealed the cab was climbing to the top floor. The blood ran out of his face at this sign their assailant had an accomplice.

They needed another way off the top floor and fast.

He spotted a wood railed stairway and motioned to Gina to follow him toward it. They hurried down the steps two at a time, rounding the atrium that bordered all four sides of the stairs on each floor.

CHAPTER 5

Joe ran down the stairs and around the atrium at every floor level, with Gina right beside him. *Other gunmen might have already staked out the building's exits. Using those doors could be suicide.* But he had an idea for a different escape route.

"We're going to the basement," he said between hurried breaths.

"We can't go there," Gina shrank back. We'll be trapped."

"No, we won't. Trust me."

They descended the stairs to the lower level and trotted through the doorway to the Castle's utility room. It seemed deserted except for the hum of electrical equipment. Large grey circuit breaker boxes lined one white limestone block wall. Fluorescent lights, pipes and wiring, hung from the ceiling.

"There's another way out." Joe's eyes darted around the room. "Greg told me about a little-known exit, the Castle Tunnel, a year ago. The doorway's in here somewhere." Joe walked the length of the space, searching for the aged passage's entrance. Sure enough, down the hall stood a wire mesh steel door fastened to a metal frame, leading to the tunnel.

"This must be it." He grunted, tugging hard on the door's round latch. The door opened, he walked through the narrow opening and found himself in a dark underground tunnel. Gina slid through the doorway a moment later. The shaft's low ceiling had them both ducking their heads.

He felt around inside the doorway, his eager fingers finding an industrial style light switch on the wall. He flipped it on. Wire cage lights attached to the wall lit up the tunnel at regularly spaced intervals. The bulbs' beams illuminated a gray dusty narrow cavern four-feet wide and five-and-a-half-feet high, with stone block walls and a rough concrete floor. Large utility pipes lined both walls on either side.

"Are you sure you know what you're doing?" Gina asked. Where does this thing go?"

Why didn't I think of that before? Joe looked down and away. "Greg didn't say. He'd never been in it 'cause it was off limits."

"I'm game, let's do it."

A different exposed light bulb appeared every twenty yards, the distance meant sections of the tunnel in between the fixtures appeared dim and shadowy. Occasional bugs scurried across the floor. Puffs of dust followed Joe and Gina's steps while the dank air hung like a vapor in their lungs. Joe put his hand on one of the pipes in the narrowest part of the tunnel, feeling the heat it generated. His foot slipped on a slick spot causing his head to miss by a whisker a sharp steel pipe's bracket jutting out from the wall. Gina recoiled when a brown spider dropped down from the tunnel's ceiling mere inches from her head.

They had run the length of a football field when the sound of hard soled footsteps clattered in the distance behind them.

"It's him," Gina said. "He must have seen the lights in the Castle utility room and found the tunnel entrance. We've got to move faster."

Up ahead in the distance, light leaked through the steel mesh door at the tunnel's opposite end. They pushed the dusty metal door open, its hinges offering resistance from lack of regular use. The door opened into a different utility room with a discarded metal sign which laid against one wall. It read, 'Smithsonian Museum of Natural History.'

"The tunnel must have taken us from the Castle, underneath the Capitol Mall, to the Natural History Museum," Joe said. "We're on the opposite side of the Mall, now."

Gina swung the tunnel door shut behind her, causing a clanking sound as the door hit the doorframe. The utility room appeared Spartan with more utility boxes, exposed pipes and wires. Joe jammed a thick metal arm chair against the tunnel door handle to block their assailant's entry.

They scurried out of the room and up the marble stairs to the Natural History Museum's ground floor. The air smelled fresher here and Joe could breathe easier. Their street shoes clicked loudly on the steps, echoing off the walls.

This noise makes us easy to follow. His worry was interrupted by the sound of the tunnel door crashing open. Their assailant must have entered the second utility room. The crash was followed by the screech of a metal chair flung across the concrete floor, scraping against the solid surface. After a minute, the lights flickered in the stairway before going completely out.

He's cut power to the building. We're dealing with a pro... we'll be lucky to get out of here alive.

Gina grabbed Joe's sleeve and pointed at the exit sign. "Hurry, the front door's this way."

"He's too close. There's no time."

Gina pointed to the stairs leading up to the second floor. "This is our only other choice. What are we waiting for?"

Joe slowed from exhaustion as they climbed up the long stairway, his muscles burning by the time they reached the second floor. *I'm not sure how much longer I can keep this up.*

Two gunshots rang out from the first floor. They turned to look behind them at the bottom of the stairs below, spotting a uniformed museum security guard who stiffened before falling to the floor. Tomas had run out of the basement and shot him. The guard had distracted Tomas enough that he lost track of where his real prey had gone.

Joe and Gina ran to a deserted exhibit area lit only by emergency lights, but it shone enough to illuminate their path. They stopped to catch their breath near a glass case holding a huge gemstone. Gina panted, casting curious looks at the dazzling rock.

"It's the Hope Diamond," Joe said. "The largest blue diamond in the world. 45 1/2 carats."

"It's beautiful," she gasped, still breathing hard.

"Marie Antoinette wore it while her subjects starved," Joe explained, his chest heaving. "They beheaded her during the French Revolution."

"I hope the stone was worth it to her," Gina said, still panting.

"They say it's cursed. I've had enough bad luck today." He saw no percentage in lingering around an unlucky stone to pick up even more trouble. Nor time to bring up her lavish spending and the 'Let them eat cake' quote. He glanced around, searching for their next move. "We can't stay here... we've got to get out of this place. This way."

They took off, darting down a different stairway into the museum's huge Rotunda. Its massive domed ceiling reached five stories high and could hold 500 people.

Gina spotted an enormous stuffed male African bush elephant in the Rotunda's center. Her eyes did a double take. The 14 feet tall pachyderm stood on a large rock formation three feet above the Rotunda floor. He surveyed his dominion with trunk lifted triumphantly in the air. His legs' position made him appear to move at a fast pace even though he stood still. Nearby, concrete tree limbs simulated his native driftwood habitat.

Joe caught a glimpse, out of the corner of his eye, of motion in the hallway at the Rotunda's opposite side. Tomas crept out of the shadows into the rotunda with his gun drawn, searching for his prey.

"In a few seconds he'll see us." Joe whispered as he nudged Gina and nodded in Tomas' direction. *We can't stay in the open like sitting ducks.*

Gina motioned for Joe to follow as she sprinted toward the huge elephant for cover. Three gunshots rang out. The bullets whizzed by his head as he ran. *Jesus, that's close.* They jumped up on the rock formation, flattening their bodies behind the animal's enormous front legs.

Tomas pulled the trigger again. The gun clicked twice, revealing an empty chamber. He threw the offending weapon down on the floor in disgust. He hoisted his body up on the huge rock and glared at them. "I don't need a gun for you."

Joe and Gina ran to the rock's opposite side, jumping down to the tile floor. Tomas dashed across the uneven rock after them. He jumped from it with outstretched arms to tackle Joe below, but as he leaped his foot tripped on the jagged concrete surface. He fell forward, landing with his left arm jammed in between two gray concrete driftwood limbs, his anguished scream reverberating through the huge hall.

The shriek stopped Joe and Gina dead in their tracks They spun around to face Tomas. He leered at them like a caged animal. His free right hand tugged on the trapped left arm in an unsuccessful attempt to liberate it from the unforgiving concrete.

"I'll get you." His lip curled as he jerked his left arm hard against the limbs. "It's just a matter of when."

Joe turned to face his disarmed assailant, raising one eyebrow. The sight of Tomas trapped of his own doing, after what he and his accomplice had put them through, warmed Joe's heart. He gave Tomas a two-finger salute, using only his middle and index fingers. "We'd love to stay and chat... but you seem stuck in your work."

Joe and Gina sprinted from the Rotunda toward the museum's back door fire exit. Gina pressed on the exit's push bar, the lock clicked, and the door swung open setting off the fire alarm. They made a quick dash through the dark staff parking lot behind the Museum to a nearby intersection under a street light. They stopped to catch their breath. The Museum and the wide Capitol Mall stood between them and the Castle.

"I hear sirens," Joe said. "Since there's a dead body by the Castle's front door, the police might be there by now."

"My phone has a police radio scanner app," Gina said. "It'll tell us if they arrived and what they're saying. It's a useful tool to have in cyber security."

Joe's forehead wrinkled. "You work in cyber security?"

"I work at an international security firm. We help corporations protect their computer systems against hackers." She touched her app's icon and the officers' crackly voices came over the speaker.

"We found the murder weapon in Richmond's desk. Looks like he's our man. But he's not here," the first voice said.

"Well, find him," said a second voice. "His co-workers were shot with the same gun as the dead Ambassador. He could be a serial killer."

Joe's face turned pale. "They think I did it. God, no."

"We can't go back there." Gina swiped her finger across the phone to switch off the app. "They'd arrest you. And I need you free to help me solve this."

"Where do we go from here?"

"Remember the scales of justice clue? I figured it out while we were running through the tunnel." Gina gave him a cocky wink. "There's a blind justice statue in Antonio's Villa Firenze study."

"Won't the authorities already be in there?"

"They've probably already been there and gone. It's been seven hours since the murder, and they would have sent a team there first thing. Investigators usually gather whatever they want and take it back to their headquarters. It's not the murder scene, so it has limited value. But we'll still have to be careful."

Gina hailed a passing taxi. They climbed into the cab's back seat, gave the driver the Ambassador's address and told him to 'step on it.' The cab drove off down the street as the dawn's first rays peeked over the rooftops.

CHAPTER 6

Gina slid the taxi's clear-plastic partition window closed and flipped the intercom's switch to 'off.'

Good thinking, we don't want the driver overhearing us. Joe leaned back in the cab's back seat and sighed. The firm cushioned foam supported his spine, taking the stress off his muscles after he'd run for so long. However, his peace was short lived, as his momentary safety reminded him his officemates were not so lucky. A shadow fell over his face. "I can't believe my co-workers are gone."

"There must be a reason. Why'd anybody want to kill them?"

"I have no idea." Joe half shrugged. *This tragedy is so crazy. She might as well have asked me who killed Jimmy Hoffa.*

"Was there anything in your office worth killing for, valuables maybe?"

"It's not like we had rare jewels or Rembrandt paintings." Joe gave a dismissive wave of his hand. "We're a research department. It's mostly texts, replicas, and photographs. They're all in storage cabinets waiting to be analyzed."

"You said the Ambassador made a discovery. They murdered him to get it or keep him quiet."

"But, why kill my team?"

"You gave the Ambassador your business card. Maybe the assassins found it on him, figured he told you what he found. That's why they came to your office… they were after you."

"So, my friends were collateral damage." Joe bit his lip. *And I'm the reason they're dead.* The image of their two faces flashed across his mind's eye. He choked up since he would never see them again, never hear their voices.

"Remember the prank phone call. The assassins called your office to confirm you were there, then hung up."

"This is beyond depressing." Joe put his palm against his forehead and rubbed the temples. *It all made tragic sense now.*

"You were called away from the office. They wiped-out your team so no one could talk. But they missed you. Now, they're more determined than ever."

She saw right through the killers' ploy. Joe's face paled and his shoulders slumped, the full impact setting in. He'd been spared, in a bizarre way, but at a cost hard for him to deal with. *What could be worth so many lives?*

The intercom crackled as the burly cab driver switched it back on. "Here's your destination, folks."

The interruption snapped Joe out of his pained focus on his friends' fate. The cab pulled up to the black wrought iron entrance outside Villa Firenze's gorgeous 22-acre estate. Daylight revealed the beautiful bell curve arches and six-inch cast-iron finials topping the dual wide swinging gates. Each one appeared hinged to a tall limestone column on either side of the driveway. The carved word 'Firenze' appeared on the right-hand column. Underneath, a metal sign displayed the words 'Italian Embassy Residence' presented in black serif type.

"That'll be $24.75," the driver said, turning around to face them from the front seat and holding out an open palm face up. Joe pulled a money clip out of his pants pocket. He peeled off a couple of bills before handing them to the driver. He and Gina got out of the cab and watched its red taillights disappear down the street.

"I guess we're on our own now," she said.

The gate's locked. How are we gonna get in?

Gina pulled a tiny gray plastic remote control from her purse, pressing its white button without uttering a word. Two seconds later a faint motorized whirring sound broke the silence. The two wrought iron gates swung open wide on their hinges, beckoning them to enter. Joe turned his head toward her, his mouth wide open.

"I never turned it in after the divorce," Gina's eyes twinkled as she slid the remote back in her purse. "Antonio didn't ask for it. He hoped we'd get back together."

Gina led Joe through the gate down a secluded side path away from the front drive. On one side lay a lush garden with immaculate trimmed shrubbery and white marble statues. The sweet clean scent of pine trees filled Joe's nostrils. As they drew closer, the Ambassador's residence came into view, a two-story Tudor style mansion with stone façade and tall arched windows. Yellow crime-scene tape blocked the front doorway. An officer sat in the driver's seat of an unmarked car parked on the red brick driveway, appearing to type on his laptop keyboard.

Probably finishing a report on what they found when searching the house last night

They waited a few minutes before the patrol car pulled away from the house, it's red tail lights disappearing down the driveway.

The lush garden hid Joe and Gina from view as they followed the path around to the back of the house. They strode up to a keypad mounted on the back-door's frame

"I hope they haven't changed the code." Gina said, taking a deep breath. She pressed the buttons to enter six-digits, the keypad's red indicator light turned green and the doorlatch made a faint click sound. "We're in Luck." The door swung open and they walked through the entryway into the house.

"Which way to Lady Justice?" Joe asked.

CHAPTER 7

Tomas' face contorted as he stared at his left arm trapped between the concrete tree limbs in the museum rotunda. Bruises were already beginning to show on the skin as he continued his jerking attempts to free it.

He scowled at the limb like it was a poisonous snake. *I should have seen the branches... they were in plain sight. How could I have been so stupid.* His single-minded obsession to snag his prey had blinded him to the danger.

The throbbing pain grew more intense with every pulse beat as his arm swelled around the bruises. He groaned, tugging the arm several times to free it without success. One last desperate jerk liberated the appendage from its spear-like trap. The discolored arm trembled as he massaged it with his other hand.

I've got to find the Ambassador's secret. I'm running out of time.

He ran out the back door, circled around the building and crossed the National Mall before climbing in his black sedan's driver's seat. Police vehicles surrounded the Castle but officers focused on the crime scene, paying no attention to Tomas. The car started, responding with a deep throated humming sound as it drove off at high speed en route to Villa Firenze.

He reached into the glove compartment, grabbed a bottle of pain killers and swallowed a double dose. As he tilted his head back to gulp, he glanced at a faded photo clipped to the windshield visor serving as a constant reminder of his tragic past. It was a snapshot of his fellow soldier and best friend. Tomas never went anywhere without it.

That was the worst day of my life. If I could only go back and do it over.

Tomas had been a highly-decorated sniper in the second Gulf War, where he and his friend were assigned to the same unit. The thermometer read over one-hundred eight degrees the day they went out on assignment. The oppressive heat made him disoriented, causing him to feed the wrong coordinates into their vehicle's GPS. He quickly realized they'd landed in enemy territory and tried not to panic.

Moments later multiple rounds of mortar fire hit them. The blast's force threw him to the ground. It blew his friend to bits and the blood splattered over Tomas' face. Tomas survived, but spent months in a military hospital recovering from his injuries. The shock of seeing his friend decapitated made the struggle against post-traumatic stress disorder a bigger challenge than his physical wounds.

I'm responsible for his death. I can't run away from that.

The car's hands-free phone link rang, snapping Tomas out of his daydream. The dashboard monitor flashed the caller I.D. number for the Patron, who was no doubt calling to get a progress report.

I can't dwell on the war, now.

His boss would not warmly receive Tomas' failure to find the Ambassador's discovery. But it would only make matters worse to delay giving him the unwelcome news. After four rings he pressed the steering wheel's phone answer button.

The Patron's voice came over the speaker, "Tomas, I'm glad I reached you. I told one of my associates how you never fail. He was quite impressed."

"You're very kind, sir."

"I described how I found you. How your wartime flashbacks haunted you so much that gardening was the only job you could keep."

"Those were dark days, sir. Before I applied for your groundskeeper position."

"My estate manager told me your story shortly afterward," the Patron said. "Incredible. I lit up when I heard it. My business requires the use of force against competitors. And here you showed up on my doorstep, an incredible marksman with no criminal record, able to move easily about without attracting attention. What a find."

I'd hit rock bottom, I had nowhere else to go. "It was a golden opportunity."

"For both of us."

"You pay me well sir. You have my undivided loyalty."

The Patron cackled with pleasure. "That's what I want.

At that moment, the black sedan drove past the White House on its way to the Ambassador's residence. Tomas glanced at its white painted sandstone walls. An American flag flapped in the frigid breeze atop the tall rooftop flagpole. Underneath the White House's white exterior paint, the walls were black from fire caused by the 1814 British takeover and their burning of the Capitol. *The only time anyone other than the American people controlled it.*

"We're fortunate Claude Zorak attended the Embassy celebration tonight." Lucian's chatter brought Tomas attention back to the task at hand. "Otherwise, we'd have never known the Ambassador possessed the secret."

"How'd he find it?"

"Blind luck. Tucked inside a rare old copy of Machiavelli's book *The Discourses.* The leather cover was torn and coming apart at the bottom seam. A slim edge of yellowed paper stuck out from the tear."

"Did the Ambassador know what he'd found?"

"He knew it was huge. It contained a warning people would kill for it. Imagine that." The Patron cackled at the irony of the aged message warning of his current efforts. "He told Claude that Niccolò Machiavelli himself had signed the first page. The second page had backwards letters and numbers running from the right side to the left. It looked like Leonardo da Vinci's trademark, mirror writing."

The comment reminded Tomas how a couple years earlier, Lucian had learned of a special Roman Inquisition file in the Vatican's *Secret Archives* in Rome. The records confirmed the existence of a secret Lucian wanted to suppress at all costs. He made a large monetary gift to the Vatican, paving the way for Tomas' access to the Archives cavernous below ground facilities. Tomas posed as a researcher and found a centuries old text confirming the existence of an amazing secret banned by the Roman Inquisition. But the text did not tell them where to find it. He secretly removed the file from the Archives and returned to New York, delivering it to Lucian.

Tomas drummed his fingers on the steering wheel as he drove. *I can't stall forever, I've got to tell him now. Best to get it over with.* "Sir, I have news for you. I confronted the Ambassador at his Embassy."

The Patron inhaled sharply on the other end of the line. "Did he have the pages with him?"

"No, unfortunately he died before he could show me where he'd hidden them."

An extended silence filled the air before the Patron replied in a sinister tone. "That's unfortunate for everyone."

"I didn't have time to search his office. I had to get outta there before the police came."

"We must obtain those pages and destroy them." The Patron's voice grated with irritation. "If we don't, our entire plan will fail. They must not see daylight, hear me?"

He's obsessed. I've got to pacify him before he goes off the deep end. "I have another lead. I believe the Ambassador spoke about his discovery with someone else."

"Then you should relieve him of the burden of the Ambassador's confidence," the Patron hissed in an icy other worldly voice. "If it becomes public it'll be a disaster."

"Yes sir, I'll make the arrangements." Tomas decided not to tell the Patron that Joe Richmond had already escaped once. It would only make him angrier.

"Take whatever steps necessary. I want those items at all costs. You know what to do."

"Understood."

The Patron hung up without saying goodbye. Tomas lips tightened as he focused on his drive with a renewed sense of urgency. It might be hazardous to his health to fail again. He called his partner Hans with instructions on tracking Joe Richmond.

CHAPTER 8

A t 2:00 a.m. that morning, FBI Supervisory Special Agent Bill Davis shuffled papers at his desk in his Washington D.C. office. His hand hurried to initial the last few reports, so he could finally go home. He set the finished pile on his desk next to photos of his five grandkids and a desktop plaque from the younger agents paying tribute to "Pops." Three decades of grinding law enforcement work had given him gray hair and a weathered face, to go with his heavyset muscular body. The phone rang.

Hell, what now?

He hesitated, staring at the receiver. *It's been a long day, maybe it can wait 'til tomorrow…, they can leave a message.* It kept ringing and ringing. *Damn, the staff must have left early today, no one's picking up.* He put the phone up to his ear, grimacing while he growled into the phone receiver. "Davis, here." As he listened to the caller, he glanced at the office walls displaying framed thank-you letters signed by victims' relatives expressing appreciation. "Yeah, Uh huh." He made notes on a yellow legal pad for thirty seconds before his mouth fell open. "You're kidding? How many?" He clenched his fist. "We'll be right there."

Oh, Lord. There must be a full moon tonight. His hand holding the phone dropped to the desktop, all the strength draining from the limb. He yelled over at one of the assistant special agents on his team. "I've gotta go. Two homicides at the Italian Embassy. Take over Mack, you're in charge."

His expression hardened. He got an his unmarked car, turned on the flashing emergency grill lights and sped off past amber streetlights to the Italian Embassy.

Once there, Davis parked his car in the compound's driveway and marched into the Ambassador's office. Yellow crime-scene tape cordoned off the room while ambulance attendants examined the body. Several officers were already on the scene including Davis' young assistant, special agent Josh Jackson.

"Any clues so far who did it?" Davis asked.

"Not a thing." Josh stood next to the desk, dusting for fingerprints, "Looks like a professional job. Embassy security's top notch. But the killer got the drop on the security guard at the front gate and disabled the alarm system. He turned off the video surveillance cameras, too. He didn't leave any loose ends. Funny thing though… the victim still had his cash and an expensive watch."

Davis held up the Ambassador's wallet and frowned at his diplomatic I.D. "His foreign service status complicates things. You know we're going to have to get the Italian authorities' permission to search his residence."

"Our State Department's already contacted 'em and obtained permission A special team from Rome is flying in and they'll be here in twelve hours. We've got clearance to check the house now. They were very clear. FBI has to be in charge, not local law enforcement."

Just as well. Too many jurisdictions only complicate matters. "I want statements from everyone who spoke with the Ambassador in the last twenty-four hours."

"Uh, that will take some time." Josh's jaw dropped. "He attended a major event last night with several hundred people."

Jesus… why does everybody give me reasons they can't do what needs to be done. Why don't they just do it. "I don't care if he sat in the stands at sold-out Yankee Stadium, get the guest list and interview everyone you can find. It doesn't matter who you have to wake up. What event was it?"

"The Machiavelli-da Vinci Celebration."

The what celebration? Davis wrinkled his nose at the foreign sounding name. His busy schedule left him no time for the pomp and circumstance of Washington's diplomatic social calendar.

"It's Mach-i-avel-li like in famous Italian writer." Josh's shoulders shook with laughter. He tried to tell Davis who Machiavelli was.

"It doesn't matter." Davis rolled his eyes at this historical detail's insertion into a no-nonsense investigation. "What do we know out about the victim's comings and goings?"

"I spoke with his secretary. She said he made a special trip to New York City yesterday. Odd thing is, he seemed very secretive about why he went and what he did there."

Agent Davis pressed his lips together when he heard about the secrecy surrounding the Ambassador's recent New York City trip. *It's what people didn't want you to know that often mattered.* "Did anyone go with him? What about his wife, have you spoken with her?"

"He went alone." Josh shook his head. "There's no wife, it's his ex-wife, Gina Bocelli. We haven't contacted her yet. But we've got some background info on her, and a photo." Josh handed him her picture.

"You've got my attention. Keep going."

Josh read from a manila file folder, "Born in Rome, degree in computer engineering, pilot in the Aeronautica Militare, that's the Italian Air Force. Former computer security analyst at a corporate headquarters in Geneva. Afterward, she lived in a couple other international capitals while her husband worked in the Foreign Service.

She's got an impressive resume. "What's she do now?"

"Works as a high-level consultant at an international security firm here in D.C. Helps major corporations protect their computer systems from hackers. She's a wiz with cyber security."

"How long have they been divorced?"

"One year. Get this, her ex had an affair with Senator Benjamin Hogue's wife. It went public when a photographer caught them kissing at a hotel near the White House. She divorced him soon after."

Nothing like public humiliation to sour a marriage. "What sparked the affair?"

"The Senator's an overweight, right-wing, heavy drinker in his mid-fifties. The wife's a former model in her early thirties. She had an intense dislike for the rich-as-rajah misogynistic campaign donors he went out drinking with late at night."

"I can't imagine why," Davis chuckled, picturing in his mind an image of fat cats swilling alcohol and smoking cigars while they schemed against the public. "What about the Senator and his wife? Did they divorce?"

"Nope. Still married. He was determined to keep up appearances for his re-election campaign a few months ago.

It figures. These clowns will do anything to stay in office. "What about her?"

"She's unhappy but stays for the money and the prestige. For her it seemed easier to remain married but have an affair."

"That explains her," Davis said. "But why'd the Ambassador have an affair when he had such a great wife?"

"It was a machismo kind of thing."

"But they divorced anyway?"

"He still loved his wife… tried to win her back. She was too hurt and embarrassed to stay."

Can't say as I blame her. Nothing like being dragged through the mud. Davis rubbed his chin as he stared at the photo of Gina Bocelli. He handed the photo back to Josh. "Find the lady. I want to speak with her."

CHAPTER 9

C laude Zorak sat in his plush corner office at the conservative Dynasty Coalition, a Washington D.C. think tank, admiring the daytime view of the U.S. Capitol. Photos of him with various conservative political leaders adorned the walls. His head pounded like a pile driver, a reminder of the delayed price of the four Brandy Alexanders he consumed the night before with Senator Hogue at the Machiavelli-da Vinci celebration. He gulped down two pain relief pills and rubbed his temples, completing his review of the charts on the desk before placing them on the stack.

Glad that's finished. His phone alarm chimed with a reminder. *Time to meet with the various think-tank leaders for their corporate donors.* He leaned back in his chair and lit up an expensive fat cigar, puffing a couple of large white smoke rings that evaporated ten seconds later. The expression on his face was one of pure bliss from the experience.

The cigar still had several good puffs left when the intercom on his desk buzzed. "Sir, we're all in the conference room for the 7:00 a.m. strategy meeting," the voice said.

Christ... can't a fella even finish a good smoke. Claude pouted as he pressed the intercom button. "Tell them I'll be right there."

He walked toward his closed office door. A framed newspaper article hung on the back, revealing his photo appearing above a caption which read *Local Prayer Breakfast Recognizes Zorak As Top Conservative Political Operative*. The story described his belief a higher power guided his efforts to bring about a cultural renewal and a return to family values. He was most proud of the story.

Claude exited his office, striding with authority into the firm's large wood paneled conference room. He shook hands with the group of twelve silk-stocking types milling about the room. They were all white men between forty and sixty years old. Each one wore a tailored designer suit. The men took their highbacked leather seats.

Good turnout. All the major donor groups represented here in one room. That's the way you get things done.

"Thank you all for coming." Claude stood at the head of a long walnut conference table and opened the meeting. "I apologize for the early hour but it's the only way to avoid the press. Everyone knows why we're here so let's get started."

He pointed a remote control at the oversize video screen beside him. A map of the United States appeared with some states colored bright red and others colored blue.

"As you know, we slashed corporate taxes five years ago in these red states. Soon after, workers' wages stagnated, while their expenses for healthcare and housing shot up. Their financial picture looks grim. Our opponents are making hay over the low wages and lack of growth. It's a public relations nightmare."

Furrowed brows crossed the faces of the men at the table as they murmured uneasily.

"The stock market's at an all-time high, but state governments are broke," Claude continued. "We tell voters our experiment hasn't had enough time to work and they should be patient. But they've reached their breaking point. We have to act now."

A stern bald lobbyist jumped in. "There's only one thing to do. I say distract voters from the problem. We need a morals issue, something about sex, like gay marriage or abortion. That'll buy us more time. Meanwhile, our rich-as-Croesus clients do business as usual."

Claude winced and looked down at the table. He'd barely gotten started and couldn't even get to his main point before the first interruption. "Nice idea but overused. It doesn't work anymore. Younger voters, especially, think we're nuts for going after gays."

Claude opened his mouth to continue, but a pudgy, pasty face lobbyist at the far end of the table, beat him to the punch. "Let's play the patriotism card. We'll claim people who criticize us don't love America. That'll shut some of them up."

"That works better for promoting wars than corporate tax cuts." Claude's lips pursed, and he shoved his hands in his pockets. *That guy loves to wrap himself up in the flag.* "We need a more targeted response." *Doesn't he realize it looks bad to raise drug prices tenfold and then attack someone else for not caring about the country.*

An elegant looking lobbyist at the far end of the table leaned back in his chair. He looked over the top of his thick black rimmed glasses. "Let's accuse our opponents of engaging in class warfare. We'll say they're socialists who want to destroy the capitalist system. A damn bunch of Trotskys." His smug look revealed his bursting pride at coming up with this idea.

Claude drummed his fingertips on the table with an impatient air. *It smacked of cliché, weak... that type of thing only works at country club dinners now. He needed real solutions, not band aids.* "It has no traction on main street. You'll draw more attention to the gap between the ultra-rich and the poor."

"How 'bout if we blame welfare queens?" said a mustachioed lobbyist. It's a twofer - moochers and racism. Our base will chomp on it like red meat."

Claude's eyes rolled. *That'd be great except we already kicked the slackers off. Doesn't anyone remember the budget cuts? Does everybody here have amnesia?* "Remember, we reformed welfare several years ago. All that's left is the working poor."

A lobbyist with a thinning shock of pure white hair leaned forward with both elbows on the table. "Let's claim we haven't cut corporate taxes enough. That there's still more to cut. And if we starve the beast, we'll get real growth and jobs. It'll force our opponents to make unpopular spending cuts later. They'll get the fallout."

Claude's nose wrinkled. *Where've you been? We've been slashing corporate taxes for years. We already cut so much in one state the governor's approval rating tanked.* "The voters are tired of waiting for results. Telling them to be patient won't distract them at all. If anything, it makes them even angrier."

A grim lobbyist slammed his palm on the table. In a robotic monotone voice, he said, "Let's say our cuts encourage freedom and liberty."

Claude looked down his nose. *Yeah, right. It won't take voters two seconds to figure that one out.* "It'll take more than buzzwords to convince underpaid citizens to support us. It's shopworn."

The men argued strenuously back and forth for the better part of half an hour, over who and what to blame for their failures. One by one they were forced to admit their ideas all had fatal flaws. After they wore themselves out, an elderly lobbyist who hadn't yet spoken rose to his feet. "No, no. The answer's obvious... blame a minority group... undocumented immigrants. Racism always divides and conquers."

There were head nods and murmurs of approval all around the table.

Claude rubbed his hands together and licked his lips. *I should have suggested this from the start. Now we're getting somewhere.* "Amen. We'll do TV ads claiming immigrants take American jobs. Our radio shows will say they're criminals receiving billions in government benefits." He called for a vote on the new strategy and it passed unanimously. The group brainstormed anti-immigrant slogans and talking points to put the message out on the news networks.

Claude spread his palms on the table and grinned. "Gentlemen, we have our plan." He was all in on this one. Racism would supply the lifeline they needed.

They indulged in a round of celebratory drinks before Claude brought the meeting to a close. He had an appointment with Senator Hogue on a matter of the utmost importance, and he didn't dare be late.

CHAPTER 10

J oe and Gina stepped through Villa Firenze's side door entryway into a dark hallway. She led him straight to a large utility closet in the back. The residence's security system's yellow flashing lights lit up the space. A row of video monitors on the wall revealed live transmissions from each room in the house. Underneath the monitors sat three state-of-the-art black video recorders on a shelf.

"We've got to disable the video cameras before we do anything else," Gina whispered. She flipped open the cover of a small putty colored rectangular plastic box on the wall. The box' control panel contained a keypad, display screen, a red button and a green button. Her index finger punched the red button. causing the monitors to go dark. She glanced sideways at Joe. "We've got two hours before the cameras automatically turn back on."

"We'd better move fast, then." Joe set the timer on his phone.

Gina's eyes narrowed as Joe stared at his phone screen. "The police could be using your phone to track us," she said. "We've got to do something about that."

A worried look crossed his face. *If they can track me, I'd be like a sitting duck.* But, a moment later he stuck out his chest. "I can fix it. I'll turn my cell phone off and take the battery out. Then they can't track me." He pressed the phone's off button and tugged on its plastic back cover.

"Umm, that won't cut it." Gina eyed him curiously, a slight smirk spreading across her lips. "Smartphones have other power sources besides the main battery. Many have a non-removable battery controlling the memory. Your phone could still send a signal someone could track."

"Well, you're full of good news. What do you suggest?"

"I've got just the thing." She reached over and snatched the phone out of his hand. "Follow me."

She led him to the kitchen. Joe followed behind, shaking his head at how much he didn't know about phones. They walked past a shimmering kitchen island. She reached for a modern gray cupboard door's chrome handle, pulling a shiny stainless-steel martini shaker from the lower shelf.

"This is hardly the time for booze." Joe couldn't help but lift an eyebrow at her choice.

"I'm not mixing drinks." It was Gina's turn to roll her eyes, unaffected by his attempt at humor. Her head shook from side to side. "I'm using it like a Faraday cage. She slid his cell phone into the shaker and popped the lid closed.

"What the hell's that?"

"Cellphone transmissions are like radio signals. A Faraday cage is a steel shield stopping signals from anything placed inside. The steel martini shaker serves the same purpose. I'll show you."

She carried the vessel through the living area to the veranda above the Villa's grounds. Joe followed a couple steps behind. Gleaming starlight reflected off a rippling pond beneath the shadowy border of winter honeysuckle shrubs. The honeysuckle's lemony sherbet scent wafted through their nostrils like sweet perfume.

"Dial your cell phone number." She pulled out her phone, handing it to Joe. "Never mind why, just do it."

He hesitated before pressing the number into her phone. She held the martini shaker up to his ear.

There's no sound at all from my phone. "It worked." Joe's eyes twinkled, speculating on her clandestine activity origins. "Where did a law-abiding citizen like you learn this? Do you secretly work for the CIA?"

"Of course not." Gina shook with laughter. She grabbed a second martini shaker and dropped her phone in it. Her face turned serious after a moment, as the mention of law-abiding citizens reminded her why they were there. "The statue of blind justice is in the study. This way."

She led Joe down a narrow hall to a room resembling an old English style library with wood paneling and floor to ceiling bookshelves. In the center sat an antique oak desk where the Ambassador kept his personal papers. Nearby sat a sofa, and behind it a sofa table. She stepped to the window which looked out on the front driveway, peering through the curtain's narrow opening.

"Good news. The officers are still gone. They must have everything they want for now."

An eighteen-inch high bronze statue of Lady Justice sat on the sofa table all by itself. The blindfolded woman held a set of chain balance scales in one hand and a sword in the other. One scale floated a couple inches higher than the other.

Gina walked up to the statue to touch the blindfold. "She wears this to show she's impartial and won't bow to wealth or power. But, do you know why she holds a sword?

"To show justice is swift and final."

"Very good. Now, the clue said, 'The scales of justice must be balanced.' What do you suppose happens once they're even?"

Joe looked knowingly at her and pointed at the statue. "Do you want to do the honors?"

"Why not? No time like the present." She cocked her head to one side, her thumb shaking as she pushed down on the cold brass plate on the higher of the two scales. The scale moved downward until it hung level with its opposite counterpart. A sharp metallic click sounded behind them.

What was that? Joe turned his head slightly toward the sound's direction. A section of the wall's built-in bookshelves swung open on hinges like a door, revealing a secret passageway in the wall. He stood frozen in his tracks.

"My God, I've never seen that entrance before." Gina covered her mouth with one hand. "Antonio never mentioned it."

Joe walked over to the opening, leaning in to examine the dark space behind it. "Your ex certainly had a flair for the dramatic."

He felt for a light switch on the wall inside the doorway and flipped it on. The exposed incandescent ceiling bulb lit up like a beacon illuminating the interior. The space wasn't much bigger than a long walk-in closet. But it allowed enough room for a landing and an iron spiral staircase leading downward.

There's no way I'm staying here. I'm going down to see where it goes. He started down the stairs.

"Wait." Gina recoiled. "We don't know what's down there. It may not be safe."

Joe signaled her to follow him. "We've come this far, we can't stop now."

CHAPTER 11

Joe held on tight to the metal banister, descending the narrow staircase step by step. Gina followed a couple steps behind. At the bottom they found a comfortable carpeted windowless room with a sofa and two stuffed chairs on one side. Bookshelves and a dark-brown sofa table and stood nearby. A handful of framed paintings adorned the walls.

Looks like a comfortable place to read a book on a rainy day.

The sofa table supported a gray marble bust of two ancient Roman men in togas standing next to each other behind a podium. The first man had his arm around the other's shoulder. The second man's hand lay atop the first man's hand, which held a document.

Joe walked over to the bust, leaned over and studied the two figures. *I recognize these individuals. This explains a lot.* "Your ex had fascinating taste in art. Do you know who these two men are?'

"No, I've never seen them before." Gina shook her head.

"They're the Brothers Gracchus."

"The Brothers who?" Gina's mouth opened into a perfect 'o.'

Joe walked over to the sofa table and put his hand on the bust. "Tiberius and Gaius Gracchus. They were Tribunes, popular Roman Republic leaders, champions of the common people. The John and Robert Kennedy of their day. They lived more than a century before Christ."

"If they were so popular why haven't I heard of them?"

"You've heard of Machiavelli's famous book *The Prince*?"

"Of course, who hasn't?" She shrugged. "Everybody read it in college."

"Machiavelli described the Gracchus Brothers in his other famous book, *The Discourses*. If your ex had this bust, he probably owned a copy of that book, too." Joe scanned the bookshelves until his eyes landed on a thick volume wedged between the other tomes. *Ahh... that's it.* "He had a copy right here." He reached up to the top shelf, pulling out an old volume and laying it open on the table. The leather cover was dry and dusty, as if the book had been subjected to the desert air. The cover had a tear, creating a slit at the bottom. *The text is in the original Renaissance Italian. This copy must be several hundred years old... I wonder where he got it.*

"Antonio mentioned *The Discourses*, a couple of times... always in the context of his fraternal group. They met in various places in Europe. He said they were old buddies from school."

Old buddies indeed. If only she knew. Joe shook his head as he explained. "Ancient Rome's controlling aristocracy sent its soldiers to fight wars and conquer foreign lands, promising the soldiers ownership of the captured real estate. But Rome paid their soldiers a pittance in wages, so they had to borrow money to survive. Soon after, those greedy aristocrats foreclosed on the soldiers' debt, took their captured farms and evicted them. The aristocracy then owned almost all the land."

"That's evil. Did anyone try to stop them?"

"The Gracchus Brothers. They proposed Agrarian Laws, ordering the aristocracy to return the stolen lands to the impoverished soldiers."

"Did it work?"

"Almost. But Rome's conquests had gained control of the world's silver mines. And the generals brought back wagonloads of foreign gold coins. Rome's aristocracy became wealthy beyond their dreams."

Gina folded her arms. "Let me guess. The aristocracy used the money to bribe politicians, so those with enormous-wealth could keep the soldiers' lands."

That's exactly what they did. But they didn't stop there. "After they got the land, the aristocracy incited an angry mob to beat Tiberius Gracchus with clubs and stones until he died. They threw his body in the Tiber River. Later, the aristocrat's mob plotted to assassinate his younger brother Gaius, who committed suicide before they could get him. After his death, they reversed the Agrarian laws."

"Don't tell me… Once Rome had become corrupt, the people were easy prey for a demagogue."

That's not the half of it. "The aristocrats' greed fatally wounded the Republic," Joe said. "A few decades later, Julius Caesar claimed he could solve all the people's problems, proclaiming himself dictator for life."

"That signaled the Republic's end and the Empire's beginning."

An Empire led by a series of tyrants. Joe's eyes drifted to an old print on the wall, of a woman, her children and her friend, all dressed in ancient Roman attire. He stepped closer to get a better look as his brow creased. "Oh my God. I haven't seen that image in years."

"What is it?" Gina asked.

"That's the Gracchus Brothers' mom, Cornelia, in the center. The print is titled *Mother of the Gracchi, Pointing to her Children as Her Treasures.*

"I've heard about her. The Republic erected a marble statue in her honor. Cornelia's father, Scipio the Great was the greatest military general of all time. He defeated Hannibal for Rome. Her mother was the daughter of a Roman Consul. After Cornelia became a widow, even Egypt's King Ptolemy proposed marriage to her. She turned him down."

She wore simple dresses and no jewelry," Joe said. "Very strange for an affluent Roman woman of almost royal status. Her friends questioned her lack of adornment. But she believed that she didn't need jewelry, because her sons' outstanding character was all the enhancement she needed. They learned their values from her."

"No wonder her sons were great men." Gina stared at the Gracchus Brothers bust as if she were imagining how prosperous life in Rome would have been for the average citizen had the brothers succeeded in enacting their reforms.

"If they'd lived, they might have saved the Republic. But, after they died, the income gap grew, the Republic ended, and the dictatorial Empire began. Six years after the last brother died, the infamous Marcus Crassus was born. That set the stage."

"I've heard of Crassus," Gina said. "He was the Roman army commander who defeated Spartacus and the slave revolt. He banished political enemies, buying their property cheap and making him the wealthiest man in Rome. He turned the Republic into the Empire."

"At the time, one-third of Italy's people were slaves, hired by the greedy aristocrats to work the farms they took from the soldiers. The slaves got fed up and revolted."

"And Crassus slaughtered them."

"But slaves weren't the only ones hurt. As the ultra-rich got richer and the poor became poorer, citizens spent all their time working to earn a living."

Joe put his hand on the Brothers Gracchus bust. "I think your ex's group was more than social. It was the Gracchus League, an ancient organization that opposed tyrants. Members were very secretive out of necessity. Some powerful plutocrats would stop at nothing to eliminate them."

"You think Antonio belonged to it?"

At this point, I would bet the house on it. "The Gracchus bust, Cornelia's print and the *Discourses* book are compelling evidence of it."

"We were married for years and he never told me." Tears showed in Gina's eyes as she stared at the statue. "Now he's gone forever. You think you know someone…." Her voice trailed off.

"He couldn't tell you, for his own safety." *To say nothing of your own.*

Gina straightened her back, wiping away a tear. "We didn't come here to talk history, we came to solve murders."

Joe's nodded and started rifling through the other books on the shelves. "Keep looking for the next clue. It's gotta be here somewhere."

Gina closed the cover on the book and took a step back. Her gaze fell on a painting of New York's St. Patrick's Cathedral hanging on the wall behind the Gracchus bust. Her lips tightened. "I've never seen this painting before. It seems totally out of place in this room. Maybe there's something on the back that explains where he got it."

She pulled out on the oak frame's side to examine the painting's backside. To her surprise, the picture wasn't hung on the wall from hooks. Instead it swung out from the wall like a cupboard door, on two hinges attached to its side. Behind the painting lurked an even bigger surprise, a 15-inch square pewter gray wall safe with digital keypad. "Look what I found."

CHAPTER 12

Gina stood in Villa Firenze's secret room, eyeing the gray wall safe behind the painting swung to the side. "I never expected this."

Joe walked over to the safe and studied its digital phone style keypad up close. *This is a huge development.* "Hmmm. What do you 'spose he's got in there?"

"I'm almost afraid to find out."

"It's a risk we have to take. Any guesses about the combination?"

"I haven't the foggiest." She shook her head.

Hmmm. Joe stroked his chin. *The Ambassador wouldn't have led us this far without providing a way to open it.* "It's got to be something we'd know about after making it to this point. Maybe the combination is Firenze."

"That's too obvious. Any thief could come up with it."

"How 'bout Machiavelli?" Joe picked up the copy of the *Discourses*.

"Too long and too well known." Gina's eyes wandered around the room until they stopped at the sofa table. "Maybe the combination's in plain sight."

"Whadda you mean 'in plain sight'... you lost me.?"

She walked over to the marble bust and placed her hand on its top. "What if it's Gracchus?"

"No... it couldn't be." Joe's mouth fell open. *That would be too perfect.*

The name wasn't on the bust. It would only be obvious to someone who cared enough to study the past.

"Antonio sent me your photo, so I'd bring you here. He knew you'd know the Brothers' story. It all fits."

Joe pointed at the safe's keypad, raising an eyebrow. "You want to do the honors?"

"Here goes." Gina stepped up to the safe, using her index finger to punch eight letters on the keypad, G-R-A-C-C-H-U-S, one by one. Two seconds later they heard a 'clunk' sound as the safe's round lock bolts receded. Its thick steel door popped open.

"You're a genius."

Gina reached one hand inside the safe and pulled out a computer thumb drive. She held it up, waving it in triumph. "Let's see what's on this. There's a laptop upstairs on the desk."

They trekked back up the spiral stairway and out through the bookshelf door into the Ambassador's office. Gina plugged the thumb drive into the laptop's USB port. She clicked the mouse and the file's contents opened on the screen.

Joe watched the monitor over her shoulder as Antonio's curriculum vitae, or resume, flashed into view. A shadow crossed his face. *That's not a clue, it's career advancement information.* "This is a dead end. There's no message here."

"There has to be. Why else would he lock it in the safe with that combination?"

"Maybe the message isn't the resume's words. Maybe it's specific letters. All we'd have to do is find those letters and string them together."

"Like using every third letter to form a sentence." Gina slapped her forehead.

"Exactly, cryptography."

They tried various combinations of letters, every other letter, every third letter, every fourth letter and so on. None of their methods created anything but gibberish.

"This isn't working, there has to be another way," she said.

"There's something else we haven't tried. The Ambassador could have marked selected letters in a slightly different font."

Joe highlighted the first sentence on the page. All words were twelve-point type size and style. He clicked on the word processor's program's advanced find command, selecting twelve-point font from the options. The laptop zipped line by line through the text until it highlighted all the letters except twenty-nine.

"Those un-highlighted letters are one-half point smaller type size." Joe pointed at the screen. "The naked eye can't tell the difference."

"Incredible. A casual observer would never guess the resume contained a secret message."

You can't intercept a secret message if you don't know it exists. "It's called steganography, concealing a message within something else."

"That's ingenious." Gina typed the smaller type size letters in the order they appeared in the resume, spelling out a phrase.

Search Where Machiavelli Was Judged

"I don't get it," Gina said, her forehead wrinkling. "Where was he judged?"

"Machiavelli's trial took place in the Palazzo Vecchio, Florence's capitol building."

"That can't be it, Antonio hasn't been there in years. This could be a dead end."

Florence sat on the other side of the Atlantic. If Antonio planted the secret somewhere, it had to be close by. "Maybe the clue doesn't mean the actual Palazzo Vecchio."

"You mean, like a replica?"

The word 'replica' hit Joe like a bolt of lightning. He stood straight up. *That's it.* "There's a Palazzo Vecchio replica in the Machiavelli-da Vinci exhibit."

"At the Arts and Industries Exhibition Hall?"

"Yeah. Your ex had unlimited access to the exhibit because Italy sponsored it." *He could have slipped the clue in there at any time. That had to be it.*

"Come on." Gina grabbed Joe's arm. "We've got to get there before the killers do. Antonio's Italian sports car's in the garage. We'll take it."

Joe yanked the thumb drive from the computer, sliding it into his jacket pocket. They grabbed the martini shakers containing their phones, rushed out of the study and headed for the garage.

CHAPTER 13

Outside the Villa Firenze estate's front gate, Tomas' partner Hans Berger sat in a black sports coupe parked on the street. On the car's dashboard, the Global Positioning System screen displayed a red icon showing Joe's smartphone location at the Ambassador's residence. The red icon moved down a hall to the kitchen, before it fluttered on Hans' screen and then disappeared. Hans tapped the GPS tracking monitor's refresh button three times, but the icon never came back.

Was Richmond still in the Ambassador's residence or had he slipped away? The Patron would not be happy if he'd eluded Hans. He fiddled with the buttons for twenty minutes in a futile attempt to bring back the signal. "Dammit." His open palm slammed against the dashboard in disgust at the same time as the mansion's front gate sprang open and a red Italian sports car burst out of the opening at high speed. The Italian sportscar's engine roared like a lion on the hunt. It resembled a red streak as it raced away from the entrance.

Hans' car engine gave a raspy yowl as it came to life and he gave chase. He switched on his hands-free phone, making a call to Tomas while he drove. "I've spotted them. Yeah, I know what to do. I gotta hang up now, they're moving fast."

The red sports car weaved through town, screeching to a stop in a parking lot near the local subway station.

"Why are you stopping here?" Joe asked. *I thought we were going to the Archives.*

"There's a huge protest march scheduled for the Capitol Mall today. Parking near the Exhibit Hall will be non-existent. Plus, this car's a neon sign. The police are looking for you and the less attention we attract, the better. We only needed it to get to this station."

They left the car, taking long-legged strides down the sidewalk toward the station entrance. Hans parked and got out of his auto, shadowing them from a distance. Nearby, a white mini-van on the street suddenly changed lanes in front of another vehicle, resulting in a blaring horn honked loud and long in protest.

Joe whipped around toward the blaring sound, spotting Hans with the gun in his hand. *Damn, these people are everywhere… we can't shake em.* He nudged Gina. "It's one of them, we've got to run, NOW."

They dashed for the subway entrance a mere ten yards away. Hans dropped to one knee, aimed his gun at them and his finger pulled the trigger.

"Ziiippppp!" a bullet whizzed by Joe's head.

Hans took another shot. The second bullet ricocheted off the station's concrete wall with a high-pitched ping. Joe and Gina ducked down into the dark subway station entrance, their footsteps clattering while they rushed down the concrete stairs. At the bottom, they reached a cavernous subway platform with steel turnstiles arms gleaming like silver wands. They jumped over the turnstiles and ran to the concrete platform's next to a subway track pit. The pit held two sets of tracks. On the tracks' opposite side sat another platform and more stairs going up to street level.

The subterranean station smelled like a combination of musty condensation and burnt copper cables. Commuters stood on the platform, waiting to go into work. A loud rumbling sound warned that a subway train headed down the tunnel toward the station. The oncoming train's light looked like a small beacon. Its light pierced the center of the tunnel's circular blackness, growing larger with every passing second.

In a few seconds, it will cross the pit and cut off our only means of escape. We've gotta act now. Joe jumped down into the subway pit, motioning with one hand for Gina to follow him.

"What are you doing?" she shrieked over the oncoming locomotive's noise.

"The gunman'll be here any second. We've gotta be on the other side of the train, away from him. It's our only chance."

Gina hopped off the platform, landing next to him near the first set of tracks. A half-dozen commuters on the platform yelled at Joe and Gina to get back on the platform because the train was coming. Joe motioned her to follow him to the pit's opposite side. She stepped on the second set of tracks, her shoe slipping on its rail causing her to fall on one knee. The bright yellow train light sped down the tunnel toward her.

She screamed, "Joe… help."

He spun around to see what was wrong. She clutched her knee with both hands and struggled to get up off the rail.

"Lean on me. I'll help you stand up." Joe kneeled and bent his arm to hook it under Gina's armpit.

Hans had run down the subway stairs in time to spot Gina down on track two. He drew his gun and crept toward the platform's edge closer to his newly hobbled prey. A couple commuters spotted him and screamed, "Gun, Gun." The frightened commuters stampeded off the subway platform, back past the turnstiles and up the stairs to daylight, leaving behind only Joe, Gina and Hans.

At that moment, the train reached the station, travelling through on the first set of tracks between Hans and his prey. The powerful locomotive pushed the air hard against Joe and Gina on track two.

The roar's deafening, I can't hear a damn thing.

The train cut off Han's path. There was no way for him to cross track one while the train moved by in front of him. He clenched his fists, pacing back and forth on the now deserted platform. He'd missed her by mere seconds.

Joe caught a glimpse of Hans in the gaps between the train cars. *It must frost him we're only a few feet away, and yet out of his reach.*

Gina leaned on Joe as she hobbled off the second track. They limped their way to the pit's opposite side where he boosted her up to the vacant platform.

The speeding train's end appeared in the distance. Hans raced down the first platform toward the last car. When it passed, he jumped down off the platform into the pit behind the car, stepping across track one onto track two, hoping to get Gina. But, when he looked at track two, she had disappeared. Wrinkles of surprise appeared on his forehead. The sudden honk of a new train on track two startled him. It came out of the tunnel into the station from the opposite direction, hidden from his line of sight by the first train. The engine smashed into him, knocking him sideways to the pit's floor with a thud. The second train's roar grew softer. Its lights disappeared down the tunnel.

Joe and Gina stepped out from behind two brown and white pylons on the opposite subway platform, surveying the scene. Joe put his hands on his knees. His head bobbed up and down while he took deep breaths.

Gina bent over to gasp for breath, staring at the tracks. "That was way too close."

"You scrambled up the platform pretty quick."

"All those youth gymnastics lessons finally paid off." Her eyes twinkled.

They turned their attention to where Hans' broken bloody body lay motionless in the pit near track two. His gun lay three few feet away from his open hand. Gina's arm covered her face to hide the hideous spectacle. Seconds earlier, the place on track two where she had fallen lay underneath twenty tons of rushing steel train cars.

The train engineer didn't realize his train hit Hans, because he didn't stop. No one but us even knows it happened. Joe lifted his head toward Gina as he deadpanned, "I think I'll take the bus next time."

They climbed back down into the pit to check Hans' pulse, but found none. He was already dead.

Gina shoved a hand into Hans' pocket, pulling out his wallet and reading his I.D. "His name's Hans Berger, a former military officer." She pulled out a folded white piece of handwritten notepad paper from inside the wallet. "He wrote today's date, your name, and the name Oscar White, with a note saying he's an employee at the National Archives." Gina looked up from the page to study Joe. "Hans intended to kill both you and Mr. White today."

Who the hell is he? Haven't these monsters killed enough? "We've got to find Mr. White, if he's still alive. Maybe he knows why Hans wanted to kill us."

They pushed Hans' body up to the platform. "Let's move him out of sight. There's an elevator near the stairs… we can put him in there."

Gina held open the station elevator's door while Joe put his hands under Hans' armpits, dragging his body inside the cab. He removed Han's hard soled shoe and belt. His hand gripped the shoe, slapping the heel against the light fixture. The bulb broke and darkness cloaked the cab. He pressed the closed button, stepping out of the elevator as the brushed steel sliding doors came together. Joe's heel jammed Hans' metal buckle into the middle of the elevator door's bottom sill. The trapped buckle froze the doors a mere one inch apart. *Nobody's gonna get these doors open without a crowbar, now. That'll buy us some time while they try to find out who's in there.*

An approaching train's rumble caught their attention.

Joe looked up. "There's our ride. Let's get the hell out of here before the police arrive."

They raced to the platform's edge, the train stopped, and they stepped through its doors. Gina plopped down on a blue fiberglass bench in the empty car and Joe joined her.

"This is insane." She threw up her hands. "Why would a former military officer want to kill us?"

"There's only one way to find out. We've gotta postpone our Palazzo Vecchio scale model visit and go see Oscar White at the National Archives."

Gina whipped out her phone, checking the subway schedule for their new destination. They had no time to lose.

CHAPTER 14

Agent Davis Back was back at his FBI office still trying to finish up for the day. He glanced at his watch. *7:00 a.m., Am I ever going to get home?* Gina's photo sat on one corner of his desk when Josh walked in and spotted it.

"Her photo really piqued your interest, huh, sir?" Josh said.

Davis raised his hand like he wanted to slap him. He opened his mouth to scold Josh for his teasing, but before he could get the words out his cell phone rang.

"Oh, hell, what now?" He put the cell phone up to his ear and glowered. "Davis, here. Yeah, Uh huh." His eyes grew big. "You're kidding... three? My God. We'll be right there."

"What is it?"

"Lord, something I haven't seen in a long time." His face grew somber as he stared out the window at the manicured Embassy grounds, lit by floodlights. "They found two victims in the Smithsonian Castle and another one outside on the pavement. Metro homicide thinks there's a link between those three and the two at the Embassy." *If they're right, there may be more.*

He yelled over at another agent outside his office. "I'm outa here, we've got multiple homicides at the Castle." He aggressively ran his fingers through his hair. "Josh, have somebody find out why the Ambassador went to New York. I want a report back on it you yesterday."

A short while later his dark blue squad car screeched to a halt on the dark street near the Smithsonian Castle's North entrance. The car's revolving blue and red emergency lights flashed on the castle's red stone like an overactive disco strobe. His expression hardened as he and Josh strode up the Castle's front steps past yellow police tape tied across the murder scene's perimeter. Uniformed law enforcement officers stretched tape measures over the scene, scrawling dimensions in small blue booklets. White chalk on the concrete outlined Axel's bloody body with a ghost-like image.

Davis approached the rotund U.S. Park Police officer in charge of the scene. "What's the situation, Sarge?"

"We've got a victim who apparently fell, or was pushed, from the North Tower. He landed hard on the pavement and died."

Davis tilted his head back to gaze straight up at the top of the 145 feet tall tower. *Fell? Pushed? Whoa, that's a hell of a drop.* It stood like a cold and forbidding obelisk against the midnight blue sky and stars. They seemed to spin slowly in a circle as his body swayed in response. He slapped his palm against the stone pillar portico in front of the building, to steady himself. His gaze lowered to ground level while he turned toward the victim. *He probably bounced when he hit the concrete.*

"Who is he?" Davis grimaced at the bloody mess as he balanced on the balls of his feet and kneeled next to the body.

"Name's Axel Muller. Former soldier and muscle for hire. Worked in security for a couple major financial brokerage firms. He's been questioned a few times about violent crimes but nothing stuck. He's clean. Has no known current employer but that's not unusual in his line of work."

"Why's that?" Davis, still on bended knees, tilted his head, looking up from underneath his knitted eyebrows at the officer.

"Some firms like to keep the names of certain security personnel a secret." The Sergeant stuck out his stocky chest a little, obviously proud he understood something the FBI didn't. "In case they need them to perform some, umm... hostile act on a competitor." When Davis frowned at him, he added by way of explanation. "My first assignment was in New York."

I knew there was a reason I disliked Wall Street. Davis stood up from his crouched position. "What the hell was he doing on top of the tower?"

"We haven't figured that out yet, but the roof has marks indicating a scuffle."

"Did security video show what happened before he fell?"

"That's the problem," the Sergeant said. "Somebody disabled the surveillance system. Whoever did it, knew what they were doing 'cause it's controlled by a secure network."

"This must be a professional hit. The Ambassador's was too." Davis locked his fingers together while he stretched his arms out in front of him.

"Dispatch thought they might be connected."

Dispatch is right. This was ugly. Two bodies at the Embassy and five here at the Castle. Seven victims so far. "Where are the rest of the bodies? The call we received said there were five here."

"Yep. Two other victims in a single department on the second floor."

"Who are they?" Davis lifted an eyebrow. This had fast become the busiest night he could remember for homicides in D.C.

"The two were Consortia Department staff. They're top researchers, work at the Smithsonian."

Researchers huh? That didn't fit the normal profile of homicide victims. Something highly unusual had struck that night. Davis turned and spit on the grass near the sidewalk. "Who ever heard of such a thing? The way this night's going nothing would surprise me."

"Well prepare for one more surprise, sir." The Sergeant slapped his gun in its hip holster as he swaggered pretentiously toward the body.

"What's that?" Davis raised one eyebrow.

"A Natural History Museum security guard was found dead at the bottom of a first-floor stairwell. And, someone turned the security video surveillance equipment off there, too."

"Jesus has this city gone mad?" Davis shook his head from side to side. "Does the killer have a thing for tourist sights? What kinda psycho goes from the Embassy to the Castle to the Natural History Museum killing people?"

"A very determined one, with a nine-millimeter handgun."

"Let's go look inside." Davis put his hand on the Sargent's shoulder.

The two law enforcement officers walked away from the body and entered through the Castle's North entry door. They went up to the second-floor Consortia department where they crossed over more yellow police tape. Barbara's motionless body lay next to the receptionist's desk, surrounded by chalk markings. They stepped around her on their way to the suite's back offices. The other dead employees still lay in the spots where they'd been killed. Other investigators made notes near the bodies.

"This is crazy." Josh stood next to Davis and lowered his voice, so the others couldn't hear. "What do you make of it?"

"Hell, if I know." Davis' expression hardened. "We're dealing with a devil the likes of which this town hasn't experienced before. And D.C.'s had a lot of experience."

"I have a creepy feeling this isn't the end of it."

"Pay attention to your hunches." Davis said. *They're the difference between life and death in this business.* "What about the building's security records? Who came in and out?"

"This is where it gets interesting." Josh's eyes lit up. "The Ambassador's ex-wife entered the building shortly before the murders. So, did the man who fell to the pavement outside. It can't be a coincidence."

Now, there was a twist you didn't see every day... the deceased's ex-wife visiting the scene of another multiple murder, the same day as her ex's murder. "Jesus, what was she doing here?"

"Don't know." Josh said. "Richmond's the only department member who's still alive and might know the answer."

"Where's he now?"

"Skipped out. He's nowhere to be found."

"Damn, we can't catch a break. Does he have a record?"

"Nope, he's clean."

Sounds like he may be our most important lead. "Get me his background profile."

"We've already read it." Josh said. "It's unremarkable, except for one thing. According to an old newspaper article, he's got acrophobia."

"Afraid of heights? Why would a newspaper print that?"

"The paper said at age ten he went on a boy-scout troop hike on a high Rocky Mountain trail. Part of the path gave way. He slid down to a narrow rock ledge with a sheer drop below. A thunderstorm moved in and trapped him for hours on the wet ledge. The emergency climbing team rescued him well after dark."

"What a helluva thing to happen to a kid." Davis shook his head at the image of a child huddled on a dark mountain ledge.

"He's afraid of heights ever since."

Davis, Josh and another young agent named Ethan hustled out of the Castle back to the squad car. They piled into the vehicle and flipped a U-turn to drive back to headquarters.

"Put out an APB on Richmond." Davis' brow furrowed. "Get a warrant, search his residence and tap his phone."

"Anything else?" Josh asked

"Find out if he ever met the Ambassador. I wanna know when and where."

"You think that's why his wife came here?"

"It's no coincidence. Richmond is somehow connected to the murders. If he's still alive, we need to talk to him." Davis let out a sigh. It was the only lead he had.

"You think he did it?"

"Who knows?" Davis stroked his chin. "Put in the APB that he's a person of interest in the murders of three victims at the Smithsonian Castle." Davis strode briskly out of the Consortia suite with Josh in tow.

Davis steered his squad car through traffic, laying on the horn occasionally. The three bloody victims' images at the Castle flashed through his mind as he drove. His team had worked on dozens of depressing homicides his over the years. *The work can drag you down if you don't find some way to reduce the sadness.*

His young agents dealt with tragedy day after day across the country. They saw innocent people who had been gunned down in the prime of life. These twenty-something guys were the best investigators he'd worked with in all his years on the force. They had a less formal way of doing things what with smart phones, Twitter, and Instagram. He needed their talent very badly right now on these multiple homicides.

Davis clenched his jaw and tightened his grip on the steering wheel. Frankly the whole job left a bad taste in his mouth. "We've got a lot to work on with these new murders."

The car's two-way radio buzzed, interrupting their conflict with a call from Dispatch. He pressed the audio button on the steering wheel. "Davis, here."

The female dispatcher's voice crackled over the speakers. "We've got another new homicide. They found the victim in the subway station a few blocks from the Ambassador's residence."

"We'll be there shortly," he said before signing off. "Guys, coffee break's gonna have to wait. We've gotta make another stop."

The car's interior became quiet and faces looked somber. Davis turned the squad car around and sped off toward the new crime scene.

CHAPTER 15

J oe and Gina trudged up the sidewalk toward The National Archives' Pennsylvania Avenue entrance. The Archives had just opened for business that morning. They approached a seated marble sculpture of an old man dressed in ancient Greek style robes, in front of the building. He held a scroll in one hand and a closed book in the other. The inscription on the sculpture's base instructed those passing by to study the past.

"That's the Past sculpture," Joe said. "It's one of four, one on each side of the building, called the Watchers and Defenders of Knowledge."

Behind the statue, 72 slender fluted columns each 53 feet high surrounded the Greek revival style temple. The main building resembled a giant rectangular concrete box with two 40 feet high thick bronze doors. They bypassed the front steps. Instead, they walked on to the smaller side research entrance, stepping inside.

Gina grabbed a color brochure off a visitor's stand, glancing at the cover, "The Archives is the headquarters for important United States Government records."

They took a moment to admire the expansive Rotunda where two huge wall murals stared down at them. The paintings depicted the founding fathers during creation of the Constitution and Declaration of Independence.

We hold these truths to be self-evident, that all men are created equal...

Joe's eyes welled up at the sight of the Declaration's signing.

Below the murals, sat glass display cases holding the Constitution, the Bill of Rights, the Declaration of Independence and an original of the Magna Carta.

"The Magna Carta... the Great Charter of Liberties." Gina whispered in his ear.

British rebels used it to challenge the 'Divine Right of Kings' to rule," he replied. "That's where the church endorsed the king and the king protected the church. Joe wanted to linger but decided against it. *I don't have time to be star struck, we came here to get answers.* He stepped up to the research receptionist's desk and handed her his business card. "Ms. Bocelli and I are here to see Oscar White on urgent business."

She peered over the top of her half-frame reading glasses, giving them a once over like she wasn't sure she believed them. But, for reasons that weren't apparent, she didn't question it further.

She buzzed Oscar's office, speaking into her headset, "You have two visitors, a Mr. Richmond from the Smithsonian and Ms. Bocelli. They say it's urgent." She paused to listen into the earpiece. "No, they didn't. They say they'll tell you personally." She hung up, looked back over her glasses at them and pointed a skinny finger toward the hallway. "Take the elevator to the second floor. Second door on the right."

They walked toward the elevator, passing a portrait of Benjamin Franklin wearing a colonial fashion grey suit and white shirt. Gina pointed at the painting. "You know, he warned Americans that they might not be able to keep their Republic. Democracy requires a lot of citizen effort."

"Franklin had studied the Renaissance." Joe said as he kept walking. "A de facto monarchy took over the Florence Republic 250 years before the American Revolution. He realized it could happen here."

They found their way to Oscar White's office suite and tapped the chrome colored bell on the vacant secretary's desk. A high pitched melodious 'dinggg...' rang out, piercing the silence. A nervous looking pale man with thick wire rim glasses strolled into the reception area. His bald head had tufts of hair on the sides resembling a child's fuzzy earmuffs.

"I'm Oscar White, can I help you?" His face displayed a forced a smile. They shook hands and he motioned them back to his office where he sat behind a light oak executive-style desk.

Joe and Gina sat down on two hardwood button leg guest chairs five feet away. On a nearby bookshelf sat a master's thesis titled the Great Depression and Nazi Germany, by Oscar White. A photo hung on the wall showing Oscar shaking hands with an official at the Franklin Roosevelt Presidential Library in Hyde Park. A plaque hung next to the photo, honoring Oscar for ten years of Archives service

"I hear you have a matter of some urgency," Oscar said in a high-pitched nasal voice. He stared at them over his glasses. His gaze moved first to Joe, then to Gina and then back to Joe again.

"We do." Joe took the lead. "Do you know a man named Hans Berger?"

Oscar paused, and his face seemed to turn a little paler, if possible. He looked down at one hand to examine his fingernails. "Why do you ask?" Hans' name had triggered a reaction.

"He tried to kill us today." Joe said. *This guy's playing coy, and not very well.* "We found this note on him." Joe spread Hans' paper down on the desk with both Joe's and Oscar's names scrawled across the page. "Your name's next on his hit list." Oscar stared wide-eyed at the writing.

"We hoped you might fill in the gaps," Gina said. "Tell us what you know." She described to him the chase in the subway tunnel, ending with how the train struck Hans and killed him. She folded her arms across her chest and stared him in the eye.

Oscar covered his mouth with his hand while he studied the paper. His hand trembled slightly. He looked up at Gina. "You're absolutely certain it was Hans Berger?"

She slapped Hans' plastic photo drivers' license I. D. down next to the page. "Yeah, he looked exactly like the photo."

"I'm familiar with Mr. Berger." Oscar's fingers fidgeted as he looked away to one side with an air of resignation. "He barged in here a few days ago trying to intimidate me into giving him access to a sealed record."

Now we're getting somewhere. "What do you mean intimidate you?" Joe asked.

"He said things would go better for me if I cooperated." Oscar leaned back in his chair and breathed a heavy sigh. "He casually mentioned my neighborhood and my family members, making a not-so veiled threat. Frankly, he scared me."

"What sealed records?" Joe lifted an eyebrow at the phrase. *Could it explain why Hans' tried to kill them*

"Rules are rules. I'm not at liberty to say." Oscar's prissy voice dripped with condescension as he pressed his fingertips together.

Oscar's hiding the killer's motivation behind bureaucratic red tape. The little weasel. Joe clenched his fist. "My God, man, you're next on Hans' list. He's not acting alone. He's got one badass associate who's no doubt looking for you as we speak. We're trying to help, but you've gotta tell us what you know."

"I can't tell you which records he was after, even if I wanted to." Oscar tapped the desktop with his fingertips. "I could get in serious trouble. Congress ordered them permanently sealed... they have been for decades." He appeared torn between the rules and his own self-preservation.

Times running out. I'll have to push Oscar harder. "Dammit, we don't have time to screw around and neither do you." Joe slammed his open hand palm down on the desk with a thump. The pens on Oscar's desk bounced half an inch above the desktop. "These people tried to kill us. They've already killed several others."

"All right. Calm down." Oscar swallowed a gulp. He looked around as if fearing he might be watched. Tiny beads of perspiration formed on his forehead. "Hans wanted The House Un-American Activities Committee records on *The Business Plot.*"

The Business Plot. Puzzled silence filled the room. *It sounded like some sort of corporate stock scheme. Had he heard Oscar correctly?* "Never heard of it." Joe's forehead creased while his head cocked to one side.

"I'll probably regret this but come with me. I'll show you." Oscar's shoulders slumped in resignation as he stood up from his desk, motioning with one hand for them to follow him.

They trailed him out of his office suite, down a long narrow hall to an old-fashioned charcoal gray vault door marked "Restricted Area". He unlocked the door with an electronic key card. It opened into a wide file room with sets of floor-to-ceiling steel storage shelves. Halfway down the second aisle, he stopped in front of a faded white cardboard file storage box. Stamped black stenciled letters read 'Permanently Sealed by Order of The House Committee on Un-American Activities.'

"What does 'sealed' mean?" Gina said.

"Sealing a record means it's unavailable to the public," Oscar said. "We store sealed files in a secure locked storage room that's separate from regular files."

"The seal looks broken," she pointed to the torn signet.

"Certain authorized staff have access to this room. I've viewed these files before… that's why."

That's interesting. He's admitting he broke the seal.

Oscar pulled out the box from the shelf, carrying it to a nearby putty colored table, and lifting its lid. A puff of dust from the box wafted into the air before disappearing. Inside were old reddish-brown expansion wallets with elastic cords holding protective flaps tightly around the wallets.

"These files have been sealed for over 80 years," he said. "The public's never seen them. They contain sworn testimony about a conspiracy to overthrow President Franklin Roosevelt and replace him with a de Facto dictator."

"I don't believe it," Joe said, shaking his head. *It sounded like something out of a movie. But still, the story intrigued him.*

Oscar removed the wallet, opening a faded manila file and laying its contents open on the table. He pointed to a weathered page. The typed title, *The Business Plot of 1934*, scrolled across the top in bold black ink on peach colored paper.

"The conspirators' names are typed on this page. Prominent witnesses implicated some of them."

"Why a coup?" Gina asked. "That's pretty drastic."

"They opposed Roosevelt's New Deal to help unemployed families." said Oscar. "The program required the aristocracy to pay higher taxes to help the poor. That's the last thing the conspirators wanted to do."

"The public needs to know this," Gina said. "Why did the Committee seal the files?"

"To protect the conspirators' names." Oscar's shoulders shrugged. "The public's right to know might sometimes takes a back seat to other interests."

Gina shook her head at the hypocrisy. "They must have had lots of political influence."

"A decorated general testified that a man claiming to represent backers with inconceivable-wealth, approached the general to lead a takeover," Oscar said. "The General claimed the agent told him the conspirators would fund the coup with millions of dollars."

"No one would attempt such an outrageous thing." Joe shook his head from side to side. *They'd be foolish to risk their riches that way. But what if a dictator really did take over the country?*

"The takeover would have stopped Roosevelt's program in its tracks," Oscar said. "With the power of the Presidency, men with wealth-beyond-compare could fight off attempts to tax their empires. An impoverished 1930s public would be too weak to oppose them."

And, they'd be able to grow even richer.

"I've heard about a lot of conspiracy theories," Gina said. "But never anything about *The Business Plot*."

"Conspiracy theorists have misled the public for a long time," Oscar said. "Those misguided souls are always claiming danger from one false bogeyman or another. But that only distracts the public from the real threat."

"So, where's your proof about the plot?" She frowned.

Oscar turned the page and pointed to a black and white photo in the file on the table. "It's right here."

CHAPTER 16

Conservative lobbyist Claude Zorak trotted up the white limestone steps toward the U.S. Capitol building's West Front doors. Below him, stretched out across the Capitol Mall, two million citizens gathered, the biggest crowd in Washington D.C.'s history. Young, old, black, white, middle-class and poor were all there. The throng reached from the Capitol steps past the Smithsonian Castle, all the way to the Washington monument. They shouted, "Kill the bill... Kill the bill."

He paused when he reached the top of the steps, looking back at the protesters. *That's a huge march. I hope the Senate's not intimidated by their numbers. We can't let the pitchfork and torches crowd stop us now. We're so close.*

The protesters opposed Congress' sweeping new proposal to abolish Social Security, Medicare, Medicaid, and the Healthcare Act. The bill would do it all in one fell swoop. The proposal's flip side used the savings to slash taxes. The House of Representatives had passed the measure on a party-line vote, sending it to the Senate for approval.

The people stood shoulder to shoulder outside the Capitol. Their ranks spilled beyond the mall's boundaries as they listened to speakers rail against this attempt to bomb the social safety net. The worried looks across their haggard faces said it all -- their way of life hung by a thread, and they knew it.

Claude scowled at their ranks as he approached the entrance. *You can protest all you want, but this baby's gonna be a done deal. We've waited years for this chance.* He had seen the cable news reports saying hardly a single person had left the march to seek a warmer location, despite many having chattering teeth and noses blue with cold. It was that important to the people.

Senator Hogue had said he had the votes to pass it on the first ballot. But first, the Senators had the right to speak their views about the measure.

Claude entered the Capitol, trotting up the building's wide marble interior stairs on his way to the Senate spectators' gallery. *I hope I'm not too late to catch the Senator's speech.* The schedule listed Hogue's oration as the first in favor of the bill. It would no doubt set the tone for the upcoming debate on the floor. Claude strode into the gallery's long balcony looming high above the Senate floor, extending around all four sides of the rectangular shaped chamber. A beautiful white oval ceiling sported a glass eagle image in the center, capping the magnificent room. The Washington press corps' world-weary members filled the several rows of visitor seats. Their pens and notepads at the ready.

Claude found a chair nearest the balcony rail. He glanced down at the Senate chamber. *Ah, I'm just in time.* Down on the floor, Senator Hogue started his impassioned speech. He stood behind a temporary wooden lectern on his desk, his arms flailing with the fervor of a tent-revival evangelist. The mahogany desks of one-hundred U.S. senators surrounded him in an arc against a backdrop of deep blue carpet. He had progressed a mere thirty seconds into his presentation, already hitting his stride. A slow southern drawl punctuated his speech even after twenty years in Washington. Its tone became nasal and high pitched when his excitement bubbled over, like today.

"I'm bullish on Wall Street." Hogue said as he raised a small statue of a virile golden bull in one hand. "Their stock brokerage houses are our job creators. This bill's tax cuts will spur unimaginable growth that will pay for itself many times over. This is American free enterprise."

Claude stifled a yawn. He'd heard this boilerplate speech so many times he could recite it in his sleep. He looked toward the Senate President's elevated desk where two grand marble pillars rose from the chamber's floor. He spied something more interesting than the Senator's speech. A shapely blonde clerk sat in one of several executive staff chairs behind the long dark marble dais.

I'd like to sample her dividends, Claude looked her up and down. Senator Hogue coughed in the middle of a sentence as if to scold Claude's roving eye. Claude stiffened, remembering why he was here. *Discipline Claude, discipline.* He forced himself to refocus on the Senator's speech.

Hogue's oration thundered on. "I remain eternally committed to the free market and robust competition. Competition that's been strangled by wasteful spending on a social safety net we can't afford. Strangled by entitlement programs that pull money from the private sector, stifling growth and killing jobs." Hogue scowled with resentment when he spoke that last phrase.

There wasn't much remarkable about this orator in his late fifties and of average height, other than he weighed almost 230 pounds. Hogue had been a handsome man in his younger days. He still had most of his white hair but had developed large bags under both eyes. His most distinctive feature was a double chin spilling out over his shirt collar's top. He dressed in a navy-blue suit, white shirt and red tie, to appear patriotic.

His hard-drinking late-night life sure showed. But it made him the wheeler-dealer politician lobbyists loved.

Hogue pounded the lectern with his fist in righteous indignation. "We must be vigilant against the dangers of government spending that would tax the life out of corporate America. We can no longer coerce our most successful businessmen to pay for welfare that destroys human dignity and incentive to work. It's time for Americans to do what they've always done, pull themselves up by their bootstraps. Government must learn to do more with less."

Claude drummed his fingers on his seat's armrest. *It'll play well to the base. But it'll be hard to persuade swing voters that people with no boots, should pull themselves up by their bootstraps. I need to have a little talk with him about revising that part.* The speech needed serious editing to appeal to centrists, at least partially. Claude found it irritating to watch. He'd given better speeches himself numerous times during his years of media experience.

Hogue held up a copy of the new bill and waived it above his head. "But we not only must reign in out-of-control spending... we must use public-private partnerships, instead of taxes, to finance highways, bridges, water systems, prisons and schools."

Claude looked down at the floor. Turning freeways into expensive toll roads owned by corporations would alienate a lot of their base, especially when the public saw how much profit it made for big corporations. Best to soft-peddle that proposal. That's something he would rather pass when no one is paying attention, not now. Appearances were everything. *I'll have to be subtle. Maybe get him to tone that down a bit. It won't do to tell him outright, he'd be offended.*

"The 'so-called experts' and the 'liberal elites' told me we can't make these cuts," Hogue continued. "Their answer to every problem is to spend more. Well, I say they're wrong. I say their tax and spend policies have accomplished nothing. I say this bill makes us stronger."

They were both on the same team, so Claude would go easy. He'd learned a long time ago to pick his battles with care. As the speech droned on, his attention drifted back to the intern.

A couple minutes later, Hogue shouted his fiery closing line. "The time has come to embrace limited government and unleash the potential of the private sector."

The noise roused Claude out of his snooze, his head jerked up. *How long did he talk? I thought he'd never stop.*

The Senator thanked his listeners, picked up his papers and ambled down the chamber aisle, shaking the hands of four colleagues who congratulated him on his forceful presentation. A new Senator took the podium to continue arguing in favor of the bill. Once Hogue finished glad-handing, he strode toward the chamber's exit.

Claude stood up from his seat in the gallery and hurried back down the stairs two at a time. He had an appointment to meet with Hogue in his Capitol office after the speech. They planned to discuss the Patron's major new project. He trotted through the empty hallway, heading toward the Dirksen Senate Office Building. *I've got to get there before he gets involved with a longwinded constituent... or God forbid, trapped in a phone call with a blustering campaign donor. If that happens, I'll be there all night.*

CHAPTER 17

Claude sped through the Capitol tunnel to the Dirksen Senate Office Building. Senator Hogue seemed a natural choice to push the Patron's agenda to cut social programs, while increasing tax cuts. His colleagues joked that Hogue had never met a fat-cat he didn't like. He had already repealed consumer protection legislation, environmental regulations and workplace safety rules. He cast the deciding vote to revoke antitrust laws prohibiting giant corporations from forming monopolies. He was a corporate lobbyist's delight.

One thing you could say about Hogue, once he was bought, he stayed bought.

Claude caught the elevator to the second floor and hurried down the noisy tiled hall. Up ahead, a black metal office door sign with gold lettering read 'Senator Benjamin Hogue.' Claude breathed a sigh of relief. *Ah, almost there.* He turned the brass doorknob, walked into the reception area and approached a trim young brunette seated behind a dark-oak L-shaped desk.

"I'm here for my appointment with the Senator."

"Oh yes, Mr. Zorak. You're expected. He's on the phone with Senator Legree about the Social Security bill, but I'll let him know you're here."

Damn, I barely missed him. Well, I guess I'll settle in for the duration. The reception area had a half-dozen comfortable leather chairs for visitors, of which only two were occupied. Claude sat down in one of the empties and grabbed a magazine. Photos showing the Senator jawboning with various prominent public officials, looked down from the walls at Claude as he read. Hogue's interoffice door behind the reception area was open about a foot. Through the doorway Claude caught a glimpse of the Senator leaning back in his high-backed chair behind his desk with the phone receiver against one ear.

After about fifteen minutes the receptionist smiled at Claude and said, "The Senator will see you now."

Claude got up from his seat and strode into the expansive office. The Senator's wide antique mahogany desk sat in front of a tall window decorated with dark velour curtains flanked by an American flag on a pole.

Hogue grunted, pushing his bulk up out of the plush chair and making his way around the desk to pump Claude's hand. "Always good to see ya, Claude. Have a chair, make yourself comfortable."

"Thanks, Senator. It's good of you to squeeze me into your schedule." Claude sat down on a yellow antique Queen Anne sofa near a blue marble fireplace opposite the desk. Its plush comfort matched its stylishness.

"No problem. You're always welcome here." The Senator shuffled back behind the desk, plopping his frame back down in the chair.

Claude's super PAC had been a major donor to Hogue's political campaigns for years. Claude's backers funded his PAC because they were eager to expand their political clout and in turn the PAC funneled the money to Hogue. Those huge campaign donations gave Claude easy access to the Senator. Hogue functioned as the point man for distributing instructions to other Senators. His numerous political contacts and salesmanship made him a natural at this job. ←

Hogue leaned way back in his chair, rocking back and forth while he touched the yellow flame of a silver plated lighter up to his huge cigar. "Didya catch my speech?"

"Matter of fact, I did. Uh, maybe we could talk about a couple of the phrases, sprinkle in a bit more populism"

The Senator's eyes narrowed when he heard Claude's response with its hint of criticism. "You didn't like it?"

I can't believe I have to pander to his fat ass and soften the critique, or he won't hear a word I say. Claude had managed big egos among politicians for years and knew what it took. "You gave a great speech. I wouldn't do more than tweak it around the edges."

Once Hogue heard the praise, his frown turned into a slim smile. "That's more like it." He offered a cigar to Claude, hollering out to the receptionist. "Close the door Maggie, I don't wanna be disturbed for a few minutes."

"Did you see the march on the mall, today?" Claude looked over his shoulder as the door swung shut. "I can't believe how many people showed up."

"Yeah, it's unfortunate." Hogue flicked his gray cigar ashes into an ornate porcelain ash tray. "They're really riled up this time. Things could get ugly."

Claude turned toward the Senator, leaning forward on the sofa and staring him right in the eye. "Did you get the President's private schedule?"

"It's right here." Hogue leaned his portly frame over one arm of the chair, reaching down and pulling a manila file out of his desk drawer. He stretched across the desk, sliding the file to Claude with a heave.

Claude pressed his hand down on the file before it could slide off the desk's edge, picked it up and thumbed through it. The President's weekly private schedule appeared vastly different from the public schedule released to the press. It comprised his actual schedule and the only one that mattered. It remained so secret the President's aides had instructions to destroy it in "burn bags" after each day. Every page had a printed warning to mark its high-level of secrecy.

"Did the Patron say why he wanted it?"

Claude shook his head side to side and his face paled. *The Patron asked me to pick up this top security level document I'm not even authorized to have.* His boss's clandestine ventures always worried him, but the Patron called the shots and Claude always obeyed. He was a true believer in their cause. *The ends justified the means.*

"That's smart. You're better off that way." Hogue turned his head sideways to stare out the window, blowing a large smoke ring from his cigar. He waited for the ring to disintegrate before speaking his mind. "You know, we still need one more vote to defeat the Wall Street regulation bill."

"Who's the holdout?"

"Senator Love. You know... the senior Senator from the state of denial."

Claude made sure to chuckle at Hogue's old joke as if he'd heard it for the first time. "You predicted this." Love had been a thorn in their side since the day the voters elected him, and he began playing the part of the self-righteous gadfly. Nobody liked him. "What's his objection this time?"

"He thinks we haven't done enough to protect Americans from the threat of homosexuals. He's scared to death some baker's gonna have to make a gay wedding cake."

"Surely he understands that killing the Wall Street regulation bill is ten times more important."

"The man won't listen to reason." The Senator shook his head from side to side. "Doesn't have his priorities straight. How does he expect us to run Congress when he can't keep his own people in line?"

"I think I've got the solution."

"What do you mean?" Hogue leaned forward in his chair, lowering his voice.

"It wasn't easy." Claude smirked while reaching into his briefcase. "I've been working on it ever since he screwed us over on the banking bill." Claude spread out three glossy 8" x 10" photos on the desk. "They're juicy."

"Oh my." Hogue's eyes grew large as he picked up one of the photos and studied it. His back straightened.

CHAPTER 18

Senator Hogue's expression showed he could hardly believe his good fortune. Claude's photos displayed Senator Love undressed in a four-poster bed with an attractive looking young woman a couple of decades his junior. Most important of all, she was not his wife. He reveled in the throes of passion and from the look on his face he had a wonderful time.

Hogue took a sudden deep breath while he laid the photo back down on the desk. "When were these taken?"

"About a week ago… in the woman's apartment. I had a pro plant cameras and microphones on the premises."

Hogue beamed. He rubbed his hands together, spreading them palms down on the desk. "I think we just got Senator Love's vote to kill Wall Street regulation." He paused for effect and winked. "Even if he doesn't know it yet."

"How will you approach him?"

Hogue had a twinkle in his eye as he held up one finger. "First, I'll arrange to have lunch with him in at a private dining room at my club near the Capitol Building. I'll ask him about his family and how they're doing. We'll discuss what's new in his district, the normal political small talk."

"That's good. That's good." Claude relished the delicious feeling of conspiracy

"I'll casually mention to him there's a nasty rumor going around the Capitol. I'll say it's reached my ears he and a young attractive woman have been seen together." The Senator glared and shook his head as if warning his victim. "Naturally I'll tell him with election season coming up we can't have even the hint of a scandal. He'll deny the rumor. He'll claim his liberal political opponents started it, that there's no basis to it whatsoever."

Claude grinned. "To be sure. How could it possibly be otherwise?" *Never underestimate Senator Love's self-righteousness.*

"I'll look him right in the eye and say I've even heard there are photographs floating around. And they supposedly show he and the young woman in embarrassing situations. At that point, there'll be a long awkward pause as he tries to figure out how much I really know. If he has a brain in his head, he'll wonder whether I already have a copy."

Claude raised both eyebrows in mock surprise. "Surely, he'll realize you do."

"To keep him off balance, I'll say 'enough talk about personal matters.' We'll discuss current Senate business. I'll bring up the fact I'm having difficulty getting the final vote to kill the Wall Street consumer protection bill."

"Strike while the iron's hot." Claude nodded his approval.

"About that time, he'll be studying me carefully for any clue how many cards I hold to play. I'll tell him we really need his vote and I hope he'll reconsider his position."

I'm in the presence of true political genius. Claude's eyes sparked with excitement. He'd never seen anyone come up with such a clever scheme on the spot. "This sounds really good."

"He'll complain last session we traded away his anti-abortion bill for votes to let Wall Street do commercial banking. Some of his supporters are still livid about it."

"He's right. They're really upset." Claude shrugged his shoulders. He remembered the shouting and gnashing of teeth following the bill's failure. The accusations and blame had spewed hot and heavy. And it was by no means the first time Hogue's group had traded away Love's constituency's causes, to pass bills for Hogue's richest donors. It had become a Congressional ritual.

"He'll mutter he needs me to corral votes for him on the religious freedom bill. He'll say he needs that before he signs on to kill the Wall

Street regulations."

"Why wouldn't he."

The Senator winked. "I'll tell him we'll try to tackle his bill later in the session, but I can't right now. I'll say I've heard the photos depict the young woman's apartment and boudoir in detail. I'll describe the scene to him. As an old friend, I'll tell him I'd like to protect his reputation."

Claude chuckled. "Well, of course, as an old friend." He envisioned Hogue putting his hand on Senator Love's shoulder in pretend sympathy, while Hogue's eyes displayed practiced concern. It gave new meaning to the phrase 'knifed in the back.'

"At that point, he'll have a nervous expression on his face. I'll ask him directly for his vote on the Wall Street bill and he'll reluctantly agree to it. We'll finish our dessert and head our separate ways. I'll bet I don't even have to show him the photographs."

"You're a master." Claude shook his head in wonder. "Nobody does it better." *Our donors are lucky we've got this guy.*

"Why thank you Claude." The Senator looked up at the ceiling with an angelic expression on his face. "One tries." He took another big puff on his cigar.

Claude paused while Hogue basked in the moment. H*e had the perfect acting skills to carry it off, honed over years of practice.* "Now, let's talk about the big picture," Claude said. "We've got some upcoming re-election races… it's possible we could lose control of Congress."

"I know, I know." Hogue stood up. He paced back and forth with hands together behind his back. "We can't afford to lose this time, if we do it's not only our hides, it's our sponsors and the whole tax cut plan. Immigration means our days in office are numbered. We don't have the votes anymore."

"There's still hope. We can make it harder for our opponents to vote by gerrymandering more of their districts. It'll buy us some time." *But if the courts overturn our efforts… it's all over.*

"It's not only immigrants that worry me," the Senator said. "Sometimes we're our own worst enemy. Our sides got too many loose cannons who don't know when to shut up. Senator Love keeps shootin his mouth off about immigration reform like it's the great Satan. It's amnesty this and amnesty that. Hell, he even runs campaign ads about deporting them."

Claude had trouble keeping eye contact after the mention of

immigration. Hogue had a point, Claude's think-tank's plan to blame immigrants would alienate a lot of independent voters, even while it shored up the base. He decided not to mention it.

Hogue slammed his open palm down on the desk for emphasis. "Don't they realize Hispanic voters have TVs, too? They can hear what we say about 'em, calling em' rapists and criminals. How the hell are we ever gonna get their votes after that?"

Claude shrugged his shoulders. "It's hard to stop candidates from saying what they think." *I'm sure glad I didn't admit my anti-immigrant propaganda effort to Hogue. His cooperation is too important to lose.*

The Senator exhaled sharply and moved on to his next pet peeve. "And there's another thing hurting us. We've got too many yahoos obsessed with strict regulations of women. They can't resist the urge."

"It's costing us votes." Claude nodded. "We've got to broaden our base to survive."

Hogue threw one hand up in the air. "Hell, we had a tough enough time getting women to vote for us after we opposed women's rights. Now some of our people claim women can't get pregnant from rape. We can't win elections if we lose half the population."

"From your mouth to God's ear, Senator." *Male candidates speaking about women's biology is a recipe for political disaster.*

"And we've gotta stop those damn bathroom bills." The Senator was on a roll now. "The late-night comedians are crucifying us and it's killing us in the polls. We look like creeps, checking people's gender in bathrooms."

"It's a thankless job if there ever was one." Claude gave a lackluster smile. *Ah, the infamous transgender bathroom bill. How'd we ever get sucked into that one?*

"We can't put a uniformed policeman in front of each restroom, with a magnifying glass to check people's private parts." Hogue buried his face in his hands, shaking his head back and forth. "It's a bad, bad joke. You can't win elections that way."

Claude chuckled, visualizing the ridiculous image in his mind. "We've gotta adapt. It's the only way we'll survive."

"Amen brother, share it."

The receptionist poked her head in the door. "I'm sorry to interrupt, Senator. But your next appointment is here."

Hogue slapped his hand against the desk top. "Oh, damn. I completely forgot. We'll have to continue this another time."

Claude took no offense as he had become used to dealing with politicians' tight schedules. He stood up from the sofa to shake Hogue's hand as he said goodbye. Claude hurried out of the office, heading back to the Capitol.

As he approached the Capitol's West Front doors to exit the building, he heard angry voices shouting in unison, "US Senators... take a stand... save the safety net, we demand!" Their incantation reverberated within the building. The floor seemed to shake from the noise. His quick glance out the window confirmed the huge rally crowd still flooded the Mall, protesting destruction of Social Security, Medicare and other programs.

He decided to avoid the throng, instead slipping out a side exit to get his car. His right hand clutched the President's schedule, his left fist pumping the air in triumph. *The Patron will be incredibly pleased when I give this to him.* What he did with it afterward Claude didn't want to think about. But first he had to prepare for his impending appearance on a major television network news program. He was set to debate mass deportation of immigrants against a skilled opponent from the opposing side. He hurried to catch a flight to New York for the show.

CHAPTER 19

Oscar White pointed his pale index finger at a black and white photo showing a distinguished looking, middle aged man in a U.S. military officer's uniform. "A General, and two-time congressional medal of honor recipient testified that the conspirators' agent approached him to lead the takeover. He was the most highly decorated officer in American history at the time."

"They set their sights high." Gina said.

"The General said their agent promised him massive financial backing if he would lead their 50,000 troops." Oscar said. "They believed their money could recruit resentful unemployed World War I veterans for a march on Washington,"

Gina's brows drew together. "Were the conspirators trying to use the Great Depression's misery to their advantage?"

"Possibly. When people are hurting, they're ripe for a would-be savior's siren song," Oscar said.

"And the conspirators thought this could work?" Gina asked.

Oscar pulled a photo of a stern looking Italian general from the file. "It already had. An armed march worked in Italy in the 1920s where fascist organizers used military veterans to start a dictatorship."

"30,000 Fascist troops marched on Rome against the elected government," Joe said. "The show of force scared the leaders, who agreed to share power by appointing a fascist as Prime Minister. He used that springboard to install himself as dictator."

"It's possible the *Business Plot* conspirators would have been successful," Oscar said. "With the General as their front man, they could have reduced Roosevelt to an impotent figurehead."

Joe's brow creased. *This is huge. Why haven't I heard about it before?* "Well, it must not have worked, we're still a Republic."

"The General reported the conspiracy to the authorities," Oscar said. "That stopped it cold." "Congress investigated and held hearings because of his stature."

Gina leaned over the General's photo, shaking her head. "I never read anything in school about *The Business Plot*. The fact they held hearings doesn't prove anything."

"The General testified about the conspiracy under oath." Oscar turned the page to a transcript of his witness testimony. "It's here in black and white."

"This is a pretty serious charge." Joe leaned over the table and read a few lines of the testimony. He looked up at Oscar. "Did the Committee believe him?"

"The House Committee investigated for two-months before issuing their report." Oscar nodded. "They found that the coup was plotted. The conspirators had it ready to go when they needed it."

"The General's only one man," Gina said. "Why believe his word against theirs?"

"It wasn't only him. The Committee had another witness, a Veterans of Foreign Wars commander at the time.," Oscar said. "He testified that the agents tried to recruit him for a takeover, too."

"So, two men testified about the coup." Gina said. "That's still not conclusive. It's he said, she said."

"There's more." Oscar pulled out two pages from the middle of the file and waved them in the air triumphantly. "The House Committee's own investigators uncovered letters from the agent about a group of French veterans from the First World War, who hoped to overthrow the French Government. The same agent who approached the General."

It's all too terrible to be true, it couldn't be. Joe drew in a long breath. "If there was a conspiracy, it would've been in all the newspapers. You can't keep a thing like that, secret."

Oscar turned to another page and pointed at a footnote at the bottom. "The Committee noted some newspapers of the day agreed with their findings."

"Then why didn't they print the conspirators' names?" Joe asked.

"The Committee said the names were mere hearsay." Oscar gave him a slow knowing smile. "The hearings were mostly behind closed doors without any press. Then as now, men as-rich-as-Midas can have tremendous political clout. And, some newspapers might have received a lot of advertising money from the conspirators' businesses."

"O.K., so some newspapers might have been intimidated," Gina said. "But the Justice Department could still prosecute."

"Roosevelt didn't want the conspirators charged," Oscar said. "The Great Depression was already turbulent, and a trial would have caused even more turmoil."

"So, the conspirators couldn't be touched," Joe said. *A poor man shoplifts some food for his hungry family to eat during the Depression, and they put him in jail. But men with incredible-wealth plotting a government takeover go free. Incredible.*

Oscar laid a yellowed page flat on the table. It was a 1936 letter addressed to Roosevelt from the U.S. Ambassador to Germany. It described how a clique of U.S. industrialists appeared hell-bent to have a fascist state replace our democratic government. The letter said some of the clique worked closely with the fascist regimes in Germany and Italy, and one executive threatened a coup if Roosevelt continued his progressive policies to create jobs.

"My God, it's true. This is the original letter, not a copy." Roosevelt's many warnings against entrenched greed resonated through Joe's mind Now it made sense why FDR alerted us.

"Unbelievably rich American conspirators... and Nazi Germany?" Gina asked. "It sounds like a supermarket tabloid headline. How could they find enough followers for a coup?"

"Maybe this will answer your question." Oscar pulled a photo out of the file and slid it across the table to her. The 1934 snapshot showed New York City's Madison Square Garden packed to the rafters with 20,000 people at a rally. A huge Nazi swastika banner flanked a stage populated with officials sitting at the dais. "Some believe Nazi Germany's Deputy Fuhrer specifically approved this rally's funding."

Gina held the picture up to the light, staring wide-eyed at the huge crowd. "How'd the rally get that many Americans?"

Oscar set his palms down on the table. "They used U.S. workers' unemployment and desperation, the same way they used it in Germany."

"But why'd it work for Hitler?" Gina asked.

"After the Allies won World War I, some of their bankers demanded Germany repay billions the Allies spent fighting the war," Oscar said. "The massive debt repayments hit Germany hard. They started a severe austerity program, so they could make their installments. But, by 1932 German unemployment reached more than 30 percent."

"They were in ruins after World War I." Joe jammed both hands in his pockets. "There's no way Germany could make those payments. *The war reparations repayment policy seemed like sheer lunacy from the very beginning. A few bankers as-rich-as-the-Medici discovered how to get repaid for the money they lent for the war, without raising unpopular taxes on Allied citizens.*

"The German government had run out of options," Oscar said. "Their desperate, hungry people longed for a savior. They were easy marks for Hitler's claims only he could save them. The Nazi's won the German elections and he became Fuhrer soon after. You know what happened next."

"Wait." Frustration crinkled Gina's eyes as she raised her hand in the universal 'stop' gesture. "Germany's problem wasn't austerity, it was inflation. They printed too much money. It took baskets full of German Marks to buy a loaf of bread."

Oscar smiled like a patient school teacher with a student who hadn't done her homework. "Germany's hyperinflation problem ended in 1924… long before Hitler became Fuhrer in1933.

Gina's face reddened while she stammered. "I guess I was off by a few years. So, austerity did help Hitler rise to power. But what happened to *The Business Plot* conspirators?"

"They died off, but a new generation of men with unbelievable-wealth exist now. Some of whom may have takeover ideas." Oscar said.

"So, how do you defeat them?" Gina asked.

"There are rumors they're searching for a lost secret about riches," Oscar said. "And if you could find it before they did then you could defeat them." His desk phone rang, interrupting their conversation. He explained he was the only one in the department and excused himself from the room to take the call.

After he left, Gina took photographs of thirty pages from the files with her smartphone. "I want a copy of these. It may come in handy later." She slid her smart phone back in her jacket pocket after she finished.

A couple minutes later Oscar returned with a face turned pale. "We'll have to move quickly. The telephone call was the front desk notifying me the police are in the building looking for you."

But nobody knows we're here," Joe said. *How the hell did they find us? We didn't tell anybody we were coming.* "

"They must have identified you from the closed-circuit security cameras in the lobby."

"We've got to get out of here fast," Gina said.

Oscar headed for the door, beckoning with his hand for them to follow. "We need more time to discuss Hans and his associates. Come with me. We'll go to the sub-basement storage facility where you can see the rest of the Committee files. No one will look for you there." He led them out his office suite's side door to a service elevator they rode to the sub-basement. The elevator doors opened into a deserted hall next to three walk-in concrete vaults with stainless steel doors.

Joe eyes bugged out while he pointed at the safes. "What the hell are those for?"

"They're nighttime vaults where the Constitution, the Bill of Rights and the Declaration of Independence sleep," Oscar said. "We display the documents under bulletproof glass on the main floor during the day. But at night they're mechanically lowered to these below ground vaults for safety."

Gina rolled her eyes skyward. "I take it visitors aren't usually allowed down here."

"That would be an understatement," Oscar said.

They continued down the hall to an old storage room three times larger than the one they'd left upstairs. The air smelled of musty paper and coffee, the latter from researchers who fueled their bodies to stay awake. Oscar grabbed a white cardboard file storage box off the gray metal shelves, plopping it on a long wood table. Joe and Gina pulled faded manila folders out of the box, spreading them on the table to display the pages inside.

Oscar glanced at his watch and turned briskly to head for the door. He looked back at them over his shoulder. "I've got to make a call. I'll be down the hall for ten minutes. If anyone's coming, I'll warn you." The thin metal door closed behind him with a click.

Joe leaned back in his metal chair and exhaled in one breath. He looked up at the fluorescent light fixtures and deadpanned. "Luxury accommodations, huh?"

"Yeah, but what do you expect from a storage area." Gina looked back down at the *Business Plot* file on the table, using her phone to photograph a page. After repeating the process several times, she shook her head and sighed. "God, there's a lot of material here."

A light lit up on the extension phone on the desk, showing a new line was in use. Joe straightened, "Do you suppose that's Oscar?"

"There's only one way to find out." She pressed an index finger against the phone's lighted extension button and then hit the speaker button.

Oscar's voice came over the speaker. "It's me. Yeah, I've got the records and I'm ready to make a deal. I want five million cash on delivery."

CHAPTER 20

Joe and Gina's faces looked worried as they listened to the speaker phone broadcast the voices on Oscar White's phone call.

The man on the other end of Oscar's line yelled back at him. "Five million. That's outrageous… highway robbery. You think we were born yesterday?"

Joe envisioned Oscar wincing and moving the phone six inches away from his ear in response to the shouting. The yeller's voice sounded eerily familiar, but he couldn't place it.

"It's worth a thousand times more than that to you," Oscar replied.

"You piece of …"

"Tut, Tut. You curse at me like that and I'll give it to cable news," Oscar said.

"Nooo, no, no. Don't go off half-cocked. We'll get the money… but if word leaks out your ass is grass."

I've got two meddlers here who also want the records. How much are they worth to you?"

Two meddlers. Joe's eyebrow raised. *He's talking about us. He wants to sell us out for cash… after we warned him his life was in danger. What a piece of shit.*

"I think we can come to an arrangement. But, before I make an offer, I must talk to my Patron. I'll get back to you later."

"But…" Oscar said.

"No buts about it. And I don't have to tell you what'll happen if you double-cross us."

Oscar's crestfallen response sounded so soft as to be almost unintelligible. "Understood." He muttered something else into the phone and hung up.

As soon as she heard him end the call, Gina nudged Joe with her elbow and whispered, "We've gotta escape before Oscar feeds us to the lions. Follow my lead and play along."

Joe licked his lips and nodded. *I hope her plan's a good one.*

"Grab that fire extinguisher from the wall," she said. "Then stand behind the door and be ready," she said.

Joe reached above him to grab the red compact canister attached to the wall. A metal bracket held its cold smooth steel securely in place. His fingers fumbled with the unit while he searched for the latch to unsnap it. *Ah, found it.* The bracket clicked, the latch released, and the hard cylinder fell into his hand before it could drop to the concrete floor. The file room's metal door flew open a moment later and Oscar marched in.

Gina leaned forward over the floor and held her stomach like she was about to throw up. "Oooooh God. I think I'm gonna be sick. Ugh," she moaned.

"It's the fluorescent lights," Joe said from behind the door

Oscar spun around toward the door's shadow, scowling with irritation that Joe had surprised him from behind. Joe aimed the fire extinguisher's black nozzle at Oscar's face, pressing the discharge lever down hard. A white cloud of harsh dry chemical whooshed out of the nozzle directly in Oscar's face.

"Owww… ow. I can't see," he screamed, frantically trying to wipe the stinging white powder out of his eyes. He tripped, falling over his own feet in his haste to get away from the spray. His head hit the table as he fell, and he passed out on the gray concrete floor.

Gina walked over to Oscar and leaned over him. "You deserved that, you Benedict Arnold." She reached down and fished his wallet out of his pocket, finding credit cards, cash and a business card with a name, phone number and address. She held it up for Joe to see. "He had Tomas Lobo's card."

"Should have known," Joe said. "Oscar must have thought he had to cut a deal to survive. He didn't realize Tomas was never going to let him just walk away."

"We'll worry about these records later," Gina said. "Let's get outta here before Oscar wakes up."

They raced up the stairs to the main level, stopping at a side door near the building's loading dock. A white government van sat parked in a space right outside the door. Its driver pushed a loaded dolly out of the van's cargo area into the building and disappeared. Gina made a run for the driver's side door and jumped into the cab while Joe did the same on the passenger side. The keys were still in the ignition. She gunned the accelerator, the tires squealed and the van tore away from the dock. Two security guards with guns drawn ran out on the loading dock platform and fired shots at the van as it drove off. The bullets whizzed by but bounced harmlessly off the pavement. The dock disappeared as the van careened down the street and around the corner.

That was way too close. If Oscar hadn't done them in, the guards might have finished the job.

The van weaved through traffic as they sped toward the Arts and Industries Building. Joe leaned back in the cold vinyl passenger's seat and tried to relax. His muscles were loose like spaghetti from anxiety and exhaustion.

"Maybe we can get some news, find out what's going on," Gina said as she turned on the radio. Instead of news, music played over the van's speaker. She frowned and flipped off the radio's power button.

"Why'd you turn it off?" Joe raised his eyebrows.

"That song… I can't stand it. It was playing when I first saw the photo of Antonio kissing Senator Hogue's wife at the hotel. I stood there dumbfounded staring at the newspaper. I confronted Antonio, slapped him, and told him he was a "bastard." Their affair hurt me so badly that I moved out of Villa Firenze and put my life on hold. I still loved him, but I couldn't go back. I guess that's why I'm trying to solve his clues. They're all I have left, now.

They'd driven for several minutes when Gina grabbed his shoulder. She pointed at an unmarked navy-blue squad car driving toward them in the oncoming lane. It passed by and pulled a U-turn in the median. The car sped up as it followed them in their lane, a half-dozen car lengths behind,

"They've spotted us." Gina's foot pressed down firmly on the accelerator. The van's engine hummed with power, but the heavy traffic limited their progress. She veered into the left-hand turn lane at a busy intersection where they stopped for the left-turn red light. Their van sat first in line to turn.

She glanced in the van's rear-view mirror, seeing the police cruiser pull to a stop two-cars behind. Her fingers drummed the steering wheel while she waited for the red light to turn green. Two plain-clothes officers in the cruiser opened their doors and got out of the car. They drew their guns while they strode toward the van.

"When you were a teenager did you ever play 'shoot the gap'?" Gina pursed her lips and placed both hands on the steering wheel, tapping it with her fingers.

That's a strange sounding game. "Nope, it doesn't ring a bell. What're you talking about?"

"We used it to get away from friends chasing us after soccer games. Hang on. I'll show you."

A line of oncoming cars had stopped for their red light at the divided four lane intersection. Those vehicles waited, ready to move forward. Their traffic signal light turned green. Gina's left turn arrow remained red, but today all bets were off. She gunned the van's engine, pulling into the intersection and whipping the steering wheel around hand over hand to the left.

What the hell is she doing? The fast, sharp turn forced Joe's body to lean hard to the right.

The van's engine whined while it raced to complete a U-turn ahead of the oncoming cars entering the intersection. Its rubber tires squealed in agony, skidding against the dry pavement. The van completed the U-turn ahead of the oncoming cars whose horns blared in anger Gina cut them off. The cars streamed into the intersection, blocking the vehicles waiting in line behind Gina at the stoplight. The police cruiser sat trapped in the left turn lane.

Gina floored the accelerator as the van came out of the turn. The van fishtailed, accelerating down the street and spewing a blue-gray cloud of choking exhaust. The cab vibrated hard from the engine's strain.

"Jesus are you trying to kill us?" Joe asked through gritted teeth.

"Sorry. This is the only way."

The officers watched as the van sped past them in the opposite direction. They recovered in time to race back to their car and radio the dispatcher with the van's direction.

Joe looked through the Van's rear window. The officers turned the steering wheel to the left and gunned the engine. The police cruiser bounced across the raised median island and high-centered on the concrete.

"They're stuck." Joe said.

The van crested a hill and Gina gave a sigh of relief they had escaped.

"Well, that's an experience I'll never forget." Joe released his tight grip on the arm rest, allowing the blood to return to his white knuckles. He raked his fingers through his hair. "My heart jumped into my throat twice."

"It got your attention, didn't it?" Gina grinned while she checked the rear-view mirror again to make sure the cruiser hadn't followed them.

"That's putting it mildly." Joe managed a weak smile. The smile faded a few moments later as he considered the danger he'd put her in. "It's obvious both the police and the assassins are hunting for me. I should leave so I don't get you in any deeper."

"Don't be ridiculous," Gina said, turning the steering wheel to navigate a sharp corner. "I know you're innocent. Plus, they tried to kill me, too. I'd say our chances of survival are better working together."

Joe wiped his forehead with a handkerchief. "We'd better get to the Exhibition Hall and find the Palazzo scale model before Tomas does."

Gina changed lanes and gunned the engine again. "We'll be there in ten minutes."

CHAPTER 21

As Claude Zorak walked away from the Capitol Building, celebrated civil rights leader Rev. Luther Gooding stepped up to the podium on the structure's elevated West Façade. Red, white and blue buntings on the rails flapped in the crisp air making snapping sounds. He gazed out from his lofty perch. In front of him, two million angry citizens spread across the National Mall like legions of humanity. The crowd cheered his arrival so loud he couldn't even hear the moderator's introduction. Their hopes and fears focused on him, yearning for leadership in their time of crisis. The responsibility weighed like a heavy stone upon his back. *Lord, help me find the words to help these hard-working people defend themselves from this vicious attack.*

He held up one hand to silence the crowd, before his deep voice rang out like thunder.

"The forces of avarice have infected the very bowels of this hallowed building, with their sinister scheme to abolish Social Security, Medicare, Medicaid, and the Healthcare Act. They've conspired to wipe out the social safety net in an instant and cast aside those most vulnerable. And why? To slash taxes for men with such amazing-riches they couldn't spend it all in a thousand lifetimes."

"Kill the bill… Kill the bill… Kill the bill," they chanted.

Luther waited for the marchers to quiet down before he continued. "But we know what they're up to."

"We sure do," came the response.

The greedy have rigged the rules to make themselves richer and us poorer. They accuse those in poverty of waging class warfare. Robber barons are the ones that started that war, but we're gonna finish it."

"You know that's right," dozens in the crowd shouted.

"We're one nation under God, not one nation under greed."

"Amen," shouted the crowd.

This crowd is feelin' me, don't stop now. The call and response are strong. "This is about the nation's welfare," Luther preached with a cadence.

"Glory Hallelujah."

The forces of evil are addicted to control and power. They oppose government of the people, by the people and for the people."

"They better not," shouted an elderly woman with a surprisingly strong determined voice.

"When Wall Street barons crashed the markets a few years ago, none of them went to jail," Luther said.

The marchers on the grass covered mall roared their disapproval of the big-bank bailouts. "Uh huh. You know that ain't right."

Luther paused as he caught sight of the Lincoln Memorial's white stone building gleaming in the distance at the Mall's far end. The former president's bronze statue appeared as a mere dot between its pillars. "As I look at Lincoln's Memorial, I realize he stood up to large plantation owners and their powerful commercial interests. Slavery was America's biggest business at the time, a three and a half billion-dollar trade. It was worth more than the banks, factories and railroads put together."

"Don't stop now, Rev." The crowd member's sudden comment brought Luther's gaze back from Lincoln's statue to his audience.

"Standing here before you, I'm reminded of those famous words 'Inasmuch as you did it to one of the least of these my brothers, you did it to me.' But this bill doesn't help the poor or the helpless. No, it only further enriches the bill's billionaire backers, doing it as fast as possible."

"'Tell it, brother, tell it."

"In the richest nation on Earth, a few men as-rich-as-a-platter-of-gravy can't have it all while our children go hungry. Their greed has got to end. This is the biggest moral issue of our time."

"Glory Hallelujah."

"But they won't give up their greed without a fight." Luther tightened his fist. "They never have, and they never will."

"That's all right! We're ready."

His previous words reminded Luther that men of phenomenal-wealth had approached him earlier in the week. They tried to win the battle by buying him off.

"Two men, representing a group with enormous wealth, came to my office, offering me a bribe to support their heartless bill. They planned to disguise their payola to me as profit from a real estate sale. They intended to sell me a building worth ten-million-dollars, for a sale price of only four million dollars. Their bank would loan me the money to buy it. Later, a friend of theirs would buy back the building from me for ten-million dollars. I'd gain six million dollars from what looked like a legal sale."

"Tell 'em no, Rev," chanted the crowd

"I didn't just tell 'em no, I said hell no. Told them what they could do with their offer. They became angry when I turned them down and made not-so-veiled threats against me."

"They're evil."

"They believe they can buy and sell people the way they buy and sell their stocks. Well they can't buy us. And the one thing their hardened hearts can't stand is that our morals limit their power. Morality is beyond their understanding. They think it's quaint... something to laugh at behind their golden doors while gorging themselves under great crystal chandeliers."

"They're so wrong," an elderly woman called out.

"Evil often tries to tempt good men, to get them to sell out for riches. The Devil tempted Christ in the Wilderness. Satan took him to a high mountain showing him all the kingdoms of the world and their glory. Satan offered him all these things, if he would do the Devil's bidding against mankind. But Christ said 'no.' He said, 'get behind me Satan'."

"Don't give in, Rev," shouted a young man.

"Christ's temptation was a warning against greed... mountainous greed, treacherous greed."

Some marchers held signs displaying warnings against avarice, on sticks bobbing up and down in time to their chants.

"Some of those in power want to turn off the lights on hope and leave us in darkness," Luther said.

"No, no, never," the crowd shouted. "Let those lights shine."

"They don't care that their love of money makes the pie smaller," Luther said. "But, we're not gonna let that happen. We're gonna make that pie bigger."

"Praise the Lord."

"They think they're self-made men, bastions of self-reliance. Well, I've got news for them... they didn't do it all by themselves."

"Ain't it the truth," came the response.

"Their money-lust increased financial hardship on families, squeezing them until husbands blame wives, wives blame husbands and children blame parents. All that human suffering for something ordinary people didn't cause and never wanted. Well, it ends here."

"Share it, brother," shouted the crowd.

"Their pride goes before a fall. Are we prepared to take on those greedy men who try to destroy the safety net?"

"Yes, yes, yes," they chanted in unison.

"Then let's send Congress a message so loud and clear they'll hear it in every corner of the Capitol."

"Kill the bill... Kill the bill... Kill the bill," they shouted.

Luther waved at the crowd and stepped back from the podium to a thunderous ovation. He shook hands with the other dignitaries at the dais and took a seat near the podium. *I've done all I can, I hope some good comes from this message, it's in the Lord's hands now.*

The event's organizer closed the protest by thanking all those who attended, and those who spoke to the crowd. The mall became less dense as the throng dispersed. Luther and two other speakers exchanged stories as they strode together to the parking lot where their cars awaited. Luther opened his red Lexus' car door, threw his leather portfolio in, slid behind the wheel, closed the door and pressed the key fob turning the engine over. "Kaboom!" The car exploded as it erupted in yellow flames stretching twenty feet above its roof, licking at the sky.

The blast knocked down the other two speakers standing next to their nearby cars. After a moment of stunned paralysis, they picked themselves off the pavement, running from their cars toward the blaze. Their hands palms-forward in front of their faces to protect their eyes from the intense heat. But the searing temperature drove them back. They peered around their hands, grimacing at Luther's once vigorous body now charred into an ashen corpse.

Sirens wailed in the distance as police and fire vehicles rushed toward the scene.

The taller speaker punched a trash can on the sidewalk two car lengths away, denting the smoky-gray container with a loud bang. "Those bastards." He tilted his head back and stared up at the sky through tear-filled eyes. "When they couldn't buy him off, they killed him."

Down the street, a long black antique limousine with smoked glass windows pulled away from the curb. A faint satanic cackle oozed from the vehicle as it changed lanes and disappeared into traffic, the voice carried by the wind. The town car held the man who made Luther an offer most people couldn't refuse.

CHAPTER 22

O scar White's eyes fluttered as he caught a hazy glimpse of black wires and aluminum ductwork attached to an unfinished ceiling. *Where am I?* He shook his head to remove the brain fog and glanced down at his torso. Bright white powder covered his shirt like a layer of spilled flour. His back ached against the cold and unforgiving gray concrete floor where he lay. The memory of the fire extinguisher spray came back to him.

I'm still in the Archives sub-basement.

A knife-like pain shot through one side of his head and caused him to place his palm against it. A quarter inch high raised bump on his skull pushed against his hand, reminding him of his fall against the table before he passed out. The pungent scent of ammonia wafted into his nostrils. He raised his head, sniffing the air to find the odor's source. His nose led him to a red fire extinguisher sprawled on the floor six feet away, its white powder-tipped nozzle hanging limply to one side.

That smell... it came from the fire extinguisher's dry chemical, ammonium phosphate.

Oscar rose to his feet with a loud groan, both hands brushing the powder off his clothes. The white dust flew up in a cloud tickling his nose. He sneezed twice. When the cloud subsided, he stumbled down the hallway to the service elevator, riding it up three levels to his office.

He marched to the adjacent file room. The faded white storage box marked 'Permanently Sealed by Order of The House Committee on Un-American Activities' still sat on the same table where he'd shown it to Joe and Gina. *Nothing had been disturbed. That's a relief.* He wiped his hand across his forehead.

Oscar grabbed the *Business Plot* files, setting them next to a large black satchel. He sifted through the box selecting which papers to put into the pouch when his cell phone rang. A quick check of the phone's caller I.D. screen displayed the caller's name, Tomas Lobo. A frown crossed Oscar's face. His relaxation was short lived.

He swiped the screen with his index finger to reject the call. There was zero chance Tomas would take the news of Joe and Gina's escape with any degree of restraint. The best route would be to gather the coveted files then make a quick departure. But he would have to hurry.

CHAPTER 23

Tomas' black sedan pulled up to the curb on the street one floor below Oscar's office window, He sat behind the wheel of his parked car, staring at the employee entrance through dark sunglasses. He needed to get inside the building without alerting the front desk. Employees hurried in and out of the doorway where they waved electronic key cards against the door frame's black box card reader. A plump middle-aged woman dressed in a gray twill suit strode out of the building and passed his car on the way to her parking lot.

He got out of his car, following the woman at a distance into a dimly lit parking garage. She descended the stairs to a below-ground level and walked toward a late model four door sedan. Tomas watched from the shadows as she pressed her key fob to unlock the door and climbed in to the drivers' seat. The garage smelled of mold and gasoline exhaust collected from years of tailpipes belching. She inserted her key into the ignition. He stepped up next to the driver's side door, pointed his gun at her head and gave her a cold hard stare. "Don't say a word. Hand over your building key card."

"Are, are… you going to… to shoot me?" Her hands trembled as she rolled down the window and opened her purse. She fumbled for the security card, handing it to Tomas. All color drained from her face.

"What do you think?" Tomas smiled a cruel smile.

She sat frozen, too terrified to answer. He squeezed the trigger followed by one quick 'pop' sound breaking the silence. Her torso slumped forward. His experienced hands caught her shoulders before chest could hit the steering wheel horn. He pushed her shoulder sideways. Her upper body fell over the console and passenger seat. She dropped below the passenger side window's line of sight and her head hit the passenger side arm rest with a clunk.

Tomas holstered the pistol. A half-inch blood spot on his right hand remained from the shooting. His eyes narrowed.

Why do I always get splattered? For once I'd like a completely clean hit."

He wiped the hand with a white cotton handkerchief and shut the car door, locking it in the process. His left hand still clutched the woman's electronic key card as he trekked out of the underground lot. It took a couple moments for his eyes to adjust to the bright sunlight on the sidewalk. A few more steps took him to the National Archives building's side door where he swiped the key card through the security lock and strolled into the hallway.

The Archives' file room door squeaked briefly. Oscar White sat at the table, his empty black satchel ready to be filled, sitting next to the *Business Plot* file box. He looked up from his work. Tomas stood in the doorway, the black hole of his nine-millimeter pistol barrel pointed directly at Oscar's face.

"Wha, Wha... what do you want?" Oscar dropped the selected papers he held back into the file box and snapped the empty satchel shut.

"You know." Tomas walked over to the table and put his hand on the satchel's handle. "You didn't answer my call. Were you trying to double cross me?"

"No, you've got it all wrong. Richmond and Bocelli, they knocked me out and escaped." Oscar held both hands up palms open. He pushed the file box toward Tomas. "Here... I had gathered these papers to bring to you."

"I don't think so." Tomas sneered. "Instead, you were going into business for yourself, looking for the highest bidder. Or, you'd go to the police, hoping to get a big reward for turning us in?"

"No, No... that's not it at all. I'm not selling you out. You've gotta believe me."

"You could have been a very rich man, but you made a stupid move." Tomas pulled out a cigarette, lit it, and blew a smoke ring. He placed the burning butt on the table's edge. "Maybe you're a naïve do-gooder who foolishly hoped to do the right thing."

"You don't believe me 'cause you think everyone's crooked like you." Oscar scowled. "You'd sell your own mother for the right price."

He's even more stupid than I thought. Tomas paused to take another drag on his cigarette, then walked around to Oscar's side of the table "You shouldn't have said that. You made it tougher on yourself."

"You won't get away with this." Oscar spoke rapidly in a high-pitched voice. "You aren't the only one who knows."

"You mean Richmond and Bocelli. They're not long for this earth."

He stopped behind Oscar, yanked a piece of piano wire out of his pocket and deftly stretched it between his hands. With one swift movement, he looped it around Oscar's neck and pulled it tight. The wire bit into the soft skin, blood oozing from the throat's crease. Oscar grabbed with both hands at the wire while he tugged hard to try to free himself. His face turned red while he struggled. But the wire only tightened until he ran out of air. His head slumped forward on the table.

Tomas put two fingers against Oscar's wrist to check for a pulse. He found none. He grabbed Oscar's body under the armpits and drug him out of the file room, to a nearby utility closet. The closet's shelves bulged with cleaning supply bottles, brown boxes, white cleaning cloths and black trash bags. It smelled like a mixture of chlorine cleaning solution and furniture polish. Inside the closet's dark narrow confines, stood a tall cabinet holding brooms and mops which Tomas pulled out to set against the wall. He stuffed Oscar's body in the cabinet, propping it up between the cabinet's vertical walls. The cabinet door slammed shut with a thud as the latch clicked closed.

Tomas spotted a large industrial plastic trash can half-full of maintenance debris, near the cabinet. *That's how I can smuggle the documents out of here past security.*

A flash of red caught Tomas' eye when he walked out of the closet into the bright hallway. There on his shoe's toe were a couple drops of blood.

Not again. I gotta figure out what I'm doing wrong.

He pulled out his handkerchief and leaned over to wipe up the revealing liquid. His route took him back into the file storage room table where he rummaged through the *Business Plot* file box and read through several pages. Once satisfied they were the real thing, he photographed the most important documents with his cellphone.

Tomas lugged the file box to the janitor's closet, setting it down, and emptying the trash can's contents onto the floor. He grabbed a fresh black trash bag off a shelf and shook the *Business Plot* files into it. His fingers wired it shut with a long twist-tie. He placed the newly sealed bag inside the existing bag lining the trash can. Then he scooped up the maintenance trash off the floor, dumping it in the trash can on top of the sealed bag holding the documents.

To any observer it looked like a full trash can ready to go to the dumpster. *But, how to tell it apart from the other bags once it's in the dumpster?* Tomas marked the bag's outer surface, puncturing a small hole on opposite sides with a pen. His quick phone call to maintenance assured that they would pick up the bag and take it to the dumpster right away.

Tomas could pick it out of the dumpster soon afterward. After that, it was a simple matter to deliver the revealing documents to his Patron.

Tomas left the office and walked out the building's side door. He took long-legged strides back to his car. Now that he had taken care of *The Business Plot files*, he could concentrate on finding Joe Richmond right away. He dared not fail this time.

CHAPTER 24

The Archives van raced in to the empty parking lot at the Smithsonian Arts and Industries Exhibition Hall. Gina parked it in a reserved space next to the back door.

"No problem getting a spot this early," she said.

"The staff worked overtime last night," Joe said. "They must have left to get some sleep.

"Let's hope we beat Tomas here."

He and Gina hoofed it through the building's back door and entered the hall. Joe pointed to its far end. "The Palazzo Vecchio model's this way."

They passed by the doorway of a small room where the night janitor guided a loud floor buffing machine back and forth over the cream-colored tiles inside. Joe put his index finger to his lips to request silence and whispered, "Keep going. Don't say a word. He grabbed Gina's arm as they hurried past the noise."

They reached the hall's end, entering a large exhibit room filled with paintings, sculptures, drawings, books and scale models related to Machiavelli and da Vinci's collaboration. Gina stopped to stare at a portrait of a thoughtful looking Niccolò. He wore a black velvet sleeveless mantle, or surcoat, over a red undercoat. "I recognize him from my old school texts," she said.

"He wrote *the* book on political power. Nobody else even came close."

"Well, that may be, but he seemed manipulative and deceitful."

"Not really." Joe gave a dismissive wave of his left hand. "Machiavelli got a bad rap about his advice. He had served under a naïve moral leader who didn't know how to hold onto power against evil adversaries with staggering-wealth. Machiavelli's book showed future moral leaders how to survive."

"I never heard that before. Are you sure?"

"He cared about democracy, warning that a few greedy men as rich-as-Midas could destroy it." *If she only knew how much he suffered at the hands of powerful tyrants.*

Gina ambled over to a nearby painting displaying a long-bearded, beret capped Leonardo da Vinci. "Da Vinci was a great inventor and painter. Both he and Machiavelli were natives of Florence, Italy."

"But few know they worked together. Machiavelli served on Florence's War Council. The same Council hired da Vinci."

Gina gawked at an image next to da Vinci's portrait, of a strange looking drawing with dozens of curved lines. It resembled a system of human veins and capillaries. She tugged on Joe's arm. "What's this squiggly looking sketch?"

"Those aren't squiggles," Joe chuckled at the description. "It's da Vinci's map of the Arno River. It ran through Florence downstream to Pisa, their war-time foe. Machiavelli planned to change the river's course, by digging a new channel."

"For God's sake, why?"

How could she have been in the military and still miss such an obvious strategy? "Florence was hopelessly losing the war against Pisa. Da Vinci hoped diverting the river and taking Pisa's water would bring it to its knees." Some people speculated the diversion would cause Pisa's citizens would die of thirst. But he believed Pisa would surrender long before that.

"That's a long river. It would take forever to dig a new channel by hand."

"They learned that the hard way." Joe pointed at da Vinci's drawing of a half-pyramid shaped wooden crane whose beams held large excavation buckets hung by cables. "Da Vinci designed this giant crane to dig the channel faster. They began building the crane, but the costs went way over budget. They needed money."

"What did they do?"

What geniuses always do… search for a solution. "They studied the time's foremost writer on greed and wealth, the famous Dante Alighieri, for insight into money," Joe said. He led her over to a copy of an aged white plaster mask. "Artists carved this death mask from his face after he died. Renaissance societies made plaster casts of famous peoples' faces to save their memory. The original's stored in the Palazzo Vecchio in Florence."

Gina touched the copy with her fingertips and then read from the plaque beside the mask. "Dante was born in Florence two centuries before da Vinci and Machiavelli. His stature was almost mythical during their lives."

"During Dante's life, Florence's giant Banks controlled much of Europe's income. Like Wall Street today, they scooped up stupendous amounts of money, creating a huge speculative asset bubble. Florence's bubble burst as they always do, markets crashed, and credit evaporated. Commerce came to a virtual stop, the European economy collapsed. It caused the worst financial depression in world history."

"I've heard of the Great Depression of the 1300s." Gina slapped her hand against her forehead. "It affected most of Europe. The Great Depression of the 1930s paled by comparison."

"Dante blamed aristocrats' greedy hoarding for Florence's depression and political corruption," Joe said. "He advocated moderation. In his poem, *Inferno,* he journeyed through the Fourth Circle of Hell where Plutus, the demon of wealth, guarded Hell's gate. Plutus oversaw demons torturing greedy hoarders' souls in unspeakable ways." The well-known story conjured an image from Bosch's famous painting *Hell* where demons punished the greedy for their deadly sin.

"I forgot about Plutus… that's where we got the word Plutocrat, right? One who rules by his riches."

Joe nodded. "It's also the root word for Plutomania, the pathological addiction to money. It's what ruins society." *Christ referred to it as 'the love of money,' an all-consuming obsession with wealth. He said it's a root of all evil.*

"Plutomania… that's why ancient Romans killed the Gracchus Brothers."

"Dante knew all about the Gracchi. In *Inferno,* he praised their mother Cornelia as a noble heroine.

"I remember. She was the wealthy woman who wore plain clothes and no jewelry."

Joe nodded. "Machiavelli and da Vinci were anxious to test Dante's idea in reverse. They posed a question -- If a few ultra-rich men hoarding money had ruined society, could circulating money cause it to prosper?

"So, what did they do?"

"Da Vinci and Machiavelli reviewed Florence's financial records going back centuries." *Machiavelli, as Second Chancellor, had custody of centuries of Florence's financial records, to test da Vinci's idea. It was a matter of running the calculations.* "They used da Vinci's scientific method of empirical observation, furiously sifting through thousands of treasury ledgers for twenty-four straight hours, looking for patterns. In the process, they made an amazing discovery."

"Like the Holy Grail," Gina said. Her words referenced the cup from which Christ's disciples drank wine representing his blood. According to legend, the elusive treasure possessed miraculous power to provide unlimited abundance.

They hurried to Florence's rulers with the results, thinking their breakthrough would be gratefully received. Instead, the aristocrats abruptly dismissed them and abandoned the crane. Machiavelli and da Vinci never spoke of their discovery again. It's lost to this day."

"So, it remains a mystery," Gina said.

"But there've been rumors the secret survived." *And it's beginning to look more and more like it's not merely a rumor.*

"And Machiavelli and da Vinci would have read Dante."

"We know they did, like most Italians." Joe pointed behind her at a life-size gold colored donkey statue nearby. "The proof's over here."

She turned toward the statue, before jerking to a stop half-way around. She did a double-take. "What's that doing here?"

"It's *The Golden Ass.*" Joe pointed to the description on the plaque standing in front of the sculpture. "The title of Machiavelli's unfinished poem."

"Where on Earth did he come up with the name?"

"It came from the ancient Roman story *The Golden Ass* written 1,500 years earlier, about a wealthy young man intrigued by magic, whose zeal results in him being turned into an ass. As a pack animal, he's sold and whipped, while watching others near him endure similar fate. He experiences firsthand the suffering that men of towering-wealth inflicted on the poor and the enslaved."

"It sounds like Karma to me. So, Machiavelli's story is modeled after one 1,500 years older."

"More or less," Joe said. "He changes the story some. In his poem, instead of a golden ass, he talks with a fat hog. The swine used to be human and now views greed as a curse that's the source of self-destructiveness, cruelty, deceit and wars. Avarice takes us away from what's good."

Gina scanned the side by side printed versions of Dante's poem and Machiavelli's poem, on a stand next to the statue. "Machiavelli must have read Dante. His Golden Ass poem uses Dante's same rhyming pattern and both stories are about rich men's greed causing pain."

"Follow me." Joe guided Gina to a black kiosk with a computer mouse and mousepad on top. A large ultra-high definition computer monitor hung on the wall behind the kiosk. It displayed a highly-magnified section of da Vinci's masterpiece the *Mona Lisa,* as well as an inset of the entire painting. The enlarged section displayed a river valley and arched stone bridge in the background near her left shoulder.

"The *Mona Lisa*'s beautiful." Gina said. "I saw it in the Louvre museum in Paris."

"She came to the U.S one time, in 1963 at the National Gallery of Art," Joe said. "Only a couple hundred yards down the street from here," *The story behind the exhibit was fascinating. First Lady Jackie Kennedy visited Paris, charming French President Gaulle with her fluent French and extensive knowledge of France's culture and history. He was so smitten he agreed to her request for the unheard-of act of loaning the Mona Lisa for temporary exhibit in Washington D.C.*

"I read about that," she said. "Thousands of Americans stood for hours in line to see her. President Kennedy spoke at the Exhibit's opening."

"Some believe the Mona Lisa holds a clue to the secret." Joe said as he clicked the mouse to zoom-in on the arched stone bridge spanning the river. "Da Vinci painted her in 1503-1504, the same time he worked with Machiavelli on the giant crane."

"You think there's a connection between the Mona Lisa and their discovery?" Gina looked perplexed.

"Probably." Joe pointed to the arched stone bridge in the painting. "That's the Burgiano Bridge over the Arno River. The area near *Mona Lisa's* right shoulder reveals a winding canal with excavated bare red dirt.

It's the partially completed dry river channel diversion." *The diverted channel held no water, showing the project's abandonment before it could connect to the existing river.*

Gina leaned in, squinting at the huge monitor. "It looks like someone dug a channel there, all right."

"Now, look at the *Mona Lisa's* mouth. Notice her tight-lipped smile, like she has a secret. She does... it's da Vinci's and Machiavelli's discovery."

"But, *Mona Lisa's* a rich silk merchant's wife." Gina frowned. "Da Vinci painted her portrait for her grand new house, not to hide a secret."

"He painted her, but not for display in her house. Renaissance portraits flaunted the social standing and affluence of their patrons, to impress others." Joe moved the mouse to zoom-in on *Mona Lisa's* dress. "But, *Mona Lisa's* quite different. She wears an ordinary dress... there's no wedding ring or jewelry. Her attire makes a clear statement about *not* displaying wealth."

"I never noticed that before." Gina peered at the image. "It's very odd for someone so well-off. And since well-heeled Cornelia also wore a simple dress and no jewelry, it's as if both she and the *Mona Lisa are* sending the same message."

"Da Vinci never parted with *Mona Lisa*. He spoke modestly about most of his paintings. But she had special meaning for him... he believed her portrait was his one truly divine work."

"That's irony on steroids," she chuckled. "A priceless masterpiece about *not* displaying riches. Maybe da Vinci had a sense of humor." Gina paused for a moment before her forehead wrinkled. "So, what's the secret?"

"Don't know. But there may be a clue in the model's name... Lisa del Giocondo. Lisa means 'God's Bountiful Promise'."

"Wow." Gina turned around wide-eyed. "You think da Vinci chose Lisa for the painting because it holds the secret to bounty... to abundance? That would be one helluva secret." As she turned, her elbow accidentally bumped Joe's arm holding the computer mouse. The screen's enlarged section shifted back to the old stone bridge with three arches spanning the rushing river. "What's that?" she stared at the screen for a moment, pointing under the bridge.

"What's what?"

"Why are there two numbers in the river under the bridge?" She stepped forward until her face measured less than three feet from the image. "It looks like a 72." She pointed a perfectly manicured finger nail at the water under the bridge's third arch.

Sure enough, there in the river appeared the number 72. Joe shook his head, doing a double-take. "That's incredible. I never noticed it before." A third and more faint character appeared after the 72, but he couldn't tell what it was. His eyes grew big. He clicked the mouse to zoom-in further.

"It must be important if da Vinci put it there. But, why paint it in the river?" Gina asked.

"He saw a divine quality in nature, believing it held answers to the World's mysteries. *So, where better to display the mystery's answer than in nature, in the water.*

"The 72 is small enough to fly under the rulers' radar. Yet it's in plain sight for anyone looking for it."

She'd said a mouthful there. "Da Vinci believed in the concept of Saper Vedere...knowing how to see," Joe said. "He made discoveries by looking at nature from different perspectives. And his friend, Machiavelli, believed the best people were those who see without being shown."

"So, da Vinci counted on us knowing how to see his message in the river."

"Exactly." *This number in the river was a major development. Da Vinci must have a reason for painting it there. But why?*

Gina suddenly straightened and looked around the room. "I almost forgot why we came... the Palazzo Vecchio scale model"

CHAPTER 25

Agent Davis stood next to Josh in the National Archive's rotunda, below the huge mural of the Constitution's creation. A half-dozen suit and tie FBI agents interviewed stunned Archives' employees in depth about Oscar White's death. Their voices buzzed across the room.

"How many murders today, seven?" Davis asked.

"I think it's six, but I lost track." Josh shrugged his shoulders.

"You know I shoulda retired when I had the chance." Davis face-palmed. "Who could dream this stuff up?"

Davis turned his attention to scanning the building security list of Oscar's prior visitors. Hans' name appeared on the roster. A cross-check of his name revealed subway station security guards had discovered his body earlier that morning.

"Alright people gather round, let's strategize." Davis said. "I wanna know why Hans Berger visited Oscar White at the Archives. What did you find, Josh?"

"Well, it's weird. When there's a professional hit man, something about the victim usually stands out. But Oscar had one of the most boring occupations imaginable."

"So, Oscar White was boring," Agent Davis rolled his eyes as he crossed his arms. "Please tell me that's not all you learned."

"No, there's more." Josh shook his head. "Oscar worked here several years. But last month Senator Benjamin Hogue pressured the Archives Director to replace Oscar. What's more surprising, Hogue's proposed replacement had no prior archival work experience. The Director refused, even though Hogue pressed him hard."

Political bigwigs like Hogue don't usually get involved in mid-level agency staffing. Something was up. "Why's he so opposed to Oscar White?"

"Nobody knows. But he wrote a glowing two-page recommendation letter to the Director, about Oscar's proposed replacement. Hogue even had the Director and his wife to dinner at Hogue's home to discuss the position."

"Damn." Davis slapped his thigh with one hand. "That's a lot of fire power over an obscure civil service job." *Nobody at Hogue's level in Washington does something like that unless there's a lot of money at stake. This is big-time.*

"There's more. Oscar's visitors included Richmond and Bocelli early this morning."

"What the hell were they doing here?" Agent Davis' eyes squinted. *Now, he absolutely knew there must be a connection between the Ambassador's murder and the killings at the Castle.*

"Security video shows they disturbed only one file, about a 1930s Hearing on the *Business Plot*," Josh said.

"What the hell is that?"

"Testimony about some rich-as-Midas individuals plotting a takeover. A General said an agent of Wall Street approached him to overthrow the President. Congress sealed the hearing records in the 1930s. The public's never seen it. But now it's missing."

"Richmond and Bocelli looked at a file that's been secret over 80 years? And it's gone. Crap, there goes our lead." Davis threw up both hands. We can't catch a break here."

"It gets weirder. We found a fourth set of prints at the scene. The first three were Oscar, Richmond and Bocelli. The fourth set matches Tomas Lobo."

"That guy turns up everywhere." *And every time he does, someone else ends up dead.* "What did you find on him?"

"He's a former army sniper," Josh said. "Worked corporate security. Don't know who he works for now. But his cell phone records show Hans

Berger, the dead subway guy, called him."

"*Damn. Everything comes back to Tomas. He's the key to answering a lot of these questions.* I wanna talk to him. Turn over every rock and bush. Find him."

"Yes sir."

CHAPTER 26

Gina walked away from the from the Monitor displaying the Mona Lisa. "Where's the Palazzo Vecchio scale model?" she asked.

"Over here." Joe pointed to a black pedestal display table beneath a three feet high scale model of a rectangular stone building. The five-story miniature fortress sported a roof with regularly spaced squared openings on its perimeter. The gaps were battlements, or crenels, through which guns could shoot. A tall rectangular bell tower loomed high above the structure's fifth story. A tiny replica of Michelangelo's original white marble statue of David stood guard outside the front entrance.

"So, they put Machiavelli on trial there in the Grand Courtroom." She said, looking the scale model up and down.

"The aristocracy seized power from the Florence Republic, then the prosecution charged Machiavelli with conspiracy to overthrow their de facto monarchy. The biased Judge found him guilty."

"Sounds like the fix was in."

Boy was it ever. It gave new meaning to the phrase Kangaroo Court. "The Judge sentenced him to the dreaded strappado interrogation. They tortured him for warning the public about the aristocracy's threat to freedom."

"What's the strappado?" Gina's brow furrowed.

Joe pointed at a painting showing two muscular bailiffs pulling down, with all their might, on a rope running through a pully attached to the prison ceiling. The rope's opposite end hung down and tied a half-naked man's arms behind his back.

"The bailiffs' rope lifted Machiavelli's arms until he hung only a few feet from the ceiling." Joe moved both hands to simulate pulling on an imaginary rope. "The pressure on his shoulders was unbearable. He cried out in pain. They loosened their grip on the rope. He fell like a sack of flour. But before his feet reached the floor, they grabbed the rope again. The sudden stop jerked Machiavelli's shoulders from their sockets."

"Oh, my god, that's hideous." Gina winced.

"He screamed. His head tilted back, his eyes closed, and his face contorted in terror. He hung with his arms stretched upwards and backwards in the most unnatural position. The bailiffs repeated the process three times. He almost lost consciousness from the intense pain."

She shuddered and covered her mouth with one hand. "It's so awful, I can't stand it."

"After the final drop, they lowered him to the floor. He collapsed in an unconscious heap. His broken shoulders were a gruesome and useless mass. They carried him to a damp dark prison cell and left him on a sparse mattress, groaning and delirious."

"It's amazing he wasn't dead." She squeezed her eyes shut.

"They interrogated him more over the next few days. But he never confessed to treason."

"Most people would say anything at that point."

"Three weeks later the Judge released him from prison. The authorities exiled him under house arrest at a distant country home. Banished for something he didn't do."

Joe stared out the window into the distance. Machiavelli's terrible suffering should never have happened.

"No one should be treated like that." She screwed her face in disgust, turning away from the painting.

Joe pointed to a scale model of Machiavelli's tomb on a nearby pedestal.

Gina read from the plaque near Machiavelli's marble vault replica. "When he died years later, his family entombed him at Florence's Basilica of Santa Croce. Michelangelo and Galileo joined him there later."

"His persecution didn't stop with his death."

"There's more about Machiavelli's persecution over here." Joe pointed to a painting of eleven Cardinals dressed in blood red choir clothing sitting in a Vatican courtroom. They sat on high-backed elaborately carved wooden chairs surrounding a long narrow table filled with books and papers. Rows of tall golden candle sticks cast flickered light on the table. The flames sent small trails of black smoke up to the high ceiling. "After Machiavelli's death, special Cardinals functioned as Grand Inquisitors to preside over the various Roman Inquisition tribunals."

"They look determined," Gina said.

"The made-of-money Florence bankers' representative met secretly with the Grand Inquisitor. The bankers' agent dressed in fine garments adorned with gold trim and rare jewelry. He carried a copy of Machiavelli's book *The Discourses*." Joe pointed to a copy of the scarred leather-bound volume displayed on a nearby pedestal against the wall.

"Why'd he bring that?"

"Machiavelli had uncovered a secret threatening the opulent bankers' power. They wanted his writings banned." *And they would stop at nothing to see it happened.*

"Must have been a pretty powerful secret," she said.

"The representative reminded the Grand Inquisitor the bankers gave a great deal of money to the Church. In return, they expected the clergy to take immediate action to protect their interests. The Cardinal protested, saying Machiavelli's books were too popular to ban. But the representative pressured him until he gave in."

"The bankers were that powerful?"

Do you even have to ask? "More powerful than you could imagine." Joe shook his head with resignation as he glanced up at the eleven men in the painting. "That day the eleven Cardinals critically reviewed Machiavelli's books. They all agreed to the ban except for the oldest priest. He found no blasphemy in the writings, only factual statements about power."

"So, there was one honest man."

"He warned the others about money's power to corrupt the Church. But, several of them came from moneyed families. They didn't listen."

"Power corrupts."

Boy, did it ever. "The Cardinals issued a new order prohibiting anyone, even the highest public officials, from possessing or reading Machiavelli's books. The penalty was jail, torture and confiscation property."

"Those must have been *some* books." Gina wrinkled her nose at Joe's description of the Inquisition's judgment. "Aren't you forgetting something? We're here to look in the Palazzo Vecchio model. Remember, the place where Machiavelli was judged."

"Oh, yeah... right. I got so involved, I almost forgot." He grabbed the scale model with both hands, tilting it over on its pedestal, so the bottom side was visible. A black hinged lid, about a tongue depressor's width and length, sealed its underside. It resembled the cover for a battery compartment on a boombox. "This small door underneath might be it."

Joe steadied the Palazzo Vecchio scale model on its side. "I'll hold it while you open the hinged door in the bottom."

"Here goes nothing." Gina reached over and gently snapped open the hinged lid. She pulled two folded pages out of the narrow compartment, spreading them out on a nearby table. The first page appeared white and new. The second page looked yellow and stained with age. She focused her attention on the first page, reading its handwritten words aloud.

Offer prayers at the Church and Barclay Street angel's bench.

The irony of telling them to 'offer prayers' was not lost on Joe. "The gunmen almost killed me. I've already offered my fair share of prayers."

"There's a Church and Barclay Street in New York City." Gina winced. "Two blocks from the World Trade Center. But I've never heard of an angel's bench there."

Joe focused his gaze on the aged second page. Its pages were crisp to the touch, like they might crackle into dust at any moment. His eyes opened wide, scanning the heading. "My God. It's a Renaissance Florence police report, describing a raid on Machiavelli's house after his death."

"Let me see." Gina nudged him over, so she could get closer to the writing. Her hand smoothed the page's creases, making it easier to read. "It says the Inquisition delivered its decree banning Machiavelli's books, to the Podestà - the Florence Police Chief. His officers jumped into a horse-drawn police carriage, driving it to Machiavelli's house to confiscate his writings."

"They worked fast."

She read aloud from the report, "The Machiavelli family's clerk stood alone in the house. Four policemen broke down the front door, rummaging through the house searching for his writings. When they found none, they arrested the clerk and hauled him to the Palazzo Vecchio for interrogation. He refused to talk. So, they tied his hands, leading him up 400 steps to the top of the Palazzo's 94-meters tall Arnolfo Tower."

"That's 300 feet high." Joe pointed to the rectangular tower on the Palazzo scale model. *They had only one reason to take a prisoner up there... torture and confession.*

"The guards stopped to catch their breath on the tower's top landing. One of them set his arquebus gun down against the spiral staircase's metal railing."

"An arquebus... it's like a primitive musket."

Gina looked back down at the page and inhaled sharply. "The guards grabbed the clerk by his feet and dangled him over the side through the square crenel openings in the tower's low stone wall. He hung upside down in the open air high above the street below. They demanded he tell them where he hid the missing manuscripts. The hapless clerk flailed his arms in the open air and screamed he didn't know."

"He must have been terrified."

Gina continued reading. "One guard let go of the clerk's right leg, telling him this was his last chance to talk before they let go of the other. The clerk screamed at them not to drop him. He told them he'd hid the manuscripts in Machiavelli's tomb in the Basilica of Santa Croce."

Joe put his hand flat on the page and pulled it over in front of him. "My turn, this is too amazing."

She stuck out her tongue at him.

He read aloud. "The guards started to pull him up when they heard an explosion behind them. They whirled around toward the blast. When they pivoted, their grip loosened on the clerk's held leg and it slipped out of their hands. They tried to catch it but were too late. His screams echoed off the stone tower while he plummeted to his death on the pavement below."

"The poor man." Gina's head shook from side to side.

"The arquebus lay on the landing's stone floor with a trail of black burnt gunpowder extending from the muzzle to the staircase. The weapon had slid off the slick metal staircase top rail and fell against the bottom rail. It sparked and exploded." *What horrible luck at exactly the wrong time.*

"More death from aristocrats' attempts to bury this discovery."

"The police searched Machiavelli's tomb but found nothing. The clerk had lied. He'd hoped they'd haul him back up on the landing, so he might escape on his way to the tomb." Joe's head shook in disbelief. He folded the yellowed pages and slid them in his coat's side pocket. His wide eyes stared straight ahead.

"They killed him to destroy a secret." Gina scowled in disgust. "A book-burning and witch hunt all rolled into one."

"The persecution's still going on five-hundred years later. Someone murdered my co-workers for it."

"My ex, too."

"*The Business Plot's* connected to it. We've got to find out how."

An electronic humming sound interrupted their conversation. Gina looked up and spotted the culprit, a motorized lens security camera hung high on the wall. Her index finger pointed up at the oscillating lens. "Someone's watching us… maybe security or the assassins. They may be on their way here, now."

"We've got to move fast." *Whoever was watching had turned the camera to follow them around the room.* Joe carefully closed the scale model's compartment before returning it to its original position on the black pedestal. A moment later, an unexpected voice startled them from behind.

"Don't move, put your hands up where I can see them."

CHAPTER 27

J oe and Gina turned their heads toward the menacing voice's origin. A man in a black European cut suit stood behind them under the room's arched cased entrance, holding a gun in one hand. He aimed it at them from the shadows. As he edged closer his face became clear... it was Tomas Lobo. An icy tingle ran down Joe's spine.

"How convenient, two for the price of one." Tomas' mouth curled into a cruel smile. "You shouldn't have come here, you made a big mistake."

"We've got to stop meeting like this," Joe deadpanned with a voice showing no fear.

"I'm good with that." Gina chimed in.

"Smartasses, it's time to pay for the pain you caused me." Tomas motioned with his gun toward the exit.

He's talking about the concrete limb trapping his arm at the Natural History Museum. "What do you want?" Joe demanded.

"I think you know." Tomas' eyes glowered. He ambled to where Gina stood under the security camera. He brushed the back of his hand against her cheek. "You're even prettier than your photo. Softer, too."

"Don't touch me, bastard." She rolled her eyes, jerking her head away from his hand.

Tomas glared at her rejection. He raised one hand to strike her.

Now's my chance while he's not looking my way. Joe picked a quarter out of his pants pocket, flipping it through the room's arched cased opening. It struck a pedestal display table in the adjacent exhibit room. The coin clanked across the tile floor.

Tomas' eyes twinkled as his hand hesitated in mid-air. He turned his back to Gina, staring at the adjacent room's cased fluted entryway with gun drawn. "So, you're not alone. Come out with your hands up."

She peeked inside her designer black leather purse for something to use as a weapon against him. Her right hand slipped inside and came back out grasping a blue travel size can of aerosol hairspray. She pointed its nozzle directly at Tomas' head. "Look out," she yelled. He turned his shocked face toward her. She pressed her index finger hard against the push button, shooting a forceful mist out of the nozzle into his eyes. It covered his face in a cloud of searing alcohol and glue-like polymers.

Tomas screamed in pain. His eyelids squeezed tight from the stinging aerosol spray. The gun dropped from his hand, its cold steel hitting the tile floor with a clatter. Both hands shot up to his face as he swept one foot across the floor, trying frantically to find the weapon.

Gina lunged for the gun on the floor. She barely escaped Tomas' kick as it passed mere millimeters from her face.

Joe glanced around desperate for a weapon to use against the wounded assailant Five feet away, the Palazzo Vecchio scale model still stood atop its supporting pedestal. Joe grabbed it with both hands and lifted it to shoulder height. He charged at the still writhing Tomas, slamming the replica down over his head. *That's for killing my friends, you sorry bastard.*

The model shattered into dozens of pieces, disintegrating in Joe's hands like a jigsaw puzzle. The blow knocked Tomas to the floor. He lay on his side, motionless.

Joe kneeled and placed two fingers on Tomas' neck to check his pulse. He looked up under his eyebrows at Gina. "He's stunned for now, but he'll wake up soon. Let's get outta here."

They ran into the hallway and out the building's side door to the van, piling into the front seat. Gina turned the key, starting the engine. The van roared off down the street where it melted into the traffic.

They'd traveled several blocks from the building before Joe's face muscles relaxed. The time in the van had given him a few minutes to think. He had an idea, but he wasn't sure how she'd feel about it. "This is too big to solve on our own. I have an old friend, Friar Dominic. He may be able to figure out the connection between the murders and the *Business Plot*."

"Tell me more," Gina said as she changed lanes to pass a slow-moving car. "How do you know him?"

"We met a few years ago when we were both panelists at a seminar. His topic was the history of wealth and power. He's been a behind the scenes advisor to D.C. politicians for decades. He should be familiar with *The Business Plot*."

"Sounds impressive. Where do we find him?"

Good, she's receptive to the idea. "At the local Monastery, about twenty minutes away. We've got to get there fast before the assassins catch us."

Gina nodded as she made a left turn at the next intersection and gunned the engine, speeding off in the Monastery's direction.

CHAPTER 28

Agent Davis stared out Oscar White's National Archives office window while one of his agents told the unusual story how the van eluded officers at the intersection. "Let me get this straight." Davis rubbed his face with his hand as he confronted his subordinate about losing them. "You got a tip from Security that Bocelli and Richmond escaped in an Archives van."

"Yes sir."

"And you caught up with the van after they stopped at an intersection, but then lost them. Is that right?"

"Yeah. We almost had 'em, but they gave us the slip. They're clever"

"How is it that you, an FBI agent with years of emergency professional driver training, couldn't keep up with a museum researcher driving a clunky van?" Agent Davis exhaled in one big huff. *Bring me up to speed, am I missing something here?*

The agent's face turned red. "Well, sir, it wasn't act-u-ally the museum researcher driving."

"It wasn't. So, who was it?"

He paused and looked down at his shoes. "The Ambassador's wife."

The Ambassador's wife? "I'll be damned. Well officer, I'd suggest you go back to driving school… and while you're at it you might want to study up on a few more tricks. Make sure you aren't outsmarted by a lady computer consultant the next time."

"Yes sir," the agent said.

"So, how'd she lose you?"

"It's a little embarrassing sir. They decided to 'shoot the gap'."

"Shoot the gap." Agent Davis scowled. "What the hell's that mean?"

The agent's cheeks turned red when he explained what it meant.

Davis leaned over into the officer's face and pushed an index finger into his chest. "So, she plain outsmarted you and then sped away. Is there anything else I should know?"

"We don't have any idea where they are now." He looked down and lowered the volume of his voice, so it was barely audible.

"Well, that's dandy, isn't it? Just goddam dandy." Davis threw both hands in the air while shaking his head back and forth. "Now can anybody tell me why Oscar White, a National Archives Clerk, met in his office with Richmond and the Ambassador's ex-wife?" Davis turned to Josh. "Why would Tomas, a suspected serial murderer, go there?"

"I don't have an answer, sir," Josh said. "But there's something else you should know. White's dead. A co-worker found him twenty minutes ago in a storage closet, strangled with a piece of piano wire."

"Any leads on who did it?"

"Not yet. But the killer gained access to the building by robbing an Archives' employee. She was on her way to lunch. He shot her in her car in the parking garage. When officers searched her purse, they found her key card missing... the same one used to gain access to the Archives. We suspect the same person murdered both her and Oscar."

So, the assassin killed Oscar before we could question him. That's par for the course.

Davis sat silent for several moments. "I want a full report on Tomas. I wanna know who he works for, where he's been, who he associates with. There's gotta be some clue why he murdered Oscar White. Turn his apartment upside down."

"Yes sir."

"I want a list of everybody he's talked to in the last month." Davis's eyes narrowed. "Run 'em down and find out what they discussed. Cross-check any connections between Tomas, Ambassador Bocelli and the Italian embassy. Get going people there's no time to lose."

Davis' long day was about to become more difficult, if possible. A call came in from dispatch as they walked out of the Archives building. Surveillance video had picked up Joe, Gina and Tomas, scuffling at the Arts and Industries Exhibition Hall. Davis and his team piled in the squad car and it accelerated toward the Hall.

CHAPTER 29

The van's engine hummed as Gina drove down busy D.C. streets toward the local Monastery. She swerved to pass other vehicles while Joe gave her directions how to get there, from his passenger seat.

"Tell me more about your friend," she said in between lane changes.

"The first thing you notice about him is he has no ego or guile. He seems completely self-assured. Probably the most well-adjusted person I ever met."

"You think he might know who'd want the *Business Plot* records?"

"Yeah. That may tell us who hired Hans and Tomas." Joe's reply satisfied her curiosity. She silently re-focused her eyes on the road.

He glanced at the dashboard clock. We've got several minutes before we arrive. His eyes blinked three times and then floated shut as the engine's constant drone lulled him to sleep. He'd been asleep five minutes when the tires bounced over a splintered pothole in the pavement, rudely awakening him. The commercial van's stiff hauling suspension recoiled like a linebacker making a full speed hit on quarterback. Joe's body flung a couple inches above his bucket seat, jarring his back as both hips came back down against the cold vinyl. "Ow! what was that?"

Gina lowered her head. "Sorry, I didn't see that pothole in time to avoid it."

His gaped mouth stare receded after a couple seconds. There was no sense blaming her. She had a lot of stress, too. They were almost at their destination by his calculations, so he breathed a sigh of relief.

They turned a corner and the Monastery's outer wall came in to view. A long row of apricot colored arched Rosary Porticos with red tile roofs stretched in a rectangle around the Monastery's grounds. Two round columns supported each of the Portico's many arches. A black wrought iron fence connected each pair.

Joe's jaw slackened as he took in the magnificent view. *It's a beautiful structure. And the grounds are incredible.*

The van turned into the main driveway. They passed through the Monastery's porte-cochère, or coach gate, a dual-arched structure which covered visitors from rain while they exited their cars. The van slowed next to a mulched flower island and parked near the side entrance. A huge silver colored dome glistened in the sunlight atop the estate's massive Neo-Byzantine style building.

They got out of the van and strode to the building's pewter colored double doors, their breath looking like white steam from a tea kettle. Joe lifted the heavy steel door knocker to rap three times. No one answered, so after a couple minutes wait, they turned away to try another door.

They had walked less than ten feet, when the door creaked halfway open behind them. A monk in a dark-brown cowl poked his head out of the doorway. His downward gaze betrayed a discomfort with outsiders.

"Peace be with you," his deep voice greeted them.

"We're here to see Friar Dominic," Joe gave a half-smile. "I'm an old friend."

The monk muttered something under his breath about guests outside visitors-hours, before waiving them through the door. They followed him down a long hallway lined with classic fine art paintings illustrating various pastoral scenes. He gave one-word responses to their attempts to draw him out of his shell.

It's a good thing the art's here to admire, because our introverted host sure isn't much for small-talk.

They arrived at an open doorway marked 'Library' with a plain brown name plate. The monk silently motioned them into the room with a wave of his hand before disappearing without a sound. The comfortable room had tall arched windows, wooden beams, fabric sofa and chairs. Joe's nostrils filled with the musty smell of yellowed pages and aged scuffed leather book covers.

He looked across the room where a trim academic-looking middle-aged gentleman dressed in a full-length habit stood, holding an open book. The man glanced up from his reading and snapped it shut when he spotted them. His eyes squinted, straining to recognize the visitors. When Joe's face came into focus, the man's mouth curved into a broad grin. He bounded forward with arm extended to firmly shake Joe's hand. "Joe, what a surprise! How long has it been?"

"Not since that Princeton seminar." Joe smiled as he returned the hearty handshake.

"Yes, Princeton. *That* was an impressive panel." Dominic raised a brow, staring over Joe's shoulder at Gina behind him. "You must introduce me to your charming friend"

"Dominic, this is Gina Bocelli," Joe extended his open hand palm up toward Gina. "Italian Ambassador Bocelli's ex-wife."

"It's a pleasure to meet you." She offered her hand to Dominic to shake.

"How do you do Ms. Bocelli?" Dominic asked, accepting her hand. "Of course, I know of the Ambassador and his distinguished career."

"Thank you for seeing us on such short notice," she said.

"Joe probably told you, he and I are old friends," Dominic had a mischievous look on his face as he turned back toward Joe. "Did you ever finish writing that book about *sex* and art in Renaissance Italy. You seemed rather *excited* about it at the time."

I *bare-ly* remember, it's been so long ago." Joe's eyes twinkled. This was the Dominic he knew, a man with intelligence and a quick sense of humor. "The *art* section was all right, but the sex part was too racy. I chose the lesser of two *easels*."

Gina did her best to stifle a smile as she rolled her eyes, groaning at the puns.

Dominic directed his kind gaze at her. "You'll have to forgive us. We have this ongoing dialogue ... its hilarity sometimes escapes others. To what do I owe the pleasure of your visit?"

"It's been such a crazy last few hours I don't know where to begin." Joe paused and looked away. How could he bring Dominic up to speed on events happening so fast Joe could barely follow them, himself?

"Well then, take your time and walk me through it." Dominic's expression softened, his fingers forming into a steeple.

Gina picked up the ball and ran with it. "We're caught up in some events we don't fully understand. It may involve men with incredible wealth and power. Joe says you know more about that subject than anyone."

"Your flattery moves me," Dominic said. His eyes lit up as he leaned in toward them. "I'll do what I can. Tell me more."

"Someone murdered the Italian Ambassador last night at the Embassy," Joe said. "It happened after the Machiavelli-da Vinci celebration. Hit-men are involved." *I'm guessing they're the same ones that tried to kill me.*

Dominic's eyes softened. He grasped Gina's hand with his. "I'm so sorry. This must be very traumatic. I can't imagine what you're going through."

Joe described how afterward he and Gina had returned from the Exhibit Hall to discover his slain co-workers. He recounted how first Axel, and later Tomas, tried to kill them.

"How tragic." Dominic's forehead furrowed as he shook his head. "But, why do you think my expertise would help?"

Joe explained about Hans Berger's death in the subway and their visit to the National Archives. "Oscar refused Hans' demand to see the sealed *Business Plot* files, sending him away empty handed. But he let us see the records. It was a real eye opener."

"You've seen the files recently?" Dominic let out a deep breath like the wind had been knocked out of him. After a couple seconds he added. "After they'd been sealed all these years

"Today, in fact. We saw the conspirators' names."

Dominic's jaw dropped. A moment later he composed himself. "How on earth did you convince Oscar to let you?"

"We showed him Hans' hit list with Oscar's name on it. Once he saw that, he was desperate to find out what we knew. In return, he shared the files." *Self-preservation can be a powerful motivation.*

"Wow." Dominic steadied himself with one hand against a bookshelf while he looked away to one side. "I never thought those files would see the light of day."

"We need your help.," Joe said. "What are we up against?"

Dominic pulled two chairs out from the table and motioned for them to sit down. "Make yourself comfortable while I show you. But, prepare yourselves to be shocked at the answer."

CHAPTER 30

Tomas stood outside the National Archives building on the busy sidewalk, peering down the street. His right hand clutched an oxblood leather satchel holding the stolen *Business Plot* files. A long black antique limousine with smoked glass windows pulled up to the curb, stopping in front of him. He stepped up to the car, opened the back door and climbed inside. The automatic door locks clicked shut. He settled in and leaned back. *God, my head throbs. When Richmond hit me with that scale model it felt like a chair breaking over my head.*

The uniformed chauffer drove the limo away from the curb, merging with the heavy traffic. Tomas sat in the back seat facing his Patron, Lucian Drake, a billionaire many times over and one of the richest men in the world. He was one of the 'hiddens'-- men using an invisible-cloak-of-wealth to avoid all photography or publicity, living in exclusive luxury compounds far from where the public could reach them. Their preferred mode of transportation were their own private jets. No commercial air flights, airport searches or invasive screenings for them. The 'hiddens' private lives were kept very private.

"You're five minutes late." Lucian's bellowing voice sounded raspy from years of smoking,

"I had some loose ends." Tomas leaned forward to shake hands, but Lucian waived him off. Tomas admired Lucian's power but found his mannerisms petty to the point of prissiness. "They took a little longer than usual."

"Did you get it?" Lucian pointed a fleshy index finger at the leather satchel sitting on the seat between them.

"Yes, Sir." Tomas reached over, patting the satchel's side three times with his hand. "Just like you asked."

"I've wanted these for years." Lucian's eyes gleamed as he reached for the satchel, yanking out stacks of paper from it, laying them on his seat. "The Archives can't be trusted. Their do-gooders might leak it to the public and ruin everything."

Lucian looks almost obsessed groping those dusty old pages. You'd think they were gold. "Well, you won't have to worry now."

Lucian stopped in mid-motion, holding a stack of files next to his chest. A fearful look crossed his face. "Did anyone see you take them?"

"Only the curator and he's dead." Tomas shrugged. *Does he think I'm a fool? I know how to pull off a job.* "The Archives has so many files they won't miss these for a while."

"Good." Lucian opened a cigar box from the limo's console, lit up a fat stogie and blew smoke rings that looked like cloudy donuts. His puffy cheeks had brown age spots marking more than six privileged decades. His demeanor turned expansive. "Have I told you about *The Business Plot*?"

"I'm afraid not sir." Tomas' expression dulled. *I'm not sure I want to know. Lucian looks so giddy over getting these documents, it's probably loosened his tongue.*

"In 1934, a retired general testified that some men of great-wealth planned a coup to replace the U.S. President with a de facto dictator. The war hero General said they recruited him to lead the takeover."

"It sounds like your current plan." Tomas raised one eyebrow. "Obviously, it didn't work back then." *So, why are you trying it, now?*

"Yeah. That's where I got it. It would have worked then... it was a good plan, one that would have made those men rich-beyond-dreams. But the General had a conscience. He reported it and Congress scheduled hearings."

"Let me guess. The hearing transcript's in this file." *God, the cab's filling with smoke... I wish he'd put the damn stogie out.*

"That's why I had you steal it." Lucian's eyes flashed with savage condescension. "The less the public knows about the 1934 conspiracy, the better."

"I see. That makes your coup a bigger a surprise."

"Exactly."

"But they failed back then." Tomas' expression changed to a scowl. "How will this time be different?"

"Their mistake was not offering the General *enough* money. Anyone can be bought for the right price." Lucian's fingers fidgeted. "But, enough about the past. How's our plan coming?"

He's probably nervous about whether we'll be ready. "Right on schedule. The downtown underground armory's finished. We moved the arms cache there yesterday. Preparations are almost complete."

"Good, Good." Lucian rubbed his hands together. "Now, who to lead the coup. We must pick the right man this time. I have a lot at stake."

"I've gone through every available name. No stones have been left unturned."

"We need someone who'll appeal to the public." Lucian smiled an evil smile before continuing. "And who shares our ideology, so he won't turn on us."

Lucian's haunted by the fear his dictator will turn on him. He can't get it out of his mind. "I found only one man who fits the bill, General George Rogers. He's a highly decorated retired general with charisma. Works for RavenSpire Industries, a military contractor. He's ideologically opposed to the President."

"Could he rally soldiers to march on Washington, in large numbers?"

"Like no one else."

What about morals?" Lucian crossed his arms. "Would he have a problem doing this for money? You know, I hate pesky morals. They interfere with profit."

It's not just morals, you hate anything that interferes with profit "No. He's a military contractor executive. He should be receptive to a lucrative offer."

"Excellent." Lucian rubbed his hands together in glad anticipation.

"There's a noon luncheon today at RavenSpire Industries for active and former military brass. General Rogers will be there along with other Gulf War big shots. You can recruit him then."

"I'll be there." Lucian took another puff on his stogie. "RavenSpire owes us money. That should help." A faraway look entered his eyes at the Gulf War reference. "Do you remember how the 1990 Iraq War started?"

"Not really. Just that we ran into a lot of opposition beforehand."

"That's right," Lucian licked his lips. "The public was worn out from decades of Middle East wars. Do you know what changed their mind?"

What the hell is he getting at? "No. Should I?"

Lucian was so into his story he ignored the jab. "My people planted the story Iraqis turned off Kuwait's maternity ward incubators to kill babies. It was a huge lie. But that's all it took to persuade the public to go to war. It worked."

"You're kidding, right?" Tomas' eyes widened. *"Why would you make up a lie like that to start a war?"*

"I'm dead serious. I had an interest in a military arms manufacturer that had serious financial trouble. We'd committed financial fraud and looted the company. A pending annual audit would have discovered it. We needed a giant cash infusion to hide the loss, right away."

"So, it was all for money." *That's diabolical. I know people who died in that war.* Tomas made a mental note about this potential blackmail tool.

Lucian was on a roll and barely heard Tomas' comment. "The war provided us with no-bid military contracts providing huge profits to hide what we'd stolen. My corporation owed billions to creditors, so they too supported the war to get paid. If we'd gone bankrupt, they'd have received only pennies on the dollar. Their lobbyists and politicians gave us complete backing, in addition to our own. We got whatever we needed from them." His face took on a smug look as he folder his arms.

Tomas gasped. *Lucian's treachery sounds evil even to me, a professional assassin. But a moment later Tomas realized it might be even more wicked than he'd thought.* "Did you trick us into the 2003 second Gulf War, Desert Storm, too?"

"What do you think?" Lucian chuckled. "I'd already decided to go back into Iraq in 2003 to recharge their balance sheets. The 9/11 World Trade Center attack gave us the perfect excuse. The public didn't even realize the terrorists weren't from Iraq."

"I know." *They were from Afghanistan and Saudi Arabia.*

"It was the easiest con ever. Like taking candy from a baby."

"You can't be serious." Tomas pained look on his face showed as he backed away from Lucian. *Brave U.S. soldiers died. Civilians lost their lives in those two wars. The country racked up huge government debt. If not for that damned second war, my best friend would be alive today, instead of rotting in a dirt grave.*

"Profits require sacrifices." Lucian examined his manicured nails before looking down his nose at Tomas.

'But the Gulf war led to ISIS. We're more vulnerable to terror now than ever." Tomas could barely believe what he'd heard. For a moment, he considered turning Lucian in. *But who would believe me?* The public wouldn't want to admit they were played, it would be too humiliating. Many would choose to ignore being duped, to save face. He'd be like the 1934 *Business Plot* General, sounding the alarm, putting himself on the line. They'd label him a Cassandra, issuing accurate warnings no one listened to nor believed. But in the end, would anything change?

"A few moral souls pointed that out, but no one paid them much mind." Lucian sneered, pouring himself another drink. "And ISIS' new terror lays the groundwork for future profitable wars. It's the gift that keeps on giving."

"But it also means a big anti-war movement."

"I handled that. We called them un-patriotic. It shut them up, drowning them out with criticism."

"That's insane." Tomas shook his head in disbelief. "You didn't need to start a bogus war to make money. You're a multi-billionaire."

Lucian waived him off. "It's never enough. I want sure things with high profit."

"But think of the human suffering, the misery."

Lucian chortled, as if he hadn't even heard Tomas' last statement, like human suffering was trivial. "I'm lucky the *Business Plot* General's long dead. After the hearings were over, he gave speeches criticizing the conspirators. He pointed out how they made billions off the war machine. Called it blood money. His forgotten warnings could have spoiled both Gulf Wars for me."

Spoiled them for you? Is that all you think about? Tomas recoiled. Lucian's self-absorbed comment left him temporarily speechless.

"The public fell for this scam twice. They'll be ready for it. We'll have to come up with a new lie next time."

Boy you just don't quit, do you?

"There's a sucker born every minute." Lucian murmured the words while he scanned the next page from the file.

Tomas eyes narrowed at Lucian's reference to suckers tricked into war. *I was a soldier during the last Gulf War. Does he think I'm one of his dupes?* Tomas knew how to give as good as he got and decided now was the time. "The *Business Plot* General had principles and intelligence. That's hard to manipulate. The conspirators should have figured it out."

"How dare you." Lucian's nose curled while he snarled, "It wasn't their fault."

"Don't go any further." Tomas's eyes blazed as he stiffened, clenching both fists. Lucian had insulted him without realizing it. *I don't take abuse from anybody. Not now, not ever.*

"Of course." Lucian took a deep breath and shrank back. Tomas had killed multiple times for hire, an expert at the world's deadliest craft. It would not do to make him angry. Lucian forced a thin smile and laid on the sugar. "Your point's well taken. We'll not make the same mistake twice."

Tomas nodded silently, staring out the window. He hated Lucian's Gulf War scam down to its core, but the conciliatory statement was a relief. *No, going public wasn't the answer. Instead, he'd stay quiet.* After all, Lucian hired him when almost nobody else would, and paid him very well. He'd collect his money and hope to save enough to retire somewhere far away. Then, he could escape this line of work and put the crappy memories behind him. In the end, he rationalized it all away for money.

Lucian pressed the button on his smart phone, calling his secretary and putting the unit up to his ear. "Set up a meeting for me with RavenSpire Industries' CEO Jim Astor, right away. Tell him it's of an urgent nature… but don't tell him what it's about. And get me everything you can find on RavenSpire executive, General Rogers. I want it yesterday."

CHAPTER 31

Gina increased the pitch in her voice as she repeated Joe's question. "What *are* we up against?" She ignored Dominic's offer to sit down in the library to be comfortable. This was too important.

"You must first understand greed." Dominic chose his words with care. "The wisest men who ever lived spent years studying it – men like Aristotle, Plato, Plutarch and Solon."

"Where do we start?" she asked.

He pointed to a cream-colored scroll with five biblical verses written in bold color Old English font. "Right here... read the first verse," Dominic said. "It's the most important."

Joe read out loud from the top of the scroll.

For the love of money is a root of all kinds of evil

"The *love of money*? Gina's forehead wrinkled. "I thought it was just *money*."

"That's a misquote from framed cross stitches sold at fall festivals," Joe said. "They changed "The Love of Money" to "Money" to save on stitching. The revision completely changed the verse's meaning. Money by itself isn't bad." He knew the difference well from the research for his book *There's the Public Line, and Then There's the Real Story*.

"I wondered why the crafts said it that way. It made no sense," Gina said. "

"Indeed, it didn't." Dominic replied. "Money's needed to buy food, clothing and housing. Evil doesn't come from money. It comes from the *love* of money… *the pathological addiction* to money."

Wow, that's a powerful distinction. A lightbulb went off in Joe's head. "The evil occurs when men lust blindly after it. When they're never satisfied."

"But my church didn't spend time on the love of money." Gina shrugged. "They preached against murder, lying and stealing. If you're right, then how could so many churches get it wrong?"

"There's a reason," Dominic chuckled. "Churches rely on members' donations to survive. It's their lifeblood. The biggest donations may come from the wealthiest parishioners. Any church preaching too loud about "the love of money" might see donations dwindle. Those well-heeled members may be lured away down the road by a less truthful, but more fawning pastor."

"I've never thought about it that way." Gina tilted her head to one side. "That's a built-in financial incentive to downplay the money changers' greed."

"The prosperity gospel can be used to accommodate the greedy. But, it's a slippery slope." Dominic said. "If churches twist Christ's teaching to fatten their coffers, they become little more than businesses selling a mislabeled product. In such cases, their members may seem more like retail customers rather than Christ's followers."

A pastor would have difficulty building a fancy megachurch without lots of money. How much influence would the wealthiest donors wield? Joe scratched his head. *Is that why Christ had no fancy church building, because it gave him more freedom to preach the truth?*

"Greed is the World's biggest problem." Dominic had a knowing look as he laid his book down on the table. "It's the underlying cause of those other sins that get more press. That makes it the vilest one of all. Now, read the scroll's second verse."

It sure sounded like Dominic had done his homework. Joe looked at the scroll and read further.

It is easier for a camel to go through a

*needle's eye than for a rich man to enter into
the Kingdom of God.*

"Everyone's heard that one," Gina said.

"Scholars think it's one of the few verses Christ actually said," Dominic replied. "A wealthy young ruler asked how to gain eternal life. Jesus told him to sell whatever he had, give the money to the poor and follow him. But the young ruler refused because he loved his riches too much."

Joe knew scholars had hotly debated the verse. Many authorities believed the 'needle' was a small gate in Jerusalem's wall used by travelers at night to enter the city after the larger gates closed for protection from enemy attack. A camel would have to unload its valuable cargo to fit through the narrow passage to enter the city. Others believed the verse referred to a metaphorical sewing needle eye through which you could pull thread, but not a camel. Regardless of which interpretation they used, most agreed it meant those with towering-wealth had extreme difficulty living the type of virtuous life allowing them entry into heaven.

"That's all very interesting, but what does it have to do with us?" Gina said.

"You'll understand soon." Dominic waved his hand toward the half-dozen framed prints hanging from the library walls. Each looked like a copy of a famous biblical scene from an old masters' painting.

Joe scanned the prints and shrugged. "I'm not sure how this helps." *The answer may be clear to Dominic, but it's not to me.*

"I'll explain." Dominic pointed his right index finger upward. "Christ used violence only one time in his life. Do you know when?"

"Jesus was peace loving." Gina folder her arms across her chest. "I don't remember him being violent."

"He was once... as an adult." Dominic exhaled with exasperation, trying not to raise his voice. "When he overthrew the money-changers' tables and drove them out of the Temple. They had turned it into a den of robbers." He pointed at a dark color print in which Jesus swung his arm at a half-dozen men in biblical robes. They scurried to get away from him.

Joe stepped within two feet of the print to peer at the image's layers of color texture. "The money-changers' look afraid and surprised. You can feel the panic. They're trampling each other to get out of his way." *Christ really did have them on the run.*

Dominic described how Temple rules required the poor to buy sacrificial doves, threatening those poverty-stricken souls with damnation if they didn't purchase quickly. "The money-changers bought the doves low and sold high, charging a huge markup. This rapacious overcharge of poor widows enraged Christ, prompting his action."

Gina leaned her head closer, studying the painting for a couple moments. "What's he holding?" She squinted, pointing a finger at Christ's hand in the painting's upper right-hand corner.

"It's a cat-o'-nine-tails, a whip of cords. You need more light for a better look." Dominic pulled down hard on the window blind's cord to open it. Sunlight rays streamed in to illuminate the painting. "He's whirling it above his head at the money-changers. He overturned their tables and dumped their coins on the ground."

"You can see the anger in his eyes," Gina said. "He meant business."

"Christ's physical reaction shows how evil they were." Dominic's jaw clenched as he read the verse from a black gold leaf Bible in one hand. "The Temple bankers didn't take this lying down. After he told them don't make my Father's house a marketplace, and called them a den of robbers, they began looking for a way to *kill* him." Dominic slapped his open palm on the table.

"They crucified him soon after." Joe stepped back from the painting, thinking about Christ's trial. "All because of their pathological addiction to money."

"Wait, back up." Gina shook her head back and forth. "I thought they killed him because he healed the sick on the Sabbath. Not because he called them robbers."

"No, my dear." Dominic shook his head while putting his hand on her shoulder. He had the look of someone who'd seen reactions like hers many, many times before, fueled by decades of religious misdirection. "They killed him because he hurt their *profits*. Many churches gloss over that part. They prefer a less threatening reason for the crucifixion... for obvious reasons."

"No, no." Gina wasn't giving up yet. "They crucified him because he claimed divinity, as the son of God. His words clashed with Temple law and challenged Caesar's rule."

"That's not entirely true." Joe recognized the gaping hole in her theory, and jumped in. "Christ had claimed divinity before. But they didn't crucify him until after he expelled the money changers. It was a crucial distinction."

Joe rubbed his forehead. Dominic's revelations had raised new unsettled questions in Joe's mind. *How ironic it would be if Christ was crucified because of greed.* Some televangelists packed the TV channels, claiming God financially rewarded those with presumed moral superiority. They piously banged the pulpit repeatedly with their fists, professing the poor had only to improve their righteousness to flourish. Those preachers strung out their pronunciation of Christ's name into four syllables for added dramatic effect. "Ja-ee-a-sus wants you to be rich." Their message promoting the very greed Christ warned against.

"The Temple bankers took their cue from powerful financial organizations throughout history," Dominic said. "They killed when someone threatened their income stream."

"You're too hard on the money changers," Gina's hand gave a dismissive wave. She wasn't quite ready to give up the comforting interpretations she'd held for a long time. "They were well-to-do men charging what the market would bear. They weren't greedy, that's commerce... free enterprise... the magic of the marketplace."

"Threatening poor widows with eternal damnation if they don't buy rapaciously priced doves, is not free enterprise. It's extortion by moneyed men who have no empathy for the poor."

"I don't think greed's the biggest problem." Gina's brow furrowed. "Churches preach a lot about sins of the flesh. Aren't those worse than the love of money?"

"No," Dominic said with a twinkle in his eye. "Christ spoke more strongly against greed. But, sins of the flesh may arouse more congregational excitement, and thus more donations. That may cause some Churches to persecute people more for their sexuality and sexual orientation, than for their money-lust."

Joe notice Gina's eyes staring off into space. *Dominic's arguments are wearing her down.*

"If that's true, are there other things my church didn't bother to tell me?" She sighed and pressed her lips together. She'd voiced a troubling question.

"Dominic may be onto something." Joe picked up a Bible off the table and opened it to Genesis. "Greed was the original sin. Adam and Eve

GARY RAPPARD

coveted everything in the Garden of Eden, even the tree's forbidden fruit. Greed got mankind kicked out of paradise." *And the intriguing question was whether man would get back in if he conquered avarice?*

Dominic spoke as if he read Joe's mind. "Reducing greed will help man return." He pointed to an oil painting of civil rights leader Martin Luther King, Jr. on the wall. "Remember the old Negro spirituals talking about the promised land and paradise. They were on to something. People are happier when their community is less greedy and has more shared respect. Humans long for it."

If Dominic's right, the Business Plot would have taken evil to a whole new level. Joe cocked his head, remembering their original purpose for this visit. "But who are we up against? That's why we're here."

"I'm getting ready to explain. This is a foe like you've never faced before."

CHAPTER 32

Lucian's black antique limousine pulled up outside RavenSpire Industries' reflective glass office building in Washington, D.C. and parked near the curb. The company's headquarters stood only three blocks from the Capitol Mall. Lucian didn't want to be late for his private meeting with RavenSpire's energetic CEO, so the uniformed chauffer arranged their prompt arrival.

The doorman, dressed in a long burgundy coat, opened the luxury car's back door and helped Lucian out onto the sidewalk, through brass framed glass double doors into the red-carpeted lobby. A quick elevator ride took them to the top floor. Once, there, a perky blonde secretary ushered Lucian into CEO Jim Astor's plush executive office.

"Lucian, it's a pleasure to see you." Astor came around from behind his modern glass and chrome executive desk to greet Lucian with a warm handshake and charming smile. "Make yourself comfortable." He motioned with an extended palm up toward an oversized black leather guest chair.

"I always do." Lucian sat down and leaned back in the seat. Astor's secretary leaned over, her top's snug V-neck defying gravity as she handed him a Perrier water. Lucian's gaze dipped to her décolletage.

"How's New York. I haven't been there since last year?"

Lucian's head jerked back up in response to Astor's query. "Oh, it's crowded with Christmas season tourists, you know, the whole Rockefeller Center thing. There's a surplus this year. I could do with a lot less."

"We haven't seen you in a while." Astor took a seat in the companion leather chair. "Your secretary said it was urgent."

"I came to talk about RavenSpire's obligation to our investment bank."

"Oh-h-h… that," Astor pressed his lips together. "I apologize. We've been late with the last few payments. We make our money off wars, but all we have now are small military actions. The President isn't interested in another big one, so it affects our cash flow."

"I understand." Lucian's eyes gleamed with deviltry. "I'm here to make you a proposition." *One you can't refuse.*

"What did you have in mind?" Astor lifted an eyebrow.

"I can temporarily suspend your obligation to my bank. That would buy you time." *I'll bet I've got his attention, now.*

"I'd be grateful of course," Astor twisted the gold ring on his finger. His eyes narrowed as he pondered the motive behind Lucian's sudden generosity. "But, what do you want in return?"

"Nothing much. I'd merely like you to persuade one of your executives, General Rogers, to help me with a project."

"He's working on some important projects for us. I'm not sure we can spare him right now."

"I'd pay him an impressive salary. And I'd compensate RavenSpire handsomely for any inconvenience. I'll make sure you're both satisfied." *He probably thinks this sounds too good to be true.*

"I'm not sure I understand." Astor squirmed in his seat. "Why do you want him? You have all the executives you want."

"He has some special *qualifications* I need." Lucian smirked. "He shares my political outlook. And he disagrees with the President on military funding."

Astor's eyes studied Lucian, searching for more clues to what was up. "If you need him, why not approach him yourself instead of asking me?"

"My project is sensitive." Lucian looked down and inspected his fingernails. "He may have some concerns. That's where you come in… you can convince him to help. You were his upperclassman mentor at the military academy. Now you're his employer. He trusts you."

"What are your suggesting I do to persuade him?" Astor rubbed his neck, gazing out his luxury office' window.

"I want you to show General Rogers a doctored White House report saying the President intends to slash military base funding and close bases. Rogers will view the cuts as dangerous. He'll want to stop them. The only way to do that is to remove the President."

Astor did a double-take. "Jesus. You aren't kidding, are you? What the hell makes you think he'll believe the report, much less go along?"

"He'll believe it because he got it from you, and he'll go along because I'll offer him too much money to refuse." Lucian stared past Astor at the floor to ceiling window's stunning view of the U.S. Capitol Building dome. *And peer pressure from the other officers' outrage at the base closings, won't hurt.* "You're having lunch here in a little while with General Rogers. You'll have some guests of the right persuasion, retired officers who work for corporate military contractors and oppose the President."

"I guess it could be the right setting." Astor shrugged.

"After the meal, you show the guests copies of the report. Everyone in the room who reads it will be angry at the President. They'll express appropriate outrage at the faux base closing plan and demand something be done."

So, we get them all angry at the President, then what?" Astor's forehead creased. "

"When the guests are leaving, you pull General Rogers aside. You ask him to stay for a private discussion in your office. I'll be waiting here to ask him to help with our plan to replace the President. I'll tell him we have unlimited money at our disposal and can recruit troops to join us."

"My God, you really plan to do this, don't you?" Astor almost choked on his words. "It won't work. The President will never go along."

"We'll see about that. Senator Hogue will schedule a meeting with him at the White House. Hogue will bring General Rogers with him. When they're alone in the Oval Office they'll offer the President an incredible sum of money to let Rogers assume power. Once that happens, the President will function as a figurehead only."

"What if the money doesn't persuade him?" Astor cringed. "After all, he's the President. He'd be giving up all that power."

Lucian eyes blazed at the thought the ante might be raised. "If the President refuses, we'll signal military officers at a secret warehouse armory near the Capitol. They'll advance on the White House with automatic weapons and artillery. The takeover will begin."

"I'm not sure what to say." Astor stroked his chin. "The explosions alone should terrify the President. But even if he agrees, the public won't stand for a takeover."

"We won't call it a takeover." Lucian shook his head. "Senator Hogue will announce it as a temporary administration to restore honest government. To reinforce the message, General Rogers won't wear a military uniform when he addresses the public. Instead he'll wear a suit and tie."

"What about the line of Presidential succession? There's the matter of the Vice-President and the Speaker of the House"

They're a mere nuisance. Lucian rolled his eyes. "What about them? Once the President's either on our side or in custody, and we take power, they'll play ball. If not, we'll offer them so much money they can't refuse."

"What about the Fourth Estate? The media won't sit still for this." Astor said.

Lucian leaned back and put his hands behind his head. "That's already been taken care of. I've been busy buying up the major media corporations in anticipation of this. They'll treat us favorably. Any anchor who doesn't cooperate will be fired."

"You'll still have to deal with Congress and the Supreme Court?"

Lucian shook his head. "Senator Hogue assures me once we control the White House and the media, he and his associates can keep them in line."

"And you'll suspend RavenSpire's debt to your bank if I help you?"

I've got him in the bag. He has no choice. "One-hundred percent, for as long as you need."

Astor hesitated for a moment before slapping his right hand down on his chair's stuffed leather arm. "Give me the damn White House report. I'll get right on it."

CHAPTER 33

A dozen current and former high-ranking military officers swapped jokes and ribald stories in RavenSpire's executive dining room around a long white cloth covered dining room table. They had finished feasting on a sumptuous luncheon prepared by the company's personal chef. The meal included champagne, caviar and stuffed lobster tail. After lunch, Astor handed each guest a bound copy of Lucian's fabricated report about Presidential military base closings. The guests puffed on cigars as they read. Several officers groused while voicing vigorous opposition to the closings.

"Damn liberal peacenik," a bald army colonel exclaimed. "The President should take his commie ways and get the hell out of the country."

Multiple head nods and guffaws around the room followed his comment. One officer made an obscene gesture with his middle finger in the White House' direction. "He wants a base closing... *I'll* give him a base closing."

The guests debated the shutdowns' negative defense impact for more than an hour before moving toward the coat room in preparation to leave. As General Rogers reached the front lobby, Astor pulled him to one side and asked him in a low tone to come to his office for a confidential discussion. The last guest said goodbye and strolled out to his car. Astor pushed the double front entrance doors closed, walking the General to the

CEO office.

They stepped into the wood paneled room where Lucian stood near Astor's cherry executive desk pouring bourbon from a golden bottle into a clear shot glass. A white opaque engraved letter 'R" adorned its side, for RavenSpire. Lucian looked up and set the half-filled bottle down on an ornate silver tray. He extended his open hand while strolling toward them.

"General, I'd like you to meet Lucian Drake," Astor said. "He's one of RavenSpire's main financiers."

Lucian's eyes twinkled as he shook the General's right hand. Lucian's free hand pointed toward a chocolate brown leather sofa. "General, please sit down and make yourself comfortable. Jim, would you mind giving the us a moment in private." His hand waived Astor back out the door.

The General raised an eyebrow as Astor left the room and closed the door behind him. The General sat down on the sofa, ramrod straight, eyes staring straight at Lucian with suspicion.

Lucian held up a clean glass and motioned toward Rogers. "Would you like something to drink, anything at all?"

The General tossed his head and cleared his throat. "No. I'm fine. But I'm curious why you called me in here. It's not often I meet with a man of your wealth in a setting like this."

Lucian scowled at the direct reference to his fortune. But his face lightened as he remembered the importance of his goal. *This isn't the time to get upset, there's too much at stake.* "Very well, General. Since you asked, I'll get right to the point." He cleared his throat. "The military budget is under siege by this White House. The President wants to close a half-dozen military bases as part of his next budget proposal. He's not cooperating with us."

"Jim showed me the report. What makes you so sure he wants to close those bases? I haven't seen this anywhere except in the report I got here. There's nothing like that coming out from the Pentagon."

He's too suspicious. This might be more than I first bargained for. "Rest assured we have it on very good authority."

"Why are you so concerned about the President cutting the military?" The General waved his hand with a dismissive outward flick of the wrist. "From what I hear, you already have half the money on the planet. Plus, you have plenty of defense contracts. The government has to pay you regardless of cuts."

This wasn't going to be easy, the General obviously thinks for himself. "Don't you understand? You of all people should be worried about the security risks."

"It's hard to get too excited." The General examined the fingernail cuticles on his curled left hand. "Even with the cuts, our military budget's larger than Switzerland's gross domestic product. It's larger than several other developed countries, too. We'll get by."

The General must have smelled a rat. He's a good enough poker player to call my bluff. Lucian squirmed in his chair, turned his head to one side and winced. He would have to play his other cards. "My God man, where's your patriotism? You were a general for God's sake… can't you stand up for your own military?"

General Rogers leaned forward on the sofa, folded his hands and looked Lucian straight in the eye. It was time to flush out the truth from this dandy. "Why don't you stop playing your little silly-ass game and tell me what you really want?"

Lucian shrank, leaning so far back in his chair he almost tipped over before catching himself with one arm. *He's treating me like one of those sarcastic sissies in elementary school. The ones who talked big but who couldn't beat their way out of a wet paper bag.* "All right, all right, let's lay all our cards on the table. We want your help convincing the President to share power with us. We think it's high time our positions took center stage."

The General threw back his head and gave a low throated laugh. "No, that's not what you want. You want me to help you intimidate the President, so he becomes a mere puppet. Then you can put a dictator in power and crush your opposition. This is about squashing democracy, isn't it?"

"Well, you put it most indelicately." Lucian's nose wrinkled as he let out a harsh breath.

"Hell, Lucian, you're damn well asking me to stage a military takeover of the White House." The General stood up from the sofa. "There's not a goddamn delicate thing about that."

"Does that bother you?" Lucian folded his arms, tilting his head back and looking down his nose at the General, with prissy-like haughtiness.

"Do you think you're the only person in history who's tried this?" The General chuckled. "At West Point we studied the records of military coups around the globe. There have been dozens and dozens."

This guy's no pushover, I underestimated him. "I had no idea you were so well-versed in this area."

"Never mind how well-versed I am. I suspected something when Jim pulled me aside after lunch and brought me in here. You wouldn't be interested in me unless you needed me to get your opponents out of the way."

How impertinent, doesn't he realize who I am? "Don't act so high minded. You don't like the President."

"I'm not sure I like you either." The General's eyes bored a hole through Lucian while pointing the cigar at him. "But that's beside the point. How do you intend to do it?"

"Well, uh, uh... you and Senator Hogue would meet with the President at the White House to convey our very generous offer to him." Lucian wasn't prepared for the question's directness.

"And what if he refuses?" The General crossed his arms.

"Then we make him an offer he can't refuse. I can afford to rent a military. My special private contractor is supplying an army of 10,000 mercenary troops for the takeover. You can supplement those forces with however many active duty soldiers you can recruit."

"A billionaire like you probably likes privatization, huh?"

Lucian frowned at Rogers' comment. "You'll send a signal to our forces waiting in a downtown warehouse. They'll advance on the White House, overpower the security detail and occupy the building. I guarantee you he'll cooperate at that point."

"That simple, huh? I don't think so." The General rolled his eyes and shook his head side to side.

How dare he give me such an insolent look. Lucian tapped his fingertips together. "Well, there are some additional details to be worked out. But, that's the gist of it."

"And how much do you expect to make off the takeover?"

How uppity. He obviously doesn't realize he's the hired help. That's none of his goddam business. Lucian shrunk back in his stuffed chair. "I'm not sure I know what you mean."

"Cut the crap." The General slammed his open hand down on Lucian's chair's arm. "You know exactly what I mean. How much?"

"My profit doesn't concern you." Lucian turned crimson and his lips pressed.

"Dammit. How much do you expect to make?" The General curled his lips with icy contempt. "And how much are you prepared to pay me for your lousy scheme?"

"Don't worry about that, you'll be well taken care of." Lucian's voice shook, surprising even himself. "You'll have to learn not to be so inquisitive if you're going to work for me."

The General walked over to the coat tree and put his coat on. "It's been nice knowin' ya." He turned toward the door, put his hand on the doorknob and opened it. "Good luck with your plan. You'll need it."

Jesus, he's serious. He's actually gonna walk out on me. The General was halfway out the office door when Lucian called out. "Wait, wait. You're right. Come back and we'll discuss your compensation."

The General stopped in the doorway and turned toward Lucian, leering at him. "How much, you dirty little bastard?"

"How does ten million dollars sound?" Perspiration drops formed on Lucian's forehead. He had not been prepared to discuss money at the very first feeling-out meeting with the General.

"It sounds like you're full of it," the General sneered.

Damn, I can't let him walk out of here without a deal. "How about twenty million? Half now and half after the takeover." Lucian had grown as rich-as-Midas by not ever paying a penny more than he had to, and he didn't intend to start now.

"That's crap. You're worth fifty billion dollars and growing, give or take a few billion. The takeover will make you ten times richer than you are now. I want one hundred million cash up front in an offshore bank of my choosing. And one hundred million more the day after the takeover."

The General's a tough negotiator. This was not going the way I'd hoped. Lucian drummed his fingers on the chair's arm. "I can't pay that much. I'll find another general. You're not the only one you know."

"Suit yourself." The General walked through the door. "Hasta la vista baby. I'm outa here."

The General sure knew how to play a poker hand. Lucian drew in a long breath and got up from his chair. He had to keep the General in the fold, he'd disclosed his plan to him and couldn't risk a leak. "Wait. Wait. Let's not be hasty." He gritted his teeth. "O.K., one hundred million dollars in cash up front with one hundred million more to follow."

The General turned back around to face Lucian. "Astor says you have offshore bank accounts worth billions. Set up an account in trust for me in the same bank and send me the account number. Transfer the cash to it by the end of business tomorrow."

"Done." Lucian held up one hand. *Drat. I've been out negotiated on money by a pro. That hasn't happened in a long time.* "But, before you go, how'd you know I'd agree to your terms?"

"You couldn't get another general of my stature who'd cooperate with you." The General snorted. "If you could you wouldn't have come to me first."

Lucian turned his head in disgust. His stomach churned with a touch of nausea. He hated that the General had bested him.

"I've got a lot of work to do if we're gonna pull this off." The General buttoned his long black wool overcoat. "Make sure you transfer the money like I said." He pulled up the collar around his neck and disappeared out the door.

CHAPTER 34

Dominic's black framed reading glasses sat low on the bridge of his nose as he pulled an old black and white photo from a cabinet in the Monastery's library. He placed it on the table as Joe and Gina peered over his shoulder. The caption read Black Tuesday, and the picture captured the tragic events that day at Wall Street's stock exchange.

"In the 1920s, Congress passed huge tax cuts for the aristocracy," Dominic said. "The cuts resulted in wild financial speculation by some men of astounding-wealth, bidding up stock prices to unsustainable levels. The 1929 Stock Market Crash followed."

"I've read about it," Gina said. "It was the deepest in U.S. history. Stock prices completely collapsed,"

"Investors lost the modern-day equivalent of over three-hundred billion dollars," Dominic said. "That led to The Great Depression, the worst economic disaster ever to hit the U.S."

"I knew people who lived through it." Joe bit his lip and looked down at the floor. *Catastrophic unemployment and massive foreclosures spread like wildfire. Poverty swept the country.*

"The Depression spiraled down deeper with no end in sight." Dominic looked over the top of his reading glasses at them. "Incredible fear gripped the nation. In the summer of 1932, 17,000 hungry unemployed U.S. World War I veterans, plus their family members and supporters marched on

Washington demanding to cash in their delayed military service bonus benefit. Republican President Herbert Hoover refused their plea, sending General Douglas MacArthur, tanks and soldiers with bayonets and teargas, to drive the veterans from their campsite. The charge caused over one-hundred injuries, a death and a miscarriage."

"Unpopular Hoover lost the election by a landslide to Roosevelt that fall," Joe said. "In the years that followed, Roosevelt helped the veterans. He got them jobs with the Civilian Conservation Corps."

"He also had a plan to dig the rest of us out of the Depression." Dominic punched the newspaper's headline with his finger. "He created jobs for the unemployed, building roads, bridges and dams, through the Works Progress Administration, the WPA. They built projects like Hoover Dam, the Lincoln Tunnel, New York's LaGuardia Airport. Most still work. Those jobs put dollars in the workers' pockets. They used those dollars to buy homes, cars and appliances which, in turn, created more jobs. It was a tremendous success putting people on the path to financial recovery."

"But some opulent men didn't like Roosevelt's program." Joe's face turned downward. "They did everything they could to stop him, preferring he do nothing to help millions of jobless Americans." *They worried his plan might work and be popular. Especially when compared to their do-nothing policy that made the Depression's first years even deeper.*"

"Hold on a minute," Gina said. "The Depression might have ended eventually without the jobs program."

"Maybe, but most experts believe the WPA shortened it by years," Dominic said. "Some ultra-rich men hated paying tax on their massive holdings, to fund programs providing jobs for the jobless. So, they fought it."

"Hey, back up," she held up one hand as a stop signal. "Wouldn't they want whatever would shorten the Depression."

"Apparently not." Joe shook his head. "They had an ulterior motive. Oscar's *Business Plot* file said the conspirators hoped destitute people would become disillusioned with democracy and turn to the conspiracy's hand-picked dictator." *Then the conspirators could control the nation. But, unfortunately for them, the jobs program worked.*

"If the WPA hadn't succeeded, those that wanted a dictator might have won." Dominic's face took on a more solemn look and his voice lowered. "Government by the people could have vanished."

THE FOURTH CIRCLE OF HELL

"There'd have been nobody left to defeat Hitler," Gina said. "A few dictators would have dominated the whole-world."

Dominic nodded in agreement. "Some U.S. industrialists wanted to appease Hitler. They sold equipment to him. Roosevelt warned Americans about men who were more interested in their own profits than in democracy."

The 1929 Stock Market Crash, the Great Depression The Business Plot, Hitler, Franklin Roosevelt, Temple Money Changers, Christ's Crucifixion. Joe scratched his head, trying to make sense of it all. *It's shocking.* After a long drawn out silence he said, "I get it. This is the great battle between good and evil. Between compassion and greed. Christ stood up to the money changers' greed, so they conspired against him. Roosevelt stood up to some enormously-wealthy men's greed, so they plotted against him."

"It's an interesting comparison," Gina said. "How ironic that some loaded hoarders' speculation crashed the markets. And after the crash, the conspirators wanted to use the hard times as an excuse to end our social safety net, steal our freedoms and destroy our traditions. They wanted to have their cake and eat it, too. Greed mattered more to them than the public's suffering."

"More than a century ago, people didn't know viruses or bacteria spread disease," Joe said. "They couldn't stop it because they didn't understand the real cause. And before the 1929 crash, people didn't realize hoarding by some men with colossal-wealth caused a downward spiral leading to depressions. They realized it too late."

Dominic bowed his head. "You're catching on. But, there's more. And, it's eye opening."

CHAPTER 35

General Rogers' black luxury sedan rolled down Arlington National Cemetery's shrub-lined boulevard toward the steel street barrier at the main entrance. A red and white stop sign adorned the narrow barricade. It allowed barely enough room to drive past. The blue-uniformed military guard stood next to a sign informing visitors unauthorized private cars were not allowed on the Cemetery's drives. Rogers' sedan coasted to a stop and the driver's window came down.

"Hello, sir." A big smile spread across the guard's face when he recognized the man behind the steering wheel.

"Hello Albert," the General said. "How's it going?"

"Great to see you. What brings you to our neck of the woods today?"

"I came to drive around a bit. I miss the days when Arlington was under my command." *I can't tell him the real reason I'm here, but he'll buy a bit of sentiment.*

"The staff was really sad when you retired. Especially the ones who'd been here for years"

"That's kind of you to say. It means a lot."

"Everybody here still respects you. Here's your pass, you're good to go anywhere on the grounds." Albert handed the General a vehicle permit hang-tag for his rear-view mirror and waved him past the barrier with one hand.

The General's car pulled away from the guard. He turned onto a winding blacktop road running through the cemetery's rolling green hills, driving briskly while surrounded on both sides by endless white headstones. The air smelled crisp like after a rain. Up ahead, an enormous light apricot colored mansion shaped like a Greek Temple, came slowly into view. Eight giant marble painted stucco columns adorned a grand raised front portico. Two long wings with several tall arched windows flanked each side of the main house. A sign next to the driveway read "Arlington House, Robert E. Lee Memorial."

General Rogers fixed his gaze on a gray granite obelisk marking Union General Philip Sheridan's grave, on the lawn near the house. Sheridan's cavalry pursuit had led to General Lee's surrender at Appomattox, ending the Civil War.

I love this place's history.

He knew the mansion's background well. Craftsmen built Arlington House high on the plantation's hill for George Washington's adopted grandson. It looked down on the White House and the Capitol Building in the distance. The President, Senators and Representatives could gaze up at the grand residence from where they worked. Confederate General Robert E. Lee, the adopted grandson's descendant, owned the house before the civil war.

The General's car rolled slowly to a stop on the driveway near the front portico and columns. The mansion's dark windows had a bygone era's mournful look.

Good, the house looks deserted.

He walked up the portico's wide concrete steps where he passed between two huge columns. He tried the front door. It was unlocked, so he opened it and stepped inside to the long Center Hall. Framed oil paintings of George and Martha Washington lined the tall white walls. *If these walls could talk, what stories they'd tell.* A vacuum cleaner's high-pitched whine resonated from the back of the house for thirty seconds before its motor shut off. A uniformed attendant came around the corner and stepped into the Hall. He spotted the mansion's unexpected visitor and stopped short, his eyes growing big.

"Oh. hello sir. I wasn't expecting anyone but visitors this time of the day." It was Charlie, a longtime cemetery employee with whom the General had spoken many times on visits to the house. "I'm almost ready to move on to my next building."

"Don't let me slow you down, Charlie. I visited a couple of the old staff today. I didn't want to leave before coming up here for the view of the City. I'd like to sit for a while and gather my thoughts."

Charlie pulled out his oversize key ring and searched for the right one. "Sir, I've got to go, but you can stay long as you like. Hell, you oversaw this place more years than I can remember. It's like you never left. Make sure the door latches when you leave."

Charlie gathered his well-worn black Pea coat and battered gray metal lunch pail before heading for the back door where his parked car waited. He inserted a key into the bolt lock, locking it from the outside. General Rogers pulled back a white lace curtain on the tall arched window. Outside, Charlie climbed into the tired old sedan's driver's seat and shut the door.

Good, he's out of the way now. Now to get down to business.

The General turned around and strolled back across the Center Hall's squeaky floorboards toward the front door. His eye caught a shadowy movement outside the front door's side window. He peered through the glass, seeing a lone figure in a grey overcoat who stood to the doorway's right side. The General opened the door.

The figure moved toward him, speaking in a thick Russian accent. "I was beginning to wonder if you were going to make it, General. I've been waiting nearby for almost half an hour."

"Sorry Dimitri. There were some last-minute details needing my attention. I figured an experienced former Russian Intelligence officer could avoid detection for half an hour or so 'til I got here."

"Next time I will stay longer in the Russian Embassy's warmth."

The General waived him in with one hand. "Come inside. We don't want anyone passing by to see us."

They proceeded down the high-ceilinged Center Hall to the Family Parlor doorway. The General grabbed a brass clip on the doorway's burgundy velvet barrier rope, unhooking it. They stepped into the historic room and sat down at a small round wooden table. The faded fabric on the antique padded chairs gave off the musty smell of days gone by.

"Who'd believe a Russian agent would help an American billionaire take over the White House?" Dimitri chuckled while he pulled his chair up to the table.

General Rogers barely heard the last statement. *I wonder what Arlington house's former owner would think about our meeting here.* "I chose this place because of its past. It was home to the last American General to turn against the United States. Do you know the story?"

"You mean your Confederate General Lee?" Dimitri guffawed at the paradox. "This gives new meaning to the word 'irony'."

"The Union took control of his estate during the Civil War, turning it into Arlington National Cemetery. Soon, Union military graves by the thousands, surrounded the mansion. He could never live here after that. He paid a big price for supporting slavery."

"I'm sure the plantation owners appreciated his sacrifice. Slavery was America's biggest business at the time, a three and a half billion-dollar trade. It was worth more than the banks, factories and railroads." Dimitri looked down at the floor, shaking his head from side to side. "Only a war could stop so profitable an enterprise."

"The richest men often own the richest businesses."

"Your early 19th century big land companies were really clever." Dimitri shrugged, "Forcing tens of thousands of Cherokees, Creeks and Seminoles off their Indian lands in the southern states, then turning the land into cotton plantations worked by black slaves. A land grab on a grand scale. The Trail of Tears and slavery… sinister, yet incredibly lucrative. Rapacious profits by screwing two minorities at once."

General Rogers fixed his gaze on Dimitri." *He didn't have to say it that way, it sounded so evil. I like to think of it in noble terms like Manifest Destiny, our God given right.* "You know your American history.

"Russian intelligence officers, even former ones, know it better than most Americans. It's our job."

I wonder how much more he knows. Knowledge is power, and he understands us better than we do ourselves. The General looked out the window with its view of the Capitol's seats of power. "Quite an impressive sight, isn't it?"

"Stunning. Nothing like it anywhere else in the world."

"My father brought me here when I was a small boy. We came to see President Kennedy's Memorial Day Address. JFK walked up here for the magnificent view." *After his assassination, his wife Jackie buried him a hundred yards down the hill.*

"He stood up well to our Russian Premier, Khrushchev."

"An assassin shot his brother, Senator Bobby Kennedy, a few years later. I remember it like it was yesterday." *They buried him next to Jack.*

Dimitri stared out the window, acting like he hadn't heard. "I've never seen the White House from this angle. How appropriate to meet where we can see our target."

Dimitri's voice betrayed a little too much relish about the situation to suit the General. But, what the hell, he needed the Russian's crucial assistance. And the General wasn't in position to be choosy about where the help originated. "Do you have the White House security schematic?" he asked.

"Right here." Dimitri said, pointing underneath his trench coat. "I stole it as part of my espionage. But I made an extra copy. I knew it would be valuable on the black-market. How delicious you got it from a former Russian intelligence agent, don't you think?"

The General was inclined to agree but didn't want to say so out loud. "You're the only ones who have it other than our Secret Service. I could never get it from them. God knows, I tried."

"Of course, we'll need certain favors from you after the, shall we say, *transition*." Dimitri gave him a cocky wink.

"Understood." General Rogers nodded. "Now that's out of the way, let me see it"

Dimitri pulled a manila file folder from underneath his gray trench coat, laying it open on the small table. He slid twenty white pages across the surface toward the General, who studied them to confirm they were as promised. The diagrams displayed rooms labeled with icons for infrared LED rays, infrared receivers and closed-circuit cameras.

It's even embossed with the contractor's seal. These are the real deal. "They're in order." The General slipped the file easily into his thin soft sided leather portfolio.

Dimitri raised an eyebrow. "Aren't you forgetting something?"

"Oh, right, Sorry," The General mopped his brow with a white cloth handkerchief. "I'm a little distracted. I'll only be a minute, the money's in my car trunk." He disappeared out the front door and came back a couple minutes later with two brown hard-shell suitcases. He flipped them open to reveal stacks of green cash that filled each to the brim.

Dimitri picked up a couple inch thick stacks, rifling through them with his fingers. A thin smile crossed his lips as he satisfied himself they weren't counterfeit. He snapped the suitcase lids shut and carried one in each hand. I've accomplished what I came here for," he said. "It's time to go,"

They walked back to the front of the house, passing below the Robert E. Lee's oil paint portrait. General Rogers looked up at the image. *Lee took a lot of risks to join the Confederacy. If the South had won, I wonder if his potential reward would have been as big as mine. I can relate to what he was going through.*

They stepped through the front doorway and onto the concrete portico. Dimitri pumped the General's hand vigorously before trudging away into the shadows between the trees. The General strolled toward his luxury sedan, still clutching the manila folder.

Inside the house, a white lace front window curtain moved six inches. A face appeared behind the glass and watched the sedan drive away. It was Charlie. He'd been suspicious about the General's unexpected visit and returned in time to hear every word they said.

CHAPTER 36

B ack at the Monastery library, Joe's own words echoed in his mind. *This is the great battle between good and evil. Between compassion and greed. But Dominic said there's more.* Joe wouldn't have to wait long to learn what he meant.

Dominic pointed to an old masters painting of Christ sitting next to a stone well across from a woman holding a rope and a jar. She prepared to draw water from the well.

"Does this image ring any bells?" Dominic asked

"I know this story." Gina leaned in to scrutinize the frame's dark scene. "It's Christ and the woman at the well."

"She was from Samaria." Dominic nodded. "He grew tired from his journey and sat down at the well to rest. When the woman came to draw water, he asked her to give him a drink. She refused to share the water with him because Jews had no dealings with Samaritans. He told her if she would share the well's water, he in turn would give her water that would become in her a well of water springing up to eternal life."

"What's so special about springing water?" Gina asked.

"It circulates. It's an analogy to circulating resources or money." Dominic said.

"There's no proof Christ meant circulating money." Joe rolled his eyes. "He was referring to spiritual gifts" *Why can't Dominic accept the less upsetting interpretation?*

"There's plenty of proof. His command to circulate resources appears throughout the scripture. 'Go, sell whatever you have, and give to the poor.' 'Whatever you desire for men to do to you, you shall also do to them.' 'Inasmuch as you did it to one of the least of these my brothers, you did it to me.' 'You shall love your neighbor as yourself."

Gina shook her head side to side. "The verses do say that. But, how can you be so sure circulation's what he's talking about?"

"It's easy. All you have to do is look." Dominic pointed to a painting of his disciples handing out food from baskets to a large crowd in a solitary grove. "It's called the Feeding of the Five Thousand."

"I know that one," Joe said. It's the famous story of the loaves and fishes." He remembered it well from his years as a child with his family attending Sunday School services, Sunday Morning Worship services and Sunday Evening services.

"He told his disciples to circulate their five loaves and two fishes to the large hungry crowd," Dominic said. "That generosity shamed others in the crowd into circulating their food among those who had none. As a result, everyone ate that day with twelve full baskets holding bread pieces and fish left over."

Gina's face brightened. "Circulation turned scarcity and hunger into abundance."

"There's more." Dominic pointed to a different painting displaying five men in robes from Christ's time. One of them held several silver coins in one hand. "Here's one of history's most famous scenes. Do you recognize it?"

It's Judas betraying Christ for thirty pieces of silver." Her eyes lit up as she hunched forward to scrutinize the dark image in the frame. "The Chief Priests gave Judas the coins to turn Christ over to them. They bound him, and led him away, and delivered him up to Pontius Pilate, the governor."

"Exactly," Dominic said. "After they condemned Jesus, Judas had gut-wrenching remorse and threw down the silver pieces on the sanctuary floor before the priests and departed. But the Priests said it was not lawful to put the coins into the treasury, since it was the price of blood. It was 'blood money.'"

Joe straightened with surprise. *I haven't heard the blood money link before.* His head shaking from side to side. "You're going too far with this.

Judas' was afraid for his own skin and betrayed his leader. It's not about blood and money."

Dominic gave an exasperated sigh, choosing his words with care. "Joe, with your book about the public line and the real story, you of all people should see blood and money is the true message."

I've never had my own book title used against me before. Joe's brow wrinkled.

"Judas' betrayal led to Christ's crucifixion and bleeding to death on the cross." Dominic's voice rose as he tapped his foot on the floor. "He could have been executed in any number of ways, stoning or hanging. But he wasn't. He died from blood loss by crucifixion."

"Why does it matter?" Joe asked.

Gina held up one hand. "I can answer that one. During crucifixion, the victim loses more than 20 percent of his blood, causing Hypovolemic shock." She put both hands over her heart and made a pumping action, squeezing them together every second to imitate the heart's action. "There's not enough fluid left in the arteries, veins and capillaries for the heart to pump it through his body. It lowers his blood pressure so much the blood can no longer circulate. That kills him."

Dominic's eyes sparkled. "Exactly. It's like when a water pump is being fed by a pipe filled mostly with air, it can't pump. You must put water in the pipe for the pump to work, so it can push water to faucets. There's a banking phrase called 'priming the pump.'"

Dominic's reference reminded Joe of Franklin Roosevelt's New Deal jobs programs. *When consumers have little money, the financial system's pipe empties, so its pump doesn't work. The government must prime the financial pump by creating jobs for workers, putting money back in the pipeline so it can circulate through the system again. That creates growth.*

"But the money doesn't have to go to workers to create growth," Gina said. "How about higher stock prices? Don't men as rich-as-kings generally spend lots of money, too?"

"On average, not nearly to the same degree as workers," Dominic said. "Low wage workers have to spend each extra buck they earn, to survive. That's almost half their wealth every year. Their spending puts money back in circulation, creating growth and jobs.

"So blue collar workers are society's financial engines," Gina said.

"By comparison, the average billionaire spends much less of each additional dollar of their income and spends less than five percent of their staggering riches each year," Dominic said. "Some of the money may go into financial gimmicks that create very few jobs. The middle-class generally spends far more of each additional dollar they earn. It's Trickle-Down versus Gusher-Up."

Joe rubbed his chin. *Gusher-Up... he'd never heard that one before. The phrase conjured up images of a geyser shooting water straight up into the air, or an old-fashioned oil derrick topping a torrent of black oil spurting up from the ground. Oil gushers were a sign of abundance. In contrast, a trickle was a sign of shortage and dissipation.* "The 'trickle-down crowd' will have a cow when they hear this. They'll attack the idea, claiming it's socialist, because it threatens their control."

"Putting money in hard workers' hands is the one thing that makes capitalism work." Dominic's nostrils flared. "Shifting money from them to a few men of unimaginable-wealth, eventually kills it. Circulation produces widespread abundance. Hoarding creates speculative bubbles, crashes and depressions." He pointed to a 1930s black and white photo displaying two men in suits and ties, wearing bib signs saying they needed work. They looked hungry, thin and desperate.

"So, more money in wage earners pockets, instead of in a few billionaires' pockets, means more spending and more prosperity. That's why they call Christ's warnings against greed The Good News," Gina said. "Because it sparks growth."

"Someone very powerful is trying to steal the Archive's *Business Plot* records." Dominic raked his fingers through his hair. "They fear the facts enough to kill so it won't go public. You two stand in their way. You've been drawn smack dab into the biggest struggle of all time. They'll ruin civilization if they're not stopped."

"How did they get this far?" she asked.

"It's simple." Dominic shrugged. "Demographic Necrosis."

I've never heard of it. Joe raised an eyebrow. "What the hell is that?"

"Hold onto your hat. The explanation will surprise you," Dominic said.

CHAPTER 37

Geneneral Rogers' steered his sedan onto the red brick driveway in front of his white Art Deco home in suburban Washington D.C. He parked the car and marched in the main door, straightening when he spotted the special visitor waiting for him in the living room. Tomas sat on a cream-colored sofa with his feet propped on a glass topped coffee table. A lit cigarette dangled from his lips.

He didn't stand up nor even say hello when the General entered the room. Instead, he blew a smoke ring and stared up at the General with arms crossed. "I think you have something for me."

"This is how you do business, breaking into my house while I'm gone?" The General scowled.

"The back door was unlocked." Tomas tilted his head toward the rear of the house. "I let myself in."

The bastard's trying to irritate me. Lucian told me Tomas had spent years in the service. He must know the protocol when a high-level officer arrived on the premises. The General looked down his nose. "You've forgotten how to show respect when a General enters the room?"

"I'm out of the service and so are you, you're retired." Tomas took another puff. "This is simply a business arrangement, nothing more, nothing less. You've been retained by my employer on a contract basis."

This will be more difficult than I thought. He obviously likes to play by his own rules. The General tried a firmer tone of voice. "If you want my cooperation, you'd better get a different attitude. You need my services more than I need yours. And don't forget it."

Tomas ignored the instruction, giving him a cold blank stare. "Do you have the White House schematic?"

"Not so fast." The General didn't miss a beat. He held up an open palm in the universal stop gesture. "Has Lucian put the funds in my offshore bank account?"

"It's being done as we speak." Tomas paused while he snuffed out his cigarette butt in the coffee table's ashtray. "Check your account on line if you want."

"Hell yes, I wanna check before you get the merchandise." The General leaned forward over the glass table toward Tomas. "Ya think I was born yesterday?" He sat down with his smartphone, punching in the bank's password. The small screen's ledger lit up with a string of digits for the newly delivered money. *Ah, it's all there... like I ordered.* "What about my men? They're to be paid in hard cash. Where is it?"

Tomas opened two black leather satchels revealing several dozen green stacks of large denomination bills. General Rogers reached his hand into the satchel and took two stacks out. He flipped through them.

"It's all there." Tomas crossed his arms. "You can count it if you want, but you'll see I'm right."

"My aide'll take care of it later." The General slid a manila folder across the glass coffee table top to Tomas. "I've got other things to do right now."

Tomas opened the envelope, the title atop the first page read 'Oval Office.' He pulled out a half-dozen pages holding graphic symbols representing circuits, wiring and cameras. His piercing eyes studied the color-coded ink diagrams. "This looks good." Tomas shifted his gaze to the General. "Lucian asked for the final details of your takeover preparations.

"We're meeting at the warehouse later to go over the plans. If you want, you can sit in. Then you can report back to him." The General disliked Tomas but at least he didn't try to con everyone. It was more than he could say for Lucian.

"I'll be there. But the soldiers can't know who I am. You'll have to create a cover story."

175

"And what do you suggest I tell them, lie that you're with the CIA?" The General deadpanned.

"Tell them I'm in charge of project finance. That's all you need to say."

The General put his hands on his hips. This guy acted far too flippant for his taste, but he didn't have time to argue. He had urgent business to address in the underground armory.

CHAPTER 38

Joe still wasn't sure he'd heard Dominic correctly, the words Demographic Necrosis sounded so strange. He shook his head, repeating his question. "What the hell is it? It sounds like a disease."

"In a way, it is." Dominic said. "It means society forgets the lessons of the past one funeral at a time."

"You mean, we collectively forget, as individuals die off?" Joe asked. *If that was the case, were we doomed to keep repeating the same tragic cycle over and over again, never making progress to solve the crisis?* It raised a fascinating question -- one with grave consequences for a society counting on knowing history, in order not to repeat it.

"Yeah. The Great Depression's survivors learned the hard way money must circulate. They saw first-hand the tragedy caused by a few in-the-money men hoarding. But, after they died off over seven decades later, the 2007 meltdown happened. They weren't around to sound the alarm."

"How do you know what happened." Gina asked.

"Simple subtraction," Dominic said, picking up a marker to scrawl numbers across the library's dry erase board. "The two greatest financial crashes in American history happened in 1873 and 1929." He wrote four columns side by side.

Crash	Next Crash	Time Between Crashes	Average Life Expectancy
1873	1929	56 years	56 years

"The stock market crashed in 1873 and again 56 years later in 1929, when life expectancy was also 56 years," Dominic said. "

"Wow, that's quite a coincidence." Gina's eyebrows raised.

"No coincidence." Dominic said. "Most people alive during the 1873 crash were dead by the time of the 1929 crash, 56 years later. They weren't around to warn us."

Dominic's drawing too much of a conclusion from a single instance. "That's only one time. It doesn't prove a thing,"

"But it happened again," Dominic said. "The third greatest crash was the meltdown in 2007." He added a new line at the bottom of each of the four columns.

Crash	Next Crash	Time Between Crashes	Average Life Expectancy
1873	1929	56 years	56 years
1929	2007	78 years	78 years

"Damn." Gina pointed to the board. "Look at the similarity. The markets crashed in 1929 and again 78 years later in 2007-2008, when life expectancy was 78 years."

The odds of both numbers being equal must be a million to one. It couldn't be an accident it applied for both crashes. Joe's eyes bugged out. "Are you sure about this?"

"If the 1929 crash survivors were still alive, could they have stopped the 2008 crash?" Gina asked.

"Yes. The same way they avoided a crash in the 1950s and 60s," Dominic said. "Make billionaires circulate their income by paying high taxes. Then, the U.S. Treasury can put that tax money back in circulation, paying it as wages to workers building highways, bridges, dams, the space program and schools."

"It's the first circulation step," Joe said. "After that, workers spend those wages on houses, cars and appliances creating more high-wage factory jobs." Wash, rinse and repeat the cycle. *It's called the multiplier effect, and history proved it's powerful.*

"But, tax cuts for big corporations create job growth and increase wages, too." Gina said.

"That's a big fable peddled by some talk-radio hosts," Dominic said. "Overall, big existing corporations created virtually no net new jobs in the last thirty years... even though they received the biggest tax cuts in decades. Most new jobs come from small startup businesses, not big companies."

"That can't be." Gina said. "I thought men of enormous-wealth were job creators."

"That's a myth the size of Montana," Dominic said. "Consumers are the real job creators. On average, when men as-rich-as-lords put millions of dollars into hedge funds and derivatives, they create fewer jobs than an equal amount of consumer spending."

"And meanwhile, less money circulates among the public as worker wages," Joe said. *An economy needs to stay afloat, like a ship at sea. Imagine how unstable the ship would be if its weight was at the top, near the crow's-nest, instead of in the cargo and ballast areas. It would be top-heavy and capsize.* Joe's eyebrows raised as he imagined a top-heavy ship tipping over and crashing into the sea. *It's the same with money, a small portion can be held by those at the top, but the rest must be paid to workers, like ballast, to keep the financial system from keeling over.*

"So, then, consumers can't afford to buy goods from factories." Gina said.

"When workers' wages stagnate while the cost of living increases, consumer buying power decreases and many products don't sell. It creates a vicious downward spiral of factory closings and new layoffs," Dominic said. "Like a game of musical chairs. They take away chairs, so there aren't enough left to sit in, and more players leave the game each round."

"Then, the population works harder and harder to try to make ends meet," Gina spoke faster, figuring it out as she went. "But they wear out. The speculative bubble bursts... and leads to a crash."

"It doesn't have to end that way," Dominic said raising his voice for emphasis. "We know how to stop it. Tax billionaires like we did in the

1960s to supply a transfusion for the nation's half-drained financial bloodstream. Put the money back in circulation."

"Back then, U.S. job growth was unequaled, our education system unsurpassed." Joe held his hands up and spread his arms apart to show the breadth of prosperity. "We landed a man on the moon and built the interstate highway system." *We'll have to battle to set things right. Some opulent men will spend huge sums on ads to convince the public not to tax the hoarding.* "They'll say eliminating their taxes is how we'll thrive."

"Tax cuts for men with astonishing-wealth are like eating a cup of sugar for breakfast." Dominic pointed to a chart displaying the various top tax rates on the richest-men over the years. "In the 1920s, three conservative presidents in a row slashed the top tax rates from 73 percent down to 25 percent. You get a brief high, followed by a tremendous crash. Some of these men used their tax cut for fever-pitch speculation, causing the catastrophic stock market crash of October 1929 and the Great Depression."

"It crashed the real estate markets, too," Joe said. *The foreclosures, evictions, farm sales and mass exoduses of homeless people were the stuff of legend. Except they really happened.*

"It sounds so different from what some talk-radio hosts told us. So, are there any good tax cuts?' Gina asked.

"Absolutely," Dominic said. "Tax cuts for workers. That money trickles-up from them to create growth, it's the only thing that does. Trickle-down doesn't work and never has."

Trickle. The water reference reminded Joe of the Mona Lisa's Arno river and the number painted in it under the bridge. Da Vinci painted it there for a reason. Maybe Dominic could shed light on that. "Does the number 72 have religious significance."

"Hmmm... 72. Interesting question." Dominic looked up at the ceiling, pausing for ten seconds. "The Bible mentioned it one time. Luke's Gospel says the Lord also appointed seventy others and sent them two by two ahead of him into every city and place, where he was about to come. Some other scholars think it's seventy-two, instead of seventy."

"So, the 72 preceded Christ, and then he comes shortly after," Gina said.

"There's more to his story," Dominic read from the chapter. "Christ says the harvest is indeed plentiful, but the laborers are few. He warned them he was sending them out as lambs among wolves." It's a parable about protecting workers from theft by greedy predators. Why do you ask?"

"I'll tell you later." Joe shrugged one shoulder. "I ran across it in some art." *72 disciples fending off theft by greedy predators... that's intriguing.*

"I want to show you something." Dominic motioned with his hand for them to follow him. They walked out of the library, down the hall and past the courtyard where they entered a greenhouse with lush plants. He led them past rows of vegetables and flowers.

"Plants are like the economy." Dominic pointed at the roots and the stem. "They're a system that requires care and feeding. Top-heavy is not good for either one. The root system must be properly nourished with balanced nutrition before the flower blooms at the top. Weakened roots and stem won't support a large flower head."

"I get it," Gina said. "The roots and stem represent workers and consumers. If too much money goes to a few billionaires at the top, instead of the rest of us, we won't have enough to spend. The financial system's base weakens and eventually dies."

"And nourishing the base creates the largest harvest," Dominic said.

Joe nodded. *Da Vinci would have understood that. He spent hours observing flowers' and plants' anatomical parts, so he could draw them in detail.*

Dominic led them out of the greenhouse and back to the Monastery, so he could leave for an important appointment. Joe and Gina donned their coats to be on their way. They thanked Dominic for his insight as he escorted them to the door.

He waived at them from the Monastery's side steps as they piled into the van. "Good luck and God speed." Then as they drove off, he added in a quieter voice, "Heaven knows you'll need it on this one."

Joe leaned back in the passenger seat as they drove out through the front gate. *There's something big behind the killings and I'm gonna find out what it is if it's the last thing I do.* "Let's head to Church and Barclay Street in New York. We've got to see what's there." He had a feeling what they would find there would make or break their quest.

CHAPTER 39

T he New York network TV news studio buzzed with the crew's banter as they adjusted television cameras and lights. Claude Zorak took his seat at the blue plexiglass host's desk. The show's audio technician clipped a tiny wireless microphone on Claude's lapel, babbling instructions about where to look once the camera focused on the guests. Claude rolled his eyes at the instructions much like he would a flight attendant's seat belt demonstration. *I could recite it in my sleep. I've heard it a thousand times before.*

A golden coifed anchorwoman in a sleeveless sheath dress sat down across from him as the yellow digital clock on the wall warned they would be live in thirty seconds. Claude pulled a mirror from his pocket, checking his makeup one last time. Satisfied, he returned the mirror to its place. The rectangular studio light flashed a warning that they were on air. He took a deep breath as the camera started rolling.

The anchorwoman's face appeared on the studio monitor. "Thank you for joining us. I'm your host Diane Harris. Today on our show we'll be discussing immigration reform. Special guest Claude Zorak is here to speak for the anti-immigration movement that favors building the wall. He heads the Dynasty Coalition, a Washington D.C. think-tank advancing conservative issues before Congress."

"I'm glad to be here," Claude said.

Diane continued reading from the rolling white letter words on her black teleprompter screen. "We're also fortunate to have with us Friar Dominic Circola, a political advisor to Washington policy makers on matters of interest to the Church. He opposes deportation in favor of more humane treatment of immigrants."

"Thank you for inviting me," Dominic said.

"Claude let's start with you," she said. "You've in the past called for mass deportation of undocumented immigrants. Is that still your position?"

"We aren't calling for mass deportation." Claude pulled himself up in his chair to his full height, the muscles in his face tightening. "Instead, we believe all undocumented immigrants must immediately leave the United States. Then they can apply to come back in to the country."

"Well, your plan certainly sounds like mass deportation to me," Diane said. "How's it different?"

"It's not mass deportation," Claude replied. "It's enforcing the law. I'd call it an orderly transition of non-compliant migrants."

Dominic crossed his arms. *Claude's stepping in it right out of the gate. He can't help it. Those lofty sounding phrases can't hide the distasteful racism behind them.*

"But the net effect is deporting massive numbers of hard-working men and women, isn't it?" Diane's forehead creased. "Why won't you let them stay?"

"My position's well known. They're taking American jobs."

"But, aren't those the less desirable jobs American workers won't do?"

"The American people want us to enforce the law," Claude slapped the palm of his hand flat against the desktop. "The immigrants have to leave."

Diane rolled her eyes. "I don't think you answered my question. Let's see what our other guest has to say. Friar Dominic, how do you respond?"

Dominic gave an exasperated sigh as his face appeared on the monitor. *It's amazing Claude's still able to peddle that garbage without being laughed out of town.* "Claude wants financially squeezed voters to blame people of color for a lack of jobs. He's blaming the wrong folks. Immigrants and people of color aren't the problem. Claude's flush backers hoard and that kills jobs. It strangles growth."

"So, why don't more people admit it?" Diane tilted her head.

"The sad truth is, they're afraid," Dominic said. "Big corporations might retaliate by firing them. So, some employees behave like Stockholm

Syndrome hostages, identifying with their captors to survive. Immigrants and minorities aren't as powerful. It's safer to blame them." Dominic left out the part about how Claude's think tank had schemed to change laws to make it easier to fire employees. It increased employee anxiety, making them even more susceptible to anti-immigrant propaganda. *What a perfect way to maximize their plan.*

"So, Claude's using the psychological principle of transference." Diane rested her chin on her hand. "Convincing voters to shift their anger away from the problem's cause, toward a scapegoat."

"He is... very cleverly. And immigrants aren't his only victims. He's also blamed Blacks, Jews, Gays, Women and Union Workers."

Claude blushed and cringed as he looked down at his shoes.

Dominic glanced at Claude' *I've hit him close to home on that one. The truth hurts.* "Claude should ask why these immigrants risk danger, even death, to make the long journey here. Drug gangs force young girls to be their sex slaves and force young boys to join the gang or be killed. Mothers and fathers know there's no future there, for their children. Gang threats drive them out of their countries. They flee to the U.S. like refugees asking for asylum." *And Claude turns them away in their time of dire need. How Christlike... not.*

"But, isn't that Latin America's problem?" Diane asked. "Shouldn't they take care of it?"

"It's our problem, too. America's hunger for illegal drugs supplies the billions of dollars fueling those Latin American gangs. U.S. drug money empowers the gangs, so they can buy high-power automatic weapons used to extort, rape and kill."

"So, the problem started here. Why do we turn to drugs? she asked.

"Americans are unhappy because of toxic workplaces or unemployment. They either can't find jobs, or their jobs aren't secure... their employers can fire them at any time. They get little time off... management treats them like children. Upward mobility is non-existent. It's even worse for the young. Teenagers face lower living standards than their parents, they have few prospects for the future. Economic insecurity stresses them out, they're depressed."

"Why aren't their jobs more secure?" Diane said.

"Some owners with stupendous-wealth pressure management to squeeze every nickel out of the company, demanding a bigger stock price increase every year. They downsize employees to independent contractor status to cut benefits and increase profits. Those managers succumb to the pressure, abusing and bullying workers, destroying their pride and dignity. It all comes down from the top.

Diane rubbed her hands together at the conflict her questions had generated. She swung around to face Claude. "What do you say in response?"

"Don't pull your kumbaya minority inclusiveness on me." Claude's neck veins throbbed, his voice growing higher as he stabbed his finger toward Dominic. You're starting class warfare... socialism. The left always does because they have nothing to offer."

Dominic gave Claude a steely look. *Class warfare, indeed. Your clients ship overseas every job they can, even if it only saves them a nickel per hour on wages.* His voice remained steady but sure. "I'm not the one starting class warfare. Your greedy clients started it when they declared war on the working class. They lay workers off, outsource their work, end their defined benefit retirement plans and force them out after middle age. Your backers hoard money until they financially squeeze families to the breaking point."

"That's preposterous and a flat out lie." Claude recoiled and sputtered, his face becoming red. "You're shaming men who were blessed by God with success, creating jobs and growth. They're spreading prosperity throughout the land."

"Another myth." Dominic replied. "Big corporations haven't created one net new job in decades. Consumers create many more jobs than do tax cuts for the ultra-rich. But you don't want people to know that."

Diane faced Dominic. "Why don't billionaire tax cuts create jobs?"

"It's simple. Corporations order marketing studies before they'll build a factory, to see if consumers have enough money to buy the factory's products. If consumers don't have money, then the factory isn't built. That means potential employees aren't hired, regardless of tax-cuts for men of stupendous wealth. Period."

"Wrong, wrong, wrong." Claude scowled while pushing against the plexiglass desk. "Workers don't have money because you haven't given my corporate clients' tax cuts enough time to work. Their tax cuts will pay for themselves."

Dominic rolled his eyes. *Hope springs eternal. It didn't work the other fifty times you tried it.* "Tax cuts for men as rich-as-kings rarely pay for themselves. You're using magical thinking."

The flashing red warning light informed Diane it was time to wind things up. "Dominic, you have the last word. You've got sixty seconds."

"Remember this -- Claude's trickle-down schemes haven't increased average consumers' buying power anywhere ever. It's a trick so his clients can get richer and richer, while everyone else gets poorer and poorer."

"On that note, we have to wrap it up," Diane said. "We'll be right back after this message."

The news director's hand made a slash sign across his throat to indicate the cut away to an advertisement. The video feed switched off and the off-air sign flashed. Claude stood straight up, ripping the microphone off his neck in disgust. He didn't wait to thank the host, instead storming out of the studio without speaking to anyone. The anchorwoman exchanged a knowing glance with Dominic as she rubbed her temples.

Dominic gave her a half-smile. *It's not surprising Claude left in a huff. He's invested so much in his house of cards, it's painful for him to see it exposed.*

Out in the hallway away from the studio, Claude wiped his makeup off with a clean white handkerchief, smearing tan color over it. He scowled as he stuffed the stained cloth back in his pocket. Dominic had gotten the better of him in front of a national audience, after the two of them had taken their best shots. Lucian would not be pleased with the result.

Claude barked into his phone for the garage parking attendant to bring his car around front. He had an urgent appointment with Lucian on a matter of the utmost importance to his boss.

CHAPTER 40

General Rogers strolled through the cavernous armaments room in the secret underground armory near downtown Washington D.C. He stopped to shake hands with two uniformed officers finishing plans for the takeover. Soldiers nearby chattered at each other while stocking gray metal shelves with the latest laser guided assault rifles. Uniformed servicemen unloaded yellow wooden crates filled with high-tech sonic weapons and drones equipped with automatic guns.

The General quizzed the officer inspecting lightsaber-like tasers capable of electrocuting people thirty-feet away. "You're sure these work? I don't want any screw-ups."

"Like nobody's business." The officer puffed out his chest. He picked one up, aimed and fired at a metal footlocker, making it glow with electricity.

Ten yards away, a couple enlisted men organized a shelf stacked with top-secret handheld laser flashlights that could blind the enemy. Hand-held rocket launchers filled the last shelf on the wall. They could destroy brick walls,

The General's smug look said it all. *Everything's going as planned, we'll be more than ready to handle anything White House security throws at us.*

He proceeded back to the armory's command war room and stood outside the door to greet the officers. Key high-level officers filed by one by one. They saluted the General as they passed by, a couple making derogatory comments about the President's policies.

After the staff had assembled, the General marched into the room. Everyone stood at attention. Poster diagrams graced the walls, displaying specific checkpoints at the White House. A large monitor at the room's far end featured a schematic of the Oval Office.

"At ease," he said. He took a chair.

Everyone in the room followed suit, taking seats around the long conference table. They resumed normal posture. Self-important aides armed with laptops sat against the wall, behind their respective officers. One aide set gold lettered blue portfolios titled 'Base Closing Rescue Plan,' on the table in front of each attendee. Tomas sat in a padded wooden chair at the back of the room, doing his best to go unnoticed.

The General addressed the group. "Everyone open the notebook in front of you. As you know, the President plans to close multiple military bases across the country. That would be catastrophic for our national security."

Murmurs of disapproval buzzed through the room.

"We can't let it happen," he continued. "There's only one option, confront the President to secure his cooperation. We'll pressure him to address the American people and announce he's sharing power with us. He'll reassure them this is in the nation's best interests. Any questions?"

One officer raised a cautious hand. The General pointed in his direction. "What makes you think he'll cooperate?" the officer asked. "I mean, after all, he's the President."

The General's mouth twitched. *I'd hoped I wouldn't have to go into detail on the political part of the plan. The fewer people who know about it the better. But it would raise suspicion not to answer the question, and he needed everyone on board.* "We have an ace in the hole. Senator Hogue will come to the Oval Office. He'll meet with the President, offering him too much money to refuse. Hogue will tell him some men with inexhaustible-wealth already support us."

"And if he still balks?" the officer asked.

This guy's obviously a little slow on the uptake, doesn't he realize that's why we're here. "Then we march on the White House and take whatever steps necessary to secure it for our purposes."

The officers smirked at each other around the conference table. Two of them murmured about how it was high time the hawks played a bigger role in running things.

"Let's go over the plan." The General pointed to the oversize monitor showing a color-coded diagram. "This is the White House security schematic. The red triangles are guard posts and the blue dots are surveillance cameras. We've already hacked into the Secret Service networks. We can override their communications and surveillance systems."

"How will we know the President's actually in the White House and not somewhere else?" the second officer asked.

"The President's main secret service agent never leaves his side while on duty. We'll place a tracking dot in the agent's pocket. It transmits his precise location in the building."

"Won't we need people on the inside to pull this off?" a third officer asked.

"We've got a Trojan Horse," the General said. "Two of our men will impersonate GSA heating and cooling repairmen scheduled to work at the White House. Once inside, they'll don oxygen masks. Their fake freon canisters contain sleeping gas. The gas will neutralize the sentries and secret service."

"What about outside?" the third officer asked.

"Our platoon will leave the warehouse in ordinary retail delivery trucks and pull up to the White House' main gate. The details of gaining access to the grounds are explained in your notebooks. It's up to each of you to review them and be ready to go."

A second officer with a furrowed brow, raised his hand. "What happens if we fail?"

The General swallowed hard. *I'd hoped to avoid that unpleasant question.* Getting psyched for battle required a certain level of denial about the horrific consequences of potential defeat. But there he had no way around it now. "That's easy. We'll all swing from a rope."

The murmuring around the conference table grew into a loud buzz. Officers talked over one another in a frenzy until the General held up his hand to silence the room.

"Failure's not an option. We're beyond the point of no return. Any other questions?" The General glanced around the table, but no one said a word. *Good, now we can get on with it. Less talk and more action.*

"Dismissed."

The officers filed out of the room muttering to each other how they had no room for error. Most of them avoided eye contact with the General. After they left, Tomas' stood up and ambled toward the exit. He hesitated in the doorway, staring poker-faced at the General. "This better work. Damned if I'll be tried for treason."

The General's body stiffened at the remark. "If you are, you'll have plenty of company."

Tomas gave him the evil eye and stalked out the door.

CHAPTER 41

One by one, five white male billionaires exited black limousines, dressed in tailored designer suits, ties, and elegant watches. They ranged in age from sixty to seventy-five years. The men strutted up the front steps outside Lucian Drake's French baroque chateau mansion as if they were kings on a red-carpet runway.

A dour prim butler greeted them at the residence' carved wood arched double front doors. He led them each to a diamond patterned wood paneled study on the main level where Lucian firmly shook each one's hand as they entered.

They took their seats in high-back burgundy leather chairs lining the long walnut conference table, making small talk. Lucian's ancestors gilded framed oil portraits stared down judgmentally at them from the walls. The sweet smell of Cuban cigars floated throughout the room as the guests lit up.

Lucian entered the room and stood at the head of the table, tapping a crystal glass with a spoon. His scowling pasty face amplified his forbidding demeanor. "Thanks for coming today. We're all familiar with each other, so I'll get right to the point. My researchers have discovered a new development posing a risk to all our fortunes."

Uneasy murmurs rose up from the guests gathered around the table in response to what they viewed as a fate worse than death.

He pressed a button on the sleek remote control cupped in his hand. Six pairs of eyes focused on a seventy-inch ultra-high-resolution monitor lowered from a narrow opening in the ceiling behind him. It revealed a colorful financial chart covering the last hundred years.

"Billionaires' share of the nation's income reached record heights this year. It's happened only twice before in history. In 1929 and 2007, before the infamous financial crashes."

Lucian clicked the remote button, replacing the image. A painting appeared displaying Marie Antoinette standing next to the gallows for her 1793 execution at the Place de la Révolution in Paris. The members at the table heaved a collective audible gasp at her executioner's image.

"Marie Antoinette ruled as the last Queen of France. She gained a huge share of France's national income for herself while she and other French nobles payed almost no tax. Workers paid most of the taxes out of their very meager incomes. Hungry impoverished citizens revolted, chopping off her head. Today, our share of the nation's income is even higher than hers was back then. We're at risk of a rebellion. We have to act now."

"If the peasants don't like it then let them eat cake," the monocle wearing member deadpanned while the others guffawed.

Lucian ignored the comment, clicking the remote again. *This is no time for jokes you fool, this is serious.* The screen displayed a grainy black and white photo displaying Bolshevik forces marching on Moscow's Red Square in 1917. "Czar Nicholas II commandeered a huge share of Russia's national income, impoverishing its citizens. The people responded by revolting against him in a bloody coup. They seized he and his family, holding them captive in a basement and later shooting them."

"Damn peasants mutilated and burned their bodies." The monocle wearing member tilted his head back and looked down his nose with a grimace. "Disgraceful."

"That brings us to our plan. You're all familiar with our bill to abolish Social Security, Medicare, Medicaid, and the Healthcare Act. It's been our long-term goal. The First and Second Gulf Wars expense pulled massive sums from the federal treasury, which holds the Social Security trust fund. Much of the war money was for armament purchases from our military contractor corporations."

"I never made so much money so fast before," the monocle wearing member said. "It was an incredible high."

"Now that the Treasury has amassed the war debt, voters worry about Treasury's ability to pay the trust fund benefits. They want to raise our taxes to replace the spent money. But we have a way out. If we eliminate peoples' benefits, there'll be no fund to reimburse. Plus, it frees-up billions of dollars in the U.S. budget, so Congress can slash our group's taxes to almost nothing. The House of Representatives passed the measure a couple days ago. The Senate votes on it this week."

Excited murmurs of approval came from those seated at the table. The monocle wearing member panted with wide-eyed desire.

Look at him, he's like a dog in heat. There's no limit to how far I can lead him on this. Now it's time to impress upon them the urgency to act now.

"There's only one problem." Lucian pressed a button on the remote, revealing video showing two million citizens stretched out across the Capitol Mall in protest. "Here's footage of today's massive march for the social safety net, protesting our plan. Even the dull and stupid are starting to realize our tax cuts didn't help anybody but us, while workers' wages stagnated and their buying power shrank. We must avoid a repeat performance of Marie Antoinette and Czar Nicholas, with us in the starring role"

The demonstrators' angry faces on the video revealed they knew powerful forces had schemed a full-scale attack their livelihoods. They shouted, "Kill the bill... Kill the bill," while standing shoulder to shoulder against the inhumanity bombing their subsistence.

The men at the table exchanged worried looks. Angry citizens like these had stormed the Bastille during the French Revolution, setting the stage for major change.

"We'd taken the steps we hoped would discourage any uprising," Lucian continued. "That included using some talk-radio hosts to convince the public they wouldn't need a safety net if they slashed our taxes. We told them tax cuts would make them so prosperous that a net was useless. It worked for a while. But now their income is flat or falling, their costs for healthcare and housing are skyrocketing, and they need protection. They're furious at..."

The tall gentleman interrupted, shaking a fleshy finger at Lucian. "*Your* talk-radio hosts tricked the public, not ours. Don't expect us to..."

"Ungrateful coward." Lucian's jaw clenched. He would not allow a mutiny in his ranks, it had to be stamped out now. "My tactics got you your incredible-wealth. You didn't complain then."

"It also incited this massive march," the tall gentleman said as he leaned forward over the table, pointing at the screen.

Calm yourself, don't go overboard. Lucian told himself and took a deep breath. *You catch more flies with honey than vinegar. We can't risk any other defections from the group.* His expression relaxed, as he leaned forward with his hands spread on the table. "I'm only saying we've ridden this wave as far as we can. The public's catching on. Time's running out."

"Couldn't we ride it a bit longer?" The pompadour gentleman pleaded as he tilted his head. "You know, don't abandon your yacht in mid-stream. Stay the course."

Lucian's scowl revealed a lack of amusement at the pun. "You saw the video, voters are angry." He pointed at the screen. "They're ready to take-up torches and pitchforks. We can't let them have control."

Several heads in the room nodded, mumbling their agreement.

"The President's listening to them. He's threatening in private to veto our bill if the Senate passes it. We can't let him do it. This is our one chance to be the richest men in the history of the world." Lucian had a stirring loin lust at the idea of eclipsing the record-setting-wealth of even Croesus and King Midas.

"What are you suggesting?" A line appeared between the pompadoured gentleman's brows.

"Take over the White House." Lucian gazed at his audience, searching for their reactions to his audacious announcement. "Install a dictator… Put fear into the public. When there's an economic crisis, people are ripe for a savior no matter who he is." *There, I've said it… finally. How satisfying to speak it out loud to them after planning the coup for so long.*

"You're mad." The tall gentleman stood up, glaring. "The public won't stand for this. We'll all be hung for treason. Even if it worked, your dictator might turn on us, too."

"You have no choice." Lucian had anticipated the objection, determined to keep his emotions in check this time. The great prize was too important to risk for momentary alpha-male one-upmanship. "The only other way to stop the revolt is to share a lot of your money to boost workers' wages. You'd never do that." His eye twinkled as he played to their greed.

THE FOURTH CIRCLE OF HELL

"Of course not," the monocle wearing member chuckled. "Are you insane? I'm trying to cut wages, not go the other way."

"Regardless, your scheme won't work." The tall gentleman slapped his open palm on the table. "A group tried it in the 1930s. It failed miserably."

He remembers the original Business Plot. He's smarter than I thought.

"It did." Lucian puffed out his chest. "But they made one big mistake that we won't. They chose a general who cared about democracy. Ours doesn't. He wants money, more than he could earn in ten lifetimes. That's why he'll stay loyal. And, I've got him on videotape agreeing to our conspiracy. If he rats on us, he'd indict himself."

Lucian looked across the long conference table at the other gentlemen, taking the measure of the room. Some of them were still on the fence despite his dire warnings. They were cautious when it came to anything that could threaten their fortunes. Now was the time to reveal the knockout punch he had held in reserve. It should convince any remaining doubters in the group to join him without reservation.

"Gentlemen look no further for proof this takeover can succeed!" He raised one hand in the air to point behind him.

All eyes in the room shifted again to the seventy-inch monitor hanging from the ceiling. Their eyes widened as the split screen streamed live video from both the Oval Office and the Pentagon's Command Center.

"Mary, mother of God," gasped one of the men as the monitor displayed the President signing bills into law and the Joint Chiefs of Staff deliberating weapons systems.

"Jesus Christ," said another.

"No one's ever done anything like this before." Lucian winked at the gentleman sitting nearest to him. "We're making history."

He let the images sink in for a bit before again clicking the remote control. The screen switched to live video showing Senators in their offices, taken by their computer web cams. Audio played from their live cell phone conversations. The discussions were high-level and potentially compromising.

"This is only the start," Lucian said. "We can stream private citizens in their homes and cars. Eavesdrop and blackmail our competitors. No one will be able to challenge us."

"How's this even possible?" the pompadoured gentleman asked.

"You can thank the government surveillance efforts made after the 9-

11 attacks. With this technology we can detect and squash any citizen opposition to our coup." Lucian reveled in the moment. Soon, he would be the most powerful man in the world. Maybe he already was. And after the takeover there would be no doubt about his influence.

Several of those in the room reacted with shock. "How'd you access this video?"

"It all started when my staff hacked in to a National Archives computer to suppress information about *The Business Plot.*" He clicked the remote which flashed a photo showing the Archives building. "We stole the records, so the public could never learn the truth about the conspirators. In the process, we stumbled upon a security flaw in the government's networks. It provided a backdoor into the National Security Agency's supercomputers and their highest-level surveillance."

The room buzzed with excitement as the guests anticipated the possibilities.

"There's no limit to what we can do with this." Lucian smirked. He had already calculated it could make him the richest man in the world, bar none.

He moved on to his presentation's next part, a video with detailed takeover plans. It contained the President's personal schedule and a list of politicians sympathetic to their cause. Lucian could tell the group was warming to the takeover idea, and its likely success. The video ended with a photo of the White House security schematic. Lucian paused the DVD and switched off the monitor.

"I've hired a special private contractor who will provide an army of 10,000 mercenary troops for the takeover," Lucian said. "We'll supplement our rented military with as many active duty soldiers as our General can recruit for the cause."

"I love privatization," the bald member said. "How soon can we do it?"

It worked... I've got them eating out of the palm of my hand. "One week from today. The preparations have already begun." He looked around the room at their faces. "Are you with me?" he asked. His voice had a thunderous quality.

"Yes." The members' chorused reply warmed the cockles of Lucian's money-grubbing heart. They stood and applauded their leader for twenty seconds.

They might not have applauded him quite so long if they'd known he'd secretly videotaped their responses. His butler sat in another room, remotely aiming the video recording cameras hidden in the study, to capture the individual members' comments. Lucian would need the recording for blackmail if any of the group later threatened to back out. Or worse yet, if they tried to wrestle from him control of his movement. After all, there was no honor among thieves, nor Lucian's greedy group.

The applause died down and the meeting ended. To celebrate their agreement, the exuberant group left the mansion with Lucian. In his haste to leave with the others and answer their questions, Lucian forgot to remove the DVD from the video player and lock it up. They climbed into their limos heading for his exclusive club nearby for "special festivities."

CHAPTER 42

A raucous game was well underway at Lucian's elite Long Island private club when the last of the six billionaires arrived late for the celebration. A club attendant ushered the latecomer into an elegant dimly lit room holding several plush sofas, ten-foot wall mirrors and a private bar.

The latecomer's eyes grew large at the striking view underneath a spotlight on the room's right side. There stood a replica of the United States' Great Seal from the back of the one-dollar bill. A triangle displaying the Eye of Providence, hung above a partially finished pyramid. Roman numerals for the year 1776 appeared on the pyramid's base. It stood for the year America declared its independence from Britain and opulent King George.

Lucian stepped up to the pyramid and rotated it 180 degrees, so the inverted pyramid's top was much wider than its bottom. The 1776 now appeared upside down.

"Why'd he do that?" the late member asked the tall member seated next to him, the one who had questioned Lucian's plan earlier.

"It makes the pyramid reflect our country where those at the top control the most, and those at the bottom control the least," the tall member whispered. "He turned the 1776 upside down because it represents America's independence from the King. Lucian identifies with the monarch."

In the middle of the room, sat a remote-control flatbed toy truck holding a load of miniature gold bricks. From the back, the load looked like the inverted pyramid from the rotated Great Seal, as it was much wider at the top than at the bottom. Nearby, ran a lengthy winding model car track.

"What the hell's that for?" the tardy gentleman whispered as he nudged the tall member.

The tall member leaned toward him, replying in a voice too soft for the others to hear, "It's a game they play. The members take turns piloting the top-heavy truck of gold bricks around the track at high speed. The one who finishes a lap the fastest without tipping the truck over, wins. It's like in real life, where we make money driving the V-shaped economy as fast as possible and as long as possible before it crashes."

"I get it. The truck's a metaphor for *driving the economy* until it *runs out of gas.*"

"Yeah, or until the Federal Reserve *puts the brakes on.*"

"What's the prize tonight?"

"The winner gets first pick of the women over there." The tall member pointed at a half-dozen attractive females wearing French maid outfits, black, puffy short sleeved, mini dresses with white lace aprons and black silk stockings. They served drinks to the group on silver trays.

One by one, the members took their turns with the remote control, piloting the truck. They watched the clock like hawks, each one desperate to win. When the game finished, Lucian had the fastest time without tipping over the top-heavy gold brick load. The French maids crowded around and crowned him King. He chose the female he wanted, and they adjourned to a private room where he claimed his prize.

CHAPTER 43

Agent Davis' unmarked midnight blue police cruiser slowed to a stop in front of the military base's striped front gate. A uniformed white-helmeted MP leaned out the white cube shaped guard booth's window. Davis flashed his brass FBI badge through the open car window. The MP nodded his approval, raising the yellow and black striped barrier arm on its hinge. He waived the car through.

The cruiser drove to a huge metal vehicle storage building, stopping in front of two open industrial size steel sliding doors. Inside on the wide concrete floor, a young blond-haired uniformed serviceman's body lay on his back, shot through the heart. The MP in charge of the scene walked up to Agent Davis to shake his hand.

"Thanks for bringing your team to investigate," the MP said. "We don't get much homicide experience here."

And we get more than we can handle, especially today. "Glad to help." Davis pointed an index finger at the chalk-outlined body. "Who's the victim?"

"Captain Stone. Been stationed at the base over a year. Mostly kept to himself, a few friends." The MP pointed toward a Lieutenant standing next to a military truck fifteen yards away. "The soldier standing over there got to know him. We haven't interviewed him yet. We thought you might want his statement fresh."

I'm glad somebody knows it's a mistake for the witness to repeat himself over and over. It muddles his mind and the facts. Davis walked up to the Lieutenant, flashing his badge. "Special Agent Davis, FBI. I'd like to ask a few questions."

"Sure."

"Understand you knew the Captain?"

"We're in the same unit."

"Notice anything unusual recently, any change in behavior?"

"He seemed kinda nervous the last few days," the Lieutenant said. "He'd been called away from our unit last week but didn't said why. He played everything close to the vest, recently. Rumor had it, someone high up the chain of command pulled some strings, so the Captain could work on a special project. That got my attention."

"Any idea where he went for this project?"

"Somewhere downtown. He didn't say where."

That special project must be the key. Especially since he tried to hide it. Davis finished his questions before thanking the soldier for his cooperation and walking back to the body. He stood next to the MP while scribbling on his notepad. "The victim worked for some big shot up the chain of command. I want you to find out who it was."

"I'll check on it right now. Wait right here, I'll be back in a few minutes." He marched to the door, disappearing around the corner.

Davis interviewed the few other soldiers who had talked with the victim. After finishing, he waited for the MP in the vehicle storage building. But after a half-hour he still hadn't come back with the information about who the Lieutenant had worked for.

I guess he's not coming back. No sense in hanging around any longer. Davis headed out the door to leave where he ran smack into the returning MP.

"Sorry it took so long. I made a complete inquiry. There's no record of the Captain working on a special project for anyone outside his unit."

"You absolutely sure about that?" Davis winced and pressed his lips.

"Positive. The witness must be mistaken."

"Well, what was he doing downtown, then?" Davis didn't like what he'd heard. "The witness said Stone wasn't with his unit. He had to be somewhere." The Lieutenant had sounded credible when he'd described the Captain's behavior earlier. And he had no obvious motive to lie. Davis sized the MP up, did this guy really know what he was doing?

"I don't know what to tell you. The records say he was here."

"Records can be changed."

"Well, these weren't." The MP's cellphone rang. He excused himself to answer it and pivoted to walk away

Way to stick your head in the sand, fella. Davis had run into a stone wall. He power-walked out of the building with a scowl on his face, pulling Josh to the side and lowering his voice, so the MP couldn't hear. "Something's very wrong. We're getting the bum's rush. He's covering up for somebody and they must be really important."

"There's one more thing." Josh nodded his agreement. "I spoke with the company clerk. He says someone's been stealing weaponry and explosives from area military bases. The brass buried the theft reports. They wanted to stop the news from leaking out to Congress and reducing the defense budget."

"That's bullshit." Davis gritted his teeth.

"You think the murder's connected to the weapons thefts?"

Why else would the Captain keep his project a secret at the same time the brass kept weapons thefts secret. "Probably. I want interviews with everyone who called Captain Stone in the last two weeks. Get the names of the brass who buried the theft reports. Find out if any of them had contact with Stone."

"Will do."

Agent Davis gave a half smile. "And don't let them give you any crap about your sense of humor either."

"You bet."

Josh made a few calls and came back fifteen minutes later with a list of persons who'd called the Captain. One of those phone calls lasted much longer than the others. The same caller's name also showed up on Tomas' cell phone records. *Why would Tomas and the Captain be speaking with the same person in the few days?*

"Josh, I think we'd better go have a talk with him ASAP. What's his name?"

CHAPTER 44

Claude's red sports roadster sped past the black wrought iron gate at the rear entrance to Lucian's forty-acre Long Island compound. He used the back entry to avoid attracting unwanted press attention to his arrival. He sped down the driveway outlined by manicured English garden shrubs. Up ahead, lush grounds hibernated for the winter in various shades of red and brown.

Lucian had requested they meet for a special high-priority project, but remained secretive, saying he would explain more in person. Claude's white knuckles gripped the steering wheel as he glanced at his Swiss jeweled wristwatch.

Good, I'm on time for the meeting.

His car whizzed by five white marble statues of Greek gods from Eros to Apollo, midway down the drive. They stood watch like ancient sentinels in a row. Claude's lips pursed at the sight of the decorative non-revenue producing sculptures. He was more into profit-making ventures than art.

Lucian collects priceless statues like some people collect box tops.

A gleaming orange six passenger helicopter waited behind the statues, sitting on a green heliport pad. Its propeller's orange and white stripes alternated like a toll gate's colors. One hundred yards from the pavement, an enormous church shaped yacht house with white cross-hatch barn doors, rose from a sparkling lake's shore.

He's never once invited me on his yacht, after all I've done for him.

The sedan slowed as it passed unblemished green tennis courts and a deep blue Olympic size swimming pool. It rounded a cream-colored paver circle driveway, bringing Claude to the mansion's front entrance. He parked between an ornate two-tiered marble fountain and the mansion's front entrance. The fountain's four sculpted lions spouted water from their mouths, gurgling into the generous basin. He got out of the car and scowled at the big cats.

What an inefficient use of capital.

He gazed up at the grand natural stone mansion. Masons had built its three-story structure in baroque French chateau style. It ranked among the larger residences in the U.S., built to impress in every way, and it succeeded. He trotted up six slab steps to the double doors and lifted the antique brass knocker, rapping hard three times. The sound bounced off the building's stone exterior and reverberated across the driveway.

The door opened, revealing a sour-faced uniformed butler. "He's expecting you, sir."

The butler ushered him into the foyer. A vibrant blue and green ringed stained-glass dome loomed overhead. Claude followed the servant across an exquisite parquet marble floor, past an eight feet wide grand staircase constructed of hand carved walnut woodwork and into the game room.

"The master is not yet home from his outing, sir," the butler said in his thick English accent. "But I believe he'll be here shortly." He bowed his head ever so slightly, before disappearing into the hall.

Claude plopped back in the plush oxblood leather sofa with both hands clasped behind his head. The rich scent of restored leather and old books filled his nostrils.

It's so like Lucian to keep everyone else waiting for him.

He drummed his fingers on the sofa's arm while looking around the room for a way to pass the time until Lucian arrived. A long antique billiards table stood in the room's center. Big game animal trophy heads looked down from the walls. An oversize stone fireplace and gaming table surrounded by six chairs filled out the space.

The sound of voices coming down the hall interrupted his inventory of the room. Claude stood up when he realized it was Lucian returning from his outing.

Five seconds later Lucian burst through the doorway and launched into his greeting. "Claude, thanks for waiting. Our, uh, outing at the club ran long because we had some important business to discuss." Lucian ran his fingers through his hair, straightening his tie which had shifted to one side.

"I understand." *Must have been some outing. It looks more like he just crawled out of bed.*

"I caught your news show appearance earlier. Your performance was disappointing, to say the least. He got the best of you. With the high wages I pay, I expect you to win every time, nothing less."

"I hear you. It won't happen again."

"There's been a change of plan." Lucian shifted gears, seeming strangely invigorated, almost breathless. "We're expanding our outreach ASAP. I'm tripling our media budget starting now." He rattled on ad nauseum about media buys and television news appearances.

"But... I don't understand." Claude's jaw dropped. He could hardly believe his ears. "Three weeks ago, I asked for more money. You turned me down flat." *Something's seriously off, here.*

Lucian gave a dismissive wave of his hand. "That was then. This is now."

He walked over to the billiards table, surprising Claude further by inviting him to play Snooker. The offer seemed odd. Lucian never had asked him to play on prior occasions, almost going out of his way to exclude him. Claude hadn't questioned it. The men of prodigious-wealth he knew had a caste system dictating they didn't socialize with you unless you had at least a half-billion dollars. He'd learned to live with their slights, but he never got used to them.

Lucian rang for the butler, instructing him to bring drinks... a Manhattan for Lucian, and an Old Fashioned for Claude. Lucian grabbed a billiards cue stick off the wall and chalked up his tip. Claude racked up the balls for the initial break. Lucian took the first shot and the balls scattered across the table.

Lucian aimed his stick at the cue ball to set up the next shot, recounting in detail how he'd become a multi-billionaire. He'd grown up in a rich-as-Versailles family, with parents who had no love for him. His mother cared only about her socialite status among her elitist peers, his father cared only about speculating in stocks while plotting to undercut his market rivals. The servants who raised him had contempt for the spoiled brat.

"At thirteen, they shipped me off to boarding school. But I detested my classes... so boring. Two prestigious New England boarding schools booted me out. Prestigious universities did the same."

Claude took two shots, making both. *What the hell is Lucian doing? Do I look like a priest? This isn't a confessional booth.*

"Love mattered little," Lucian said. "Money was the sole source of affection, my only solace in a cold and sterile household."

"Don't focus on the negative, it'll depress you. Instead, concentrate on the good work we've done educating the public."

Lucian lifted his glass, giving him a blank look. "Uh, hate to burst your bubble, but there's not much. That 'trickle-down austerity' we pay you to preach... it's a bunch of crap."

Claude stiffened as if he'd been poked by an electric cattle-prod. *What the hell had got into Lucian? He'd never talked like this before.* "It's not a bunch of crap, it's the free market." His effort to change the topic of conversation had failed. Claude leaned over to take another shot, scowling as the white cue ball missed its target bouncing impotently off the table's side.

"Free all right," Lucian sneered. "Free for me to get richer. And free for Joe six-pack to get poorer. I use buzzwords like liberty to justify killing workers' rights, convincing them government's so bad they don't have a choice... that it's the problem, not the solution."

Lucian must think he controls me, that's why he's not holding back. He must feel invincible. "But liberty's a good thing."

"I don't give a damn if it's good or bad... it's my red-herring to hoodwink the public, so I keep control. I use it to play others like a chess game, determining their future and fate, continuing the cycle."

Lucian was treading on hallowed ground, here, bordering on blasphemy. Claude whiffed on a shot toward the side pocket. "But individual liberty's our bedrock. We're committed to that, aren't we?"

"Only if it means less government protection for the public. When it comes to my wealth, I want more government protection, not less. Flag-waving lingo about freedom gives me cover, so I can smuggle my message in under the radar...make me look like a patriot instead of a selfish bastard. It also intimidates my opponents so they back down."

Patriotism's the last refuge of a scoundrel. Lucian needs to be reminded of the reason for shrinking government. "But... we slashed regulations, because the savings would create jobs."

"Why would I want more jobs or higher wages." Lucian gave a condescending laugh. "Employees are a necessary evil… their wages cut into my profits. I replace them with automation every chance I get. Then the rest work harder to pick up the slack, out of fear I'll fire them, too."

"That's not what we told the public," Claude said. "We told them they'd prosper. I put my reputation on the line for you."

Lucian walked around the table searching for his next shot. "There's a lot we don't tell people… like I privatize my profits and socialize my losses. If I succeed, I keep all the money. If I fail, the government bails me out. I can't lose… and the public can't win."

Claude shook his head at the irony. *Lucian, the icon for free enterprise and shrinking government, getting bailouts at taxpayer expense.*

"I'll destroy the social safety net and public education if it cuts my taxes." Lucian lined up his cue for the next shot in the corner pocket. "The nineteenth century gilded age seemed the best time for men like me. Back then we ruled a society of poor, desperate and uneducated workers."

"But you said they'd benefit from spending cuts, too."

"I lied, so sue me. But I don't want to cut the police, the CIA and the military. I'll need them to arrest the angry citizens who oppose me. They'll fill my private profitized prisons and fatten my wallet."

Claude winced. *Surely Lucian's endgame wasn't an American version of Dickensian England's debtors' prisons.* "But, shrinking the government is good. That's what we said."

"You're so naïve. When government gets smaller, private monopolies step in to fill the power void before the common man even knows what hit him. Privatization gives me more influence over the public, whose vote doesn't stop me."

"You don't mean that." Lucian's words were a frightening description of a massive power grab against democracy. "It's the alcohol talking."

"I meant every word. And, don't you worry yourself about my drinking." Lucian missed the easy shot in the side pocket, cursing the table. He drained the last of his drink. "You of all people should know better. You saw wages stagnate after my taxes were slashed. Don't be a fool."

Wage's had declined after Lucian's tax cut, Claude couldn't deny that. But there was a reason. "The cuts only need a little more time to succeed."

"Jesus, where've you been? I received the biggest and longest tax cuts in history, a few years ago. Guess what? We got the worst job creation in history and stagnant wages."

"That was a fluke." *It's only temporary, it will change very soon. It must.*

Lucian gave him a hard stare. "No. Trickle-down austerity was always destined to be a disaster at increasing wages. But it was a tremendous success at increasing my wealth."

"But our cuts jumpstarted the stock market. That's good."

"Get real. It's a temporary sugar high that doesn't last. The bubble market requires more and more sugar to maintain the high, until eventually it wears out and crashes."

"But greed is good.*" Lucian couldn't be right.*

"Not really." Lucian took another sip from his glass, wiping his mouth with the back of his hand. "Even the ancient Greeks knew that money-lust ruins a nation. Plato described how greedy men with inexhaustible-riches corrupted Greek democracy and it disintegrated. They turned it into tyranny."

Claude scowled. "That's only one man's opinion from a long time ago." *Lucian couldn't believe avarice caused society's problems instead of solving them.*

"Hmph! That's no ordinary man. Plato and Socrates both believed it." Lucian leaned his head back and looked down his nose at Claude, as if he was an unlearned child. "Even the great Greek philosopher, Plutarch, explained how severe wealth-inequality is fatal to a republic."

Claude's lower lip quivered as he laid his billiards cue against the table. "But, but... what about our think tank research? It said we'd grow the economy?"

"Who do you think paid for those studies." Lucian smirked as he lined up his next shot. "I paid a bundle to rig them. Remember the tobacco studies saying cigarettes don't cause cancer?"

"If you knew it cost people their jobs, why'd you do it? Why cause all that misery? I've spent my life supporting your ideas. I told church members it's God's plan."

"I don't know about God, but it's definitely a plan."

Claude's mouth hung open. *This was a nightmare, his worst fears come true. Had he given the public what he thought was a vitamin but turned out to be rat poison.* "You can't be serious."

"Here's how it works." Lucian took a drink and set the glass down. "I donate to politicians who slash my taxes, so government has too little money to pay workers and lays them off. I put my tax savings in speculative ventures that men with unimaginable-wealth buy and sell to each other, bidding up the price in a speculative frenzy. I sell and make a huge profit. But I don't create jobs... never will."

"But in that case the public can vote for change." Claude folded his arms across his chest.

"You forget. I rigged that too. I gerrymandered districts and culled minorities from the voter rolls. That makes it hard to kick my politicians out. Most voters who wanted change, will give up."

Claude took a shot at a red ball that banked harmlessly off the table's corner. "But those who get jobs make good wages, right?"

"That's the dirty little secret. Many don't make a living wage or have healthcare. They're the working poor, like paupers... half of all state welfare and Medicaid recipients."

"Sorry to interrupt, sir." The butler appeared in the doorway unprompted, carrying a silver tray holding another round of drinks. "Time to refresh your glasses."

Lucian eagerly reached for another glass and took a gulp. "Leave the tray on the table." The butler set it down and left the room.

I've got to bring up something Lucian can't challenge. That will snap him out of his madness. "Well, increasing your taxes won't help workers. It'll reduce your incentive to make money and create jobs."

That's the biggest whopper of all." Lucian tipped back his head and roared with laughter. "It wouldn't change my behavior one bit. Money's like cocaine to me. I'm addicted, and I'll keep scheming to make a profit no matter how much you tax me. I can't stop 'til I'm the richest man in the world."

Had his boss lost touch with reality? Lucian's creepy bellow startled Claude so much he almost choked on his drink. "Listen to yourself. If that's true you need help." Claude's hands shook as his stick hit the cue ball, which in turn struck a red ball that went nowhere near a pocket.

"You don't understand, it wouldn't do any good." Lucian's head shook side to side. "Money gives you power, freedom, control over others, the never having to want or fear of going without. That's an addictive feeling."

"But that doesn't mean you're an addict."

"I have to be the alpha male. Second place doesn't count. My circle of billionaires' gets smaller over time, like criminals dividing up stolen loot. One may get rid of the other to get both shares."

"You'd even destroy your allies, to be top dog?" *My God, I'm one of the in-crowd, Lucian's group, yet he sees me as expendable, too. We're all sacrificial lambs in his book.*

"In a heartbeat." Lucian stared right through Claude. "It's the law of the land, the haves or have nots, the attitude that no one is going to give you anything so you must take it. Compassion is weakness. If society doesn't like what I do, that's tough."

"Why'd you lead me on?" Claude chalked his pool cue. "Why didn't you tell me this before?" His mind was numb, not hearing Lucian at this point. *What a total betrayal. Money had hardened him to the point he didn't care about anyone but himself.*

Lucian leered at him with bloodthirsty and unforgiving eyes. "Would you have spread my lies if you'd known?"

"Of course not." Claude recoiled in disgust.

"There's your answer."

The butler re-appeared in the doorway with an anxious look on his face. "I'm terribly sorry to interrupt sir, but there's a very urgent call on line three."

CHAPTER 45

Agent Davis stood inside the military base's vehicle storage building as he asked Josh about who had the long phone conversation with Captain Stone before his death.

"A retired general named George Rogers," Josh said. "Handles military contracts for RavenSpire Industries."

"Let's pay him a visit. Find out what he and the Captain talked about."

They packed up their things, left the base and drove downtown to RavenSpire's glass paneled corporate headquarters. A clerk ushered them into the General's expansive office where he greeted them both with firm handshakes. Davis sat down in a leather chair, taking a good look around. Oversized framed photos of the General posing with well-known dignitaries, covered the walls. A grand cherry display case hung near his desk, holding his numerous military medals and colorful ribbons.

Humility's certainly not the General's strong point. He gives new meaning to the phrase self-promotion. Davis chuckled to himself. "Looks like you had quite a career. How long have you been out of the service?"

"About five years." The General lit a cigarette and leaned back in his executive chair. "Seems like yesterday. Even the best old war horse must one day step aside to make room for new blood. Tell me, what can I do for you?"

We're investigating Captain Stone's murder at the military base."

Davis leaned forward, his hands folded.

"Yes, I heard about it. Tragic, very tragic.

"I understand he called you last week." Davis studied the General's face, searching for any telltale signs of deceit.

The General stiffened in a motion so small as to be almost unnoticeable. "Uh, yeah, we touched base."

Hmmm. That caught him by surprise. He didn't realize we knew. "What did you talk about?"

"Nothing special." The General shrugged his shoulders. "How was he doing, any problems with his equipment, that sort of thing. I knew him from my time in the service. I keep up my relationships. Comes in handy when you're working on military contracts."

"Did he say anything unusual? Anything bothering him?"

"Nothing out of the ordinary." The General fidgeted with a pen, looking down at his desk. "Which weapons they were using. His opinion what's good and what's bad. That's all."

"Did he mention anyone who might have a grudge?"

The General crossed his arms. "Not that I recall."

He's nervous and evasive. There's something he's not telling. "The security log says you visited him at the base the next day." Davis pulled a sheet of paper out of his satchel, sliding it across the desk to the General. "What was so pressing? Why not make another phone call?"

"You don't understand." The General gave an exasperated sigh. "In my business, there's no substitute for face to face contact."

This guy's lying right to my face and thinks he's getting away with it. Davis stared a hole right through the General. "Why'd you visit him out of all the officers on the base? Was he more qualified on the weapons system than the others?"

"Not really." The General pursed his lips. "We market weapons to the military and marketing's all about relationships. Like I said, I maintained a good rapport with the Captain."

I'm getting nowhere fast. He's one cool customer. "Thanks for your time, that's all we have today." Davis narrowed his eyes and stood up. "Come on, Josh."

The General exhaled a long breath, relaxing in his high-backed executive chair. He made no attempt to walk them out. Instead, he looked down at the paperwork on his desk while scribbling notes.

Davis walked toward the door. He stopped after a couple steps, pivoting to face the General and cocking his head to one side. "By the way, you ever hear of a fellow named Tomas Lobo?"

The General bit his lip, pausing a bit too long while he decided how to respond. "No. Never heard of him. Should I?"

"You're sure?" Davis said shifting his head to one side. *I'll give him another chance to come clean.*

"A hundred percent." The General gripped the arms on his chair. "Why'd you ask?"

"We're looking at all potential leads, that's all." Davis shrugged his shoulders. "Just wondering."

"Well I haven't heard of him." The General's eyes narrowed.

Davis walked back toward the desk, handing the General his business card. "If you learn anything more about the Captain, I'd appreciate you letting me know." *He already knows more, he doesn't have to learn about it. I won't hold my breath waiting for him to spill the beans.*

"You can count on it." The General walked him to the door, flashing a tight-lipped smile and shaking Davis' hand.

Davis and Josh left the building, driving the squad car back to the office. Josh sat in the passenger seat, writing up his notes from the meeting. After a couple minutes, he looked up and asked Davis what he thought of the General's statements.

"He's hiding something." Davis' jaw muscle twitched. "No way he's clean."

"Damn straight." Josh nodded his head.

"What makes you so sure I'm right?"

"I finished reviewing Oscar White's cell phone records a while ago." Josh held up a printed piece of paper in triumph. "He called Tomas from the Archives' the same day he was murdered. Tomas called the General three minutes later. They're connected."

This breakthrough could nail Rogers' egotistical hide to the wall. There's nothing I'd enjoy more. Davis gave Josh a playful push on the shoulder. "There's a career for you in the FBI, yet son."

"I never knew you had any doubt." Josh gave a look of mock surprise.

"The General lied to us about not knowing Tomas... somehow it ties in to the murders. I want you to follow Rogers starting today. Stick to him like glue. We're gonna find out what he's up to before anybody else shows up dead."

CHAPTER 46

Lucian held the phone receiver up to his ear, glancing over his shoulder at the butler standing in the game room's doorway. "I need privacy while I take this call. I may be a while. Escort Mr. Zorak to the study." Lucian waived his hand to shoo them away, mumbling, "He can wait there 'til I'm finished."

The butler led Claude down an arched hallway to the study, before leaving to deal with other duties. Claude drummed his fingers on the conference table, looking around the room. The rhythmic beat of his digits on the wood, broke the library-like silence.

What a crock. First, Lucian returns late from his club outing, claiming it was about business. Fat chance of that. Then, he says he doesn't even believe what we've told the public. Now, he tells me to cool my heels while he makes a lengthy phone call. I don't like this one bit.

The large video monitor still hung down from the ceiling, left in position from Lucian's earlier meeting. The remote control lay on the table where he had left it.

Conservative cable news might help kill time 'til Lucian's available.

Claude picked up the remote and pressed the on button for the video monitor. The screen flickered for a moment before lighting up. The paused image of a security schematic appeared, the words 'White House' printed in bold letters at the top. Claude tilted his had to one side, staring fixated at the image. This didn't look like ordinary entertainment.

Why the hell had Lucian looked at that?

Two bars in the middle of the screen showed the machine had paused.

So, it's a video. Well, let's see what the great Lucian Drake watches in his leisure time.

Claude pressed the play button on the remote and the whirring DVD sound kicked in. His eyes widened as the recording played. He took in a sharp breath, watching in horror the detailed plans for a takeover of the White House. More details appeared, including the President's personal schedule, the conspirators' names and a list of military officers sympathetic to the conspiracy.

My God, he's plotting to overthrow the United States. That's treason. They could all be tried and executed.

Claude's hands trembled like cold jello at what he'd seen on the video. As Lucian's right-hand man, he would be a natural suspect in the scheme. But, his absence from the conspirators list might save him. T*he DVD could prove my innocence. It'll be my insurance policy if Lucian tries to make me the fall guy.* Claude pressed a button on the remote, ejecting the DVD. Once done, he slipped it into his overcoat pocket and switched off the monitor. He plopped down in one of the executive swivel chairs, exhaling sharply.

What have I gotten myself into? This is insane.

He gazed around the room, hoping for guidance what to do next. His eyes fell on a mahogany credenza against one wall, its file drawer ajar about half an inch. He walked over to it, pulling the drawer open all the way to reveal a single manila file labeled simply *"The New Business Plot."* He laid the folder open on the credenza's top. His jaw dropped as he read the first page.

It contained more information about Lucian's conspiracy, not on the DVD. A photo stuck to the first page named its subject as Dimitri Ivanovich, a former Russian Intelligence officer stationed in their Washington Embassy under cover as an aide. Paperclipped to the photo were details for transfer of White House security schematics. Included were instructions about secret locations where Lucian's henchmen and Dimitri could drop information for delivery to each other. The file held plans for a joint venture between Lucian and one of Russia's powerful billionaires. Once the coup succeeded and ended U.S. democracy, he'd make sure Russia would not interfere while Lucian took control of North and South America. In exchange, Lucian's dictator would stand by while the staggeringly rich Russian gained control of Europe and Asia. The two conspirators had hatched a diabolical plan to gain control of much of the world.

I'll bet Lucian's group of five men as rich-as-kings doesn't know about this other plan. He's gonna double cross them too, in favor of the Russian gentleman, as soon as he gets control. It reminded Claude of what Lucian told him during their billiards game, how a tyrant shuts out more and more groups, his inner circle getting smaller and smaller until eventually no one's left but himself. *That's exactly what Lucian plans to do.*

Claude gasped, the blood draining from his face. Lucian had planned the worst scenario imaginable. *How on Earth could I have supported this psychopath? He's selling humanity down the river to satisfy his pathological addiction to money.*

Claude prided himself on patriotism, yet his own think-tanks had made this traitor's mad scheme possible. Lucian didn't want free markets. He wanted a monopoly and dictatorship too powerful to challenge. And, once in power… his rule might never end.

There must be some way out of this. Claude paced back and forth on the hand knotted Persian area rug, hands clasped behind his back. The sound of voices coming down the hall interrupted his angst. He gulped, as he heard the butler and Lucian talking, after finishing the phone call. Claude grabbed the remote off the table, fumbling for the tiny off button before slapping it down on the wood surface. The monitor flickered, going black right before Lucian strutted through the doorway into the meeting room.

"That took longer than I planned," he said. "Now, where were we?"

Typical Lucian, he didn't even have the decency to apologize. Claude crossed his arms over his chest. "You were explaining why you didn't tell me about your lies before I spread them. What else haven't you told me?"

"There are things you don't need to know."

Claude decided the time had come to put his cards on the table. Lucian had placed too much at risk to hold back. He pointed at the monitor. "I saw your DVD."

Lucian's face turned pale as he glanced at the blank screen. "How much of it?"

217

"Enough. You plan to take over the country, don't you?"

Lucian ran his hand through his hair, pausing for a couple moments before sneering. "You have a problem with that?"

Even caught red-handed he's got the gall to act defiant. Did his narcissism make him feel invincible? "You're damn right, I do. You'll get us all hung for treason. This risks everything we ever had."

"Hah, you think I don't know?" Lucian grabbed the back of a high-back leather chair, squeezing it hard between his hands as if he wanted to tear into something, or someone. "You of all people, the great privatizer, should appreciate that I hired a private army for the takeover."

"I never supported treason."

"Maybe not political treason, but you supported my financial treason. You convinced politicians they'd save money by outsourcing to corporations. But after I skim my huge profit markup, they spend more than they would have on public employees for the same job."

When Lucian mauled the chair, a light bulb went off in Claude's head. *He's willing to kill whoever he needs to for his plan.* "There've been several murders in D.C. in the last twenty-four hours. You know anything about 'em?"

"That doesn't concern you." Lucian's eyes raked him with freezing contempt. "Let's just say Tomas is paid well to keep my secrets."

"Why on Earth would you do this? Your scheme involves several conspirators, any one of whom could testify you're the ringleader." *And once you're charged it would lead the authorities straight to me.*

"I told you I'm addicted... my analyst said so. I can't stop because power feels so good. You saw the video, the public's getting wise to my deception and would try to stop me."

"So, trickle-down's a lie, and you can't control yourself." Claude threw his hands up in the air. *Lucian played with peoples' lives, did he think he was God? Or, the Devil?* "All this time I thought it would increase wages and improve people's lives. I believed in your free market theory. How could you do this to me... t-to everybody?"

"How dare you question me." Lucian's expression looked almost satanic as he snarled and shook his fist in Claude's face. "Me, a bastion of finance. Why you're nothing but... the hired help. I could fire you any time I want, just like that." Lucian snapped his fingers as if to emphasize his last point.

"You're mad." Claude, still facing Lucian, backed up toward the doorway. "You used me and everyone at the think tank. We were mere whores to you, selling our credibility to make you richer than King Midas."

Lucian glowered at Claude, taking a step toward him. "You'll keep your mouth shut if you know what's good for you."

Claude glanced up at the stuffed animal heads mounted on the wall. *Lucian thinks no more of me than his wild game trophies, and I could end up just as dead. Would he display me on the wall, too? Well, I'm not staying around to find out.*

Claude bolted out the door, rounding the corner and running smack into Tomas walking down the hall. The collision's force knocked Claude sideways. But he kept his feet, continuing his dash down the hall toward the front entrance.

Tomas absorbed the blow like a linebacker, raising his eyebrows before smoothing his jacket and ambling in to the game room. He locked eyes with Lucian, jerking his head to one side in the direction Claude had run. "What's all that about?"

"Don't worry about him." Lucian gave a half shrug. "Let him go. He's got too much invested to turn on us."

Claude ran out the mansion's front door, jumped in his red sports roadster and inserted the key in the ignition. The engine coughed twice, before turning over with a deep throaty rumble. He gunned the motor, pulling away from the mansion with a roar and cloud of heavy sweet-smelling exhaust fumes.

An odd feeling of being watched fell over him as he pulled away. His eyes veered toward Lucian's game room window where Tomas stared at him laser-like from behind the tied purple velvet curtain. Claude looked away to avoid eye contact. Chills went up his spine like an ice-cold shower. *He's scary, there's no telling what he'd do for Lucian.* Claude needed help right away and knew exactly where to get it.

Back in the game room, Tomas shifted his gaze away from the window. Lucian strapped a mounted spring-loaded stiletto knife on his bare forearm, the straps hiding the blade under a shirt sleeve where it could pop out from the wrist when needed. Its thick steel wrist bracelet secured the weapon to his forearm.

Tomas smirked with contempt at his boss's attempt to arm himself.

"Where did you get that?"

"My father got it as a gift years ago. I've been saving it for a special occasion."

"And this is it?"

"I'm going to find Joe Richmond." Lucian leered as he stood up to his full height. With a bravado inconsistent with his cowardice, he added, "No one else has got rid of him. So, it looks like I'll have to do it myself."

CHAPTER 47

Gina drove the van away from the Monastery's front gate, pressing her foot hard against the accelerator. The vehicle's motor unleased a high-pitched whine under the stress "We've got to get to New York, ASAP. The Church and Barclay Street intersection's the key."

"We can't go by train," Joe shook his head, from the passenger seat next to her. "The police would stop us at the station before we could even board the coach."

"There's another way. My firm has a six-passenger private jet at the airport."

"Great idea." No sooner had the words come out of his mouth than Joe realized they had a problem. *Who would fly the plane for two fugitives?* Joe rolled his eyes. "Wait. We'd never find a pilot on such short notice. And if we did, he'd probably turn us in for the reward."

Gina's eyes twinkled. "We already have one."

"Who?" *What kind of a game is she playing?*

"I've flown it to New York many times to meet clients."

"You... a pilot?" Joe straightened. *She's full of surprises.* "You're kidding. Where'd you learn to fly?"

She stuck out her tongue at him in mock indignation. "After college, I served in the Aeronautica Militare, the Italian Air Force. I've been flying ever since."

"Well then, I guess we'll be flying the friendly skies of Gina." *She's an amazing woman. What'll she come up with next?*

She made a phone call to the airport while driving, instructing them to have the plane fueled and ready in twenty minutes. After a short drive, they pulled up to the private hangar at the D.C. airport and climbed aboard the sleek white jet. Gina strapped herself into the leather pilot's seat. Joe buckled himself into the cockpit seat next to her. The 'new car smell' of plastic and foam components filled his nostrils. Her fingers flipped instrument panel switches lighting up three colored screens with gauges and maps. He watched with big eyes as the engines roared, the plane accelerated and taxied down the runway, picking up speed. Seconds later they soared into the sky.

Down on the ground, a tall man in a dark trench coat stood next to a black sedan in the hangar parking lot, watching the jet take off. As soon as the plane left the ground, he walked into the hangar office, shot the manager and grabbed Gina's flight plan off the desk. His eyes devoured the information. He pressed speed dial on his cellphone, making a call to convey Gina's destination to an unknown party.

Up in the sky, the private jet reached altitude and leveled off. Gina flipped a switch on the plane's instrument panel, putting the plane on autopilot. She looked over at Joe. "What do you think the clue means 'offer prayers at the Church and Barclay Street angel's bench'?"

"No idea. I'm hoping when we get there it'll make sense."

"When Antonio and I first moved to D.C., we'd fly to New York for my firm's business. Or sometimes for his visits to the Italian consulate. While I met with clients, he'd go see his old buddy at Saint Patrick's Cathedral, the building operations director who died about a year ago. They belonged to the same social group."

I'd be willing to bet money it was the Gracchus League. I've been there at Christmas time when I'd go to the Macy's department store to buy gifts," Joe said. "There'd be a store Santa Claus with small children on his lap asking for toys."

"Same here," she said. "A group of carolers stood outside singing *God rest you Merry Gentlemen*. It's a contrast to the panhandlers begging for money a few blocks away. I feel very sorry for them. With the wrong breaks, any of us could be in their situation."

Joe's eyelids weighed heavily as the lack of sleep caught up with him.

I could think more clearly if I wasn't so exhausted. He looked out the window at the ground far below and his fingers dug into the seat's arm rest. A moment later his eyes clenched shut and his face took on a pained expression.

Gina looked down at his white knuckles and frowned. "Are you alright?"

He exhaled. "I'll be O.K. in a minute."

"Heights bother you, don't they?" She put her hand on his shoulder.

"I just need some rest, that's all." He nodded off, snoozing for forty-five minutes. The plane needed another ten in the air before reaching New York City's airport. Gina's hand shook his shoulder hard. He stirred, his eyes opening to a horrifying sight outside her cockpit side window. A much larger white jumbo jet flew alongside them, filling the window. The plane sported a gold-colored fuselage with a huge black letter 'D' adorning the tail. It matched their speed, like a flight escort. Thirty seconds later, the airliner accelerated to full throttle, flying right in front of them. The huge aircraft's jet engines spewed hazy exhaust, creating a major "wash" or turbulence right on their jet's nose. The small private jet's cabin creaked, twisting and vibrating from the severe strain.

What the hell is happening? This isn't good. Joe grabbed the cockpit seat's armrests to steady himself. He glanced out the window where the plane's wings rocked from the turbulence. "That's not supposed to happen."

"The bastard pulled right in front of us." Gina gripped the yoke, or control wheel, grunting through clenched teeth. "Their wash hit us head on."

Joe's heart jumped up into his throat as the plane lost altitude and went into a spin. *Was someone trying to take them down?* "What's h-h-happening... we're f-falling?"

"The wash caused a compressor stall and flameout." Gina shouted above the descent noise, hands shaking as she pulled against the vibrating control wheel, or yoke. "I can't talk now," she shouted. "I've gotta try and pull us out of this dive."

The earth whirled below them through the windshield as the small jet spiraled out of control. Odd shaped fields of green and tan spun in a circle like a game wheel framed by white cloud wisps.

Dizziness overtook Joe as he watched the images rotating at high speed.

His stomach dropped. Nausea overtook him, but he couldn't grasp the air sickness bag while the plane dived and rolled. "I think I'm gonna pass out."

Gina's knuckles turned white on the vibrating yoke, pulling back on it with all her might to regain control of the jet. It continued dropping and twirling.

"I'm so sorry," she screamed over the engine's screaming whines.

Joe's life flashed before his eyes. *Is this how it all ends? Plunging thousands of feet to the ground, followed by a sudden crash.*

She gave a desperate backward heave on the pulsing yoke and a moment later the plane's engines restarted. The spinning motion stopped. Seconds later their descent slowed. The jet gradually leveled out to a smooth horizontal path. Gina exhaled in one big breath, her shoulders relaxing. "I've got it under control now. I can't believe the asshole did that."

Joe stared through his side window as the jumbo jet changed direction, flying away in the distance. Gina's eyes glared icily at the offending craft. "I've been flying thirty years and never seen anything like that. He tried to bring us down. Who the hell would use a commercial size airliner to kill somebody?"

The jumbo jet disappeared on the horizon and she switched their private plane back on autopilot. Joe let out a sigh, sitting back in the seat and closing his eyes. Gina's words echoed in his ears.

A very good question. Who would use a jumbo jet to kill us?

They flew for five more minutes before the New York City skyline came into view. Its various height skyscrapers stretched across the Manhattan skyline like a long uneven bar chart. Their plane descended as they neared the New York airport, landing on one of the private jet runways without incident. They taxied to the small hangar. Once there, they disembarked, piling into the back seat of a cab she'd reserved.

She parroted Oscar's last clue, instructing the driver, "Take us to Church and Barclay Street. And step on it. We're in a hurry."

CHAPTER 48

The cabby cursed as he whipped the steering wheel around, weaving through South Manhattan streets packed with traffic. The rough ride made it impossible for Joe to doze in the cab's back seat. The driver hit the brakes, changing lanes with such force the back of Joe's head hit hard against the seat's firm head restraint. The blow jerked his neck to one side. He rubbed it with his hand while gripping the cab seat's arm rest with the other.

God, my neck's sore, hope it's not too much further. Joe's eagerness to reach their destination made the pain bearable. He looked up from the long street canyon at the tall skyscrapers, wondering how he might find an angel's bench once they arrived.

The cab screeched to a halt against the curb near the busy corner of Church and Barclay Street, three blocks from the New York City Hall. Joe and Gina got out of the cab, pushing their way through the crowd on the sidewalk until they stood on the corner. Their heads turned from side to side, searching the street for connections to the Ambassador's clue.

The words 'angel's bench' rolled over and over in Joe's mind. *Where the hell is it? This is the place, but there's no angel's bench, and no one offering prayers.*

Busy office workers and city employees buzzed up and down the sidewalks, going about their daily activities. An idling bus twenty feet away belched dark smelly exhaust fumes. The gray smoke drifted toward Joe, making him cough.

God, I hope this isn't a dead end.

"We need time to think," Gina said. "There's a restaurant across the street. Let's get something to eat."

They racked their brains as they ate. But no matter how they interpreted the Ambassador's clue about the angel's bench, they came up empty handed. After drinks, salad, main course, coffee and dessert, they still had no idea how to proceed any further.

"We're stuck," Joe said.

He was about ready to throw in the towel, when a tall red and white armored truck drove by on the other side of the street, laying on its shrill horn. The blast caught his attention. He swung his head toward the blaring sound. The van's side displayed the red stenciled words Galbraith Security. It drove forward next to a black and white street sign attached to a light pole. Joe squinted at the sign. Its white letters read 'Pierre Toussaint Square.'

Toussaint… that sure sounded familiar. Where had he heard that name before?

He tugged Gina's sleeve, pointing to the sign while asking her if she recognized it.

"Yeah, Antonio told me about Toussaint. He was a Haitian slave. His owners brought him to New York where he became a free man and a business success. He used the money to start an orphanage, spending his life helping the poor. People loved him so much that when he died the Church entombed him in Saint Patrick's Cathedral crypt. Right alongside the Cardinals. The people considered him an angel. The Church created a special prayer card with a prayer to him."

Angel, prayer, cathedral and crypt. Joe stared at the sign for a moment, his eyes becoming big like silver dollars. He slapped a trembling hand against his leg with excitement. "I know where the secret is. It's in Saint Patrick's Cathedral. That's where Antonio's leading us."

"What do you mean?"

"You said it yourself, Church and Barkley Street is Toussaint Square. Toussaint's an angel. He's buried in Saint Patrick's crypt."

Gina's mouth gaped. "Oh my God. Antonio's friend worked at Saint Patrick's. He showed Antonio all the Cathedral's secret places. He would have known how to access the crypt."

"It all fits. Crypt is from the Latin word crypta. It literally means hiding place."

"That's irony on steroids." she winced. "Stashing a secret in a spot whose name means hiding place."

"Once your ex found the secret, he had to hide it until he could decide what to do with it. He couldn't keep it at home, the type of person who'd want it would tear his home apart looking for it. It wouldn't be secure enough."

"He thought of the perfect hiding spot," Gina said. "A place so unusual no one would ever think to look... the Cathedral. He took the secret with him and left for New York. He had barely enough time to hide the secret, plant the clues and get back to the Embassy before the celebration."

"It's a place where no one would look." *What a brilliant clue. Joe remembered something he'd seen in Villa Firenze's secret room. Something that confirmed they were on the right track.* He grabbed Gina by both shoulders, staring into her eyes. "Remember the painting covering-up Antonio's wall-safe in his secret room?"

Gina recoiled from his sudden move, looking at him like he was slightly touched in the head. Then as she answered his question, her eyes grew big. "It was St. Patrick's Cathedral."

"I thought at the time, it seemed out of place with everything else in the room. Don't you see?"

"There's only one reason Antonio would hang it there. To point us in the right direction." She paused for a moment, frowning. "But, what about the angel's bench?"

Joe stroked his chin and looked upward. "Crypts sometimes have prayer benches for visiting relatives. *It couldn't be anything else, it all matched up so well.* We've got to get to Saint Patrick's ASAP before anyone else."

They dashed to the subway and boarded the train for Saint Patrick's Cathedral's stop.

CHAPTER 49

Dominic strolled out the network studio building's revolving front door onto a bustling New York City sidewalk. Street traffic bedlam filled the air, competing against the buzz of pedestrians hurrying to reach their destinations. An unseen police siren wailed in the distance, its pitch alternating from high, to low, to high again. The bright sunshine hit his face. Its rays invigorated him despite the chilly temperature. A group of three young male protesters in jeans and baseball caps shouted chants near the curb ten yards away. They clutched signs supporting building of the border wall and deporting undocumented immigrants.

Dominic sighed at the sight. *Ah, they're here again. Don't they every give up.*

Small immigration protest groups often camped outside the studios televising his appearances with Claude. A conservative think tank funded their protests, assuring Claude's appearances made the evening news. Dominic looked away from the picketers and trudged next door to a coffee shop to have lunch. He took his time eating, reading the local newspaper and chatting with the waitress about her difficulty making ends meet. As he left the restaurant, the protesters chanted against undocumented immigrants while they paced back and forth on the sidewalk. He would have preferred to ignore them, but their location meant he had to pass by on his way to the subway.

Why not speak to them and find out who they are? You can learn something from everyone.

Dominic walked over to the blonde-haired blue-collar protester holding the largest sign. "Why are you here?"

Frustration crinkled the protester's eyes. He growled that he'd been laid off from a large construction firm months ago and hadn't been able to find work since. Dominic said he was sorry to hear about the young man's situation, sympathizing about how difficult it must be to get by.

The protester seemed surprised by Dominic's concern. He stared warily into Dominic's eyes. "If ya really care 'bout what we're going through, why don't ya join us?"

"I would, if immigrants had cost you your job," Dominic said. "But they didn't. Somebody else did."

"That's bullshit." The blonde protester spit on the sidewalk. "Who else could do that?"

"The same gang who killed workers jobs eighty years ago during the Great Depression, long before Hispanic immigrants became an issue."

"Whadaya mean?"

I've got his attention now. Don't lose him. "In the 1930s, unemployment hit twenty-five percent, the highest ever. But documented Hispanics were only one percent of the population. Undocumented Hispanics even less. No way immigrants' fraction-of-a-percent could take the jobs of twenty-five percent of American workers. It's not mathematically possible."

"Never heard that before."

I'll bet you hadn't. Claude sure wasn't gonna tell you. "Something much bigger than immigration erased those jobs. Something still alive and sinister today, and it's causing your job problems, too."

The protester spit on the sidewalk and sneered. "What's that?"

"It's not hard to figure out. Claude's group paid you to protest here, didn't they?"

"Yeah. What of it?"

"Ask him who his boss is. Follow the money. He has an ulterior motive for bringing you here to broadcast his message."

The protester squinted as if trying to make sense of this. "What makes you so sure?"

"His super-rich backers want you to blame other poor people for your lack of a job, instead of the real culprit." Dominic said. "They distract you, so you'll do Claude's bosses' dirty work for them and won't figure out they're the ones causing your problems."

The protester looked dumbfounded. "I don't care who's behind him. He helps me."

This guy's like the fellow playing poker at the card table, who doesn't know who the mark is. That means he's the mark. He doesn't realize it's him, yet. "After Claude's boss crushes immigrants, how long before he comes after you?"

"He'll never come after us, we're part of his crowd."

"I've got news for you… you're not. He won't stop after destroying immigrants. A tyrant shuts out more and more groups, his inner circle getting smaller and smaller until eventually no one's left but himself. Being white won't save you."

"How da you know this?" the protester said.

"Heard of Nazi Germany? Hitler didn't stop with the Jews. His hit list kept growing, abusing other races, unions, Catholics."

"That's years ago. This is Amerka. I don't haveta worry," the protester said.

They really did a number on him. He still doesn't get it… how expendable he is to them. "Yes, you do. Claude's boss isn't stopping with immigrants. He's going after blacks, women, gays and union workers."

"Those aren't my groups. I wasn't union."

"But, when he attacks unions, it shows he wants to cut wages for laborers like you, too. If Claude's boss can hurt them, there's nothing to stop him from going after you."

"Ya think so?"

"The only way you're safe, is if they're safe, too."

The protester squinted down at the sign he held in front of his chest. His index finger pointed at the sign's corner where he'd drawn a crude gold cross. "My pastor told me God wants us to keep immigrants out. Who are you to question him?"

Another false prophet twisting the gospels to persecute minorities and the poor, while distracting from the real problem. "He's wrong. Christ said when we hurt those least powerful, we hurt him. That includes immigrants and refugees. He said to show compassion, not turn them away."

The protester's face flushed, his religious hypocrisy exposed. Both eyes flashed anger as he stepped forward, his fist clenched a few inches in front of the Friar's face.

Dominic didn't budge, his appearance calm and composed as if he had nothing but compassion for the young man standing in front of him.

The protester paused, staring into Dominic's eyes. After a few seconds the young man's expression changed as he slowly lowered his fist. He looked at his companions and tilted his head to one side, indicating his friends should follow him. "C'mon, let's get outa here." He scowled at the pavement, walking away until disappearing around the street corner, his two cohorts in tow.

Dominic sighed. *Unfortunately, conflict's often necessary before growth can occur. At least I confronted him with the truth.* You plant the seeds, hoping some of them grow. He'd made an impact, but it would take them a while to understand.

Dominic strolled down the street as he headed toward Saint Patrick's Rectory a few blocks away. There he could link up with some priests he'd long known and rest up before the trip back to Washington, D.C. He walked into the Rectory's main entrance and spent time visiting his friends. The conversation was winding down when his cell phone vibrated in his pocket. The name that appeared on the caller I.D. startled him. Why is *he* calling?

"Hello..." Dominic held the phone against his ear, listening to the voice on the other end of the line. "You caught me by surprise." His eyes narrowed as he heard the reason for the call. "Yeah, I understand it's urgent. I'll meet you here at the Rectory in fifteen minutes." He said goodbye, a stunned look crossing his face. The hard-plastic cell phone slipped back into his pants pocket against his thigh.

He had to meet the caller about a matter of life and death.

CHAPTER 50

Agent Josh's right foot pressed against the unmarked squad car's accelerator pedal, struggling to keep up with the black luxury sedan ahead. Its red taillights weaved in and out of traffic. The sedan whipped around a corner and entered a side street, vanishing from view. The squad car made the same motion a few seconds later. Up ahead on the dim street, the luxury sedan's red brake lights flashed. It pulled over to the concrete curb in front of an old soot darkened brick office building, where it parked.

Why the hell is he stopping here, these buildings look empty? Josh watched through the windshield while the sedan's driver's side door swung wide open. A stiff uniformed man got out, hurried through the building's masonry arched front entrance and disappeared inside. General Rogers' determined face signaled he would allow no interference.

Josh parked the squad car six car lengths behind the sedan, waiting thirty seconds before skulking up to the building's door. He tried twisting the cold brass doorknob, but found it locked. The wind whipped up, blowing an abandoned newspaper page past him on the sidewalk. The sudden unexpected motion made him jump. *My nerves are more on edge than they've been in years.* He put his cell phone up to one ear to call FBI headquarters with his location. "I'm gonna find a way inside the building," he told the dispatcher. "Send backup if I don't call back in twenty minutes."

Josh walked past the building's front, around the corner to the side where he found a separate entrance with a gray metal door. To his surprise, a ray of yellow light shone through a tiny gap between the door and its frame. *It must not have completely closed after the last person entered. The latch failed to catch.* He pushed on the door and it swung open. He slipped inside to a large first floor room with a tall ceiling, empty except for an old grey metal desk and a swivel chair. An outdated lateral file cabinet sat next to the far wall.

Josh opened the desk's center drawer, hoping to find a clue why the General would come to this building. He found nothing but a handful of old paperclips. The front door squeaked, startling him enough he ducked behind the desk. He crouched down as low as possible. The door opened, allowing a couple enlisted soldiers to parade by while he peeked around the tank's corner. They walked to the back of the room and disappeared. He couldn't see their faces because the desk blocked his view.

Where the hell did they go?

Josh waited thirty seconds to make sure the coast was clear before slinking out from behind the desk. There appeared to be only the one doorway in or out of the room, the one he had walked through to enter. He stood in the room's center, looking back and forth, puzzled how soldiers had come into the room, yet it appeared empty now.

There must be another exit but where?

He heard wood scrape against wood and dove back underneath the desk for cover once more. He peered underneath the desk, searching for the noise' source. A four-foot section of the wall at the back of the room, swung open to reveal a hidden passage. Four soldiers in military khakis marched out from behind the hidden door. The wall section swung shut behind them and they crossed the room, exiting the building through the front door.

So, that's how they did it? Clever. Josh waited until they were out of sight before crawling out from under the desk. He brushed the dust off his pants. Long-legged strides took him to the wall where the panel had swung open. An almost invisible seam split the wall where the panel's edge met it. He tried to pry the seam open with his fingers, but it wouldn't budge. He paid the price for his effort with a broken fingernail.

Ow. That cut to the quick. There's got to be an easier way.

He shook his hand trying to erase the pain. Once the hurt subsided, he tapped two fingers on the wall's surface looking for a hollow spot harboring a mechanism to open the door. *It's got to be here somewhere.* But it eluded him.

A tiny flicker of dim white light caught the corner of his eye. The gray thermostat on the wall near the panel, flashed small white numbers on its display. The numbers lit up, then switched off, then lit up again.

Something was wrong with it. Maybe a short circuit.

He eyed the thermostat with suspicion, his index finger pressing the up arrow until the temperature display read 70 degrees and lit up. Next to him behind the panel, a loud click sounded. He pivoted toward the sound. The hidden door in the wall suing wide open.

Ingenious. I never would have thought to hide the door opener in the thermostat.

Behind the open door, an unlit concrete stairwell led down to the lower level. He crept down the stairs, pausing inside the stairwell on the bottom step. The stairway opened into a huge brightly lit facility furnished with high tech computer displays and office equipment. It looked like some sort of command operations room. He stood very still. Muffled voices filtered across the room from a group of officers working about sixty feet away.

He cupped his ear, shifting his head to hear better. An authoritative male voice described plans to move a cache of military weapons to the building. Josh bent his ear even more to better make out the words. The voices had become clearer as cold unyielding steel touch his temple. His body froze.

"Turn around slowly with your hands in the air," a deep male voice ordered. Josh hesitated. "Do it now unless you want to have your brains scraped off the floor." he swung around, finding himself face to face with a chiseled face military policeman wearing a white helmet.

The MP pointed a shiny steel pistol at him. "What are you doing here? This is a restricted installation."

Josh held both hands in the air. "FBI. I'm here to serve an outstanding warrant. We received a tip there was a felon in this building who's been charged."

"I don't believe you," the MP sneered. "You'd better come clean and quick."

"There's a badge in my coat pocket." Josh hadn't expected this kind of resistance from a fellow law enforcement officer. *Something's not right here.*

The MP's free hand reached into Josh's inside pocket and pulled out his badge. His eyes narrowed in reaction to the letters FBI. "Well, you received a bad tip. This building's empty."

"It doesn't look so empty to me." Josh's jaw tightened. "There's a lot of activity here."

"Smartass. I gave you fair warning. You couldn't leave well enough, alone." The MP pulled the trigger. The crack of gunfire bounced off the walls. Blood splattered from Josh's forehead, three red drops landing on the MP's sleeve. Josh crumpled to the floor where he breathed his last gasp, his eyes staring blankly at the wall.

Two soldiers with guns drawn burst into the stairwell.

"Who the hell is he?" one soldier asked as he pointed at Josh's body.

"Never mind that." The MP holstered the weapon before wiping the blood off his sleeve. "I need you to run an errand for me. Dump his body in a grave at an isolated location on the military base." The MP poked one hand into Josh's pants pocket and pulled out a set of car keys. He tossed the keys to the heavyset soldier. "Find his car outside. Hide it in the back of the base's equipment warehouse."

Across town, a female FBI dispatch clerk glanced down at the handwritten log call-in sheet on her desk. She'd drawn a line through the name of every agent except Josh. The log showed he had not checked in at the twenty-minute mark like he said he would.

"I've got another tardy one." She curled one lip, facing the new co-worker seated next to her. "He should've checked in five minutes ago," she said in a thick southern drawl. She punched the phone keypad to dial Josh's number. Her earpiece rang ten times without an answer. She hung up, waiting only a couple seconds before trying his car radio three times. She huffed, slamming the microphone down on the desk. "Now he's got me worried." She typed instructions into her computer, "Send out officers for backup right away."

Soon afterward, two plain clothes FBI agents, in an unmarked navy-blue government sedan, pulled up to the brick office building Josh had entered earlier. Their GPS showed it as his last location. They parked on the street near the side door and entered, searching the large first floor room with the old grey metal desk, swivel chair and outdated lateral file cabinet. They walked right past the thermostat, finding nothing out of the ordinary. All traces of Josh had vanished, including the squad car. They didn't discover the secret door in the smaller room's wall. It never occurred to them to check the thermostat.

Agent Davis had taken an FBI helicopter to New York City, on a tip Tomas had arrived there earlier. Davis landed at a government heliport and was climbing into a squad car with two other officers, when his cell phone rang. His office informed him Josh had gone missing and failed to report in at the scheduled time. Davis gritted his teeth. *This case had become a nightmare and getting worse by the hour. It was more urgent than ever he find Tomas and get to the bottom of this.*

CHAPTER 51

J oe and Gina climbed up the New York City subway's fluorescent-lit concrete stairs and exited at street level. Their eyes squinted in the bright sunshine. She pointed to the right, and they dashed down the sidewalk two blocks toward Saint Patrick's Cathedral. Its magnificent Neo-Gothic-style white marble rose up into view, revealing its 100 meters-tall spires and beautiful rose stained-glass window. The sight enamored Joe so much he almost ran into a streetlight pole near the curb. He sidestepped it at the very last second.

They hurried through the double bronze doors at the Cathedral's grand front entrance, still breathing hard. Once inside, they paused while their eyes adjusted to the Narthex' low light. A dozen sightseers had lined up twenty feet away, dressed in the usual attire of tennis shoes and khaki slacks. A small sign designated the spot where they should gather to meet their guide.

"We'll need to join a tour," Gina whispered. "That'll get us close to the crypt without attracting attention. Once the tour starts, we'll slip away from the group to search for the bench."

Joe nodded without speaking. *Sounds like a plan. Nobody will notice us if we blend in.*

She picked up a copy of the Cathedral's map and guided tour schedule at the small square information desk. Her eyes scanned the pages. "We're in luck. The next one starts in five minutes."

Joe slid a ten-dollar bill into the wooden donation box near the desk. "I hope you know what you're doing."

He and Gina strolled to the back of the tour group line. The elderly white-haired tour guide led them through the Narthex pews, stopping occasionally so he could expound on points of interest. The sightseers snaked their way through the Cathedral until reaching the Sanctuary platform in front of the pews. Joe and Gina followed at the back of the group.

Joe leaned over and mumbled in her ear. "Get ready. We're close."

The group strolled across the Sanctuary's marble floor, stopping when they reached the Chapel's High Altar for the next presentation. Four angel statues adorned the four-feet tall rectangular marble slab, flanked on two sides by three large gold candle sticks. The guide finished his altar spiel and the tour moved on to their next stop.

It's now or never. "This way." Joe whispered, motioning with his hand for Gina to follow him in the opposite direction of the tour.

They scurried to the sunken Sacristy entrance behind the High Altar, where they crouched down out of sight. Next to them, the brightly colored priests' robes hung from hangars near shiny sacred vessels stored on shelves.

"Watch your head, don't forget to duck," Gina said as they descended a dimly lit marble stairway leading from the Sacristy down to the lower level.

Joe obediently followed suit. *The last thing I need is a big knot on my noggin.*

The dim light at the stairway's top landing grew fainter as they descended past the basement rooms used by the sanctuary boys. Their heels clattered on the unforgiving steps, the sound bouncing off the narrow walls. Joe's nostrils filled with the musty odor of heavy air coming from the crypt below. They continued down to the bottom of the stairs, stepping inside the crypt's doorway. They slipped into a room with red brick walls filled with rectangular box-shaped tombs stacked four high from floor to ceiling.

This place isn't dingy like some crypts. "It doesn't look as old as I thought it would. It must have been remodeled at some point." Joe read the crypt's plaque with its list of prominent individuals' names, until he came to Toussaint. His breaths quickened as they approached the tomb.

They advanced within ten feet of the tomb when Gina's arm stretched across his chest, stopping his progress in mid-stride. She pointed an outstretched index finger at a piece of wooden furniture. "There it is. That's the kneeling bench."

A gothic-revival carved-oak prayer bench stood next to Toussaint's tomb. Its top consisted of a flat wooden horizontal arm rest for a single worshiper's elbows. Under the armrest sat a desk-like closed compartment with a hinged lid that opened upward. A purple velvet kneeling cushion padded the bench's bottom.

Joe's spine turned cold as if ice water had been poured down it. *I expected to find it here, but it's still a shock to see it up close and personal.*

"This must be the 'angel's bench'," Gina said. "Bench doesn't always mean a long pew-like seat. It can fit one person like this one."

"There's only one way to be sure this is it." Joe said, grunting as he grabbed the lid's edges with his fingertips to look inside. He tugged to pull the top up, but it wouldn't budge. His second attempt had the same unsuccessful result. *Well, this is going nowhere.*

Gina reached out, grabbing his arm before he could tug on the lid a third time. "Hey, you're not gonna damage this beautiful old antique, are you?"

"If you're going to grab me like that, at least buy me a drink first." Joe gave her a crooked smile. "What kind of a guy do you think I am?"

"Oh, stop it." She pressed her lips and waived an open hand as if to swat him. "This is no time for games."

Joe playfully pulled back from her, leaning over to examine the compartment's front panel under the lid's lip. It had a keyhole allowing the lid to be locked. *Damn, you knew this wasn't gonna be easy.* His eyes searched around the room for something he could use to open it but found nothing. "You happen to have a nail file on you?"

"Dunno. I'll check my purse." She rummaged through her cross-the-body purse, after a few moments holding up a slender metal manicure tool in triumph. "I found it. Now be careful."

Moi? Of course, I will. Joe had a twinkle in his eye. "As careful as a long-tailed cat in a room full of rocking chairs."

Gina rolled her eyes. "Open the damn lid."

Joe kneeled, placing the nail file against the concrete floor. He pulled a car key out of his pocket, pressing it down against the nail file's tip to bend it at a 90-degree angle. He eased the modified nail file vertically into the keyhole. Little by little he twisted it counterclockwise until a scraping sound indicated the lock bolt moved. Another quarter turn and the lock bolt clicked.

Ah, success. Joe placed his fingers under the lid, lifting it to reveal the compartment's contents. An old weathered black Bible with gold leaf pages and lettering sat in the opening all by itself, placed there for the use of visitors. *How disappointing, all buildup and no payoff.* He exhaled in a huff. "That's a lot of work to find a Bible. We could've picked up one in the Narthex for a lot less trouble."

"There must be something more." Gina brushed her arm past Joe, reaching into the compartment to pull out the Good Book. "Antonio didn't lead us here for no reason. Maybe we should look closer." She peered into the open compartment, examining its edges before extending her outstretched hand palm up. "Hand me the nail file."

Her fingers pushed the bent file's sharp end into the thin gap between the open compartment's thin wood bottom and its side. She pried at the bottom board, raising it up a couple inches on one edge. The file pulled up on the board's edge and it came loose, revealing a shallow false bottom underneath. She took in a sharp breath at the sight. Inside the hidden cavity sat a transparent clear-plastic cover holding yellowed pages appearing to be several centuries old.

"This is it!" Gina said. "It's hidden in Toussaint's bench. Like Antonio said."

Could it be? It was almost too good to be true. Joe picked up the clear-plastic cover and its pages written in Renaissance Florentine dialect. He placed it on the prayer bench top, leaning over as he translated aloud.

> *I am the Machiavelli family clerk. The Inquisition ordered me to destroy these papers written by Machiavelli and da Vinci. I cannot bring myself to do it for they are far too valuable to mankind. So, I am hiding it with the hope a future generation will find them. Take care not to let it fall into the wrong hands. If so, they will destroy the secret forever.*

He looked up, staring with wide eyes. *It's the real deal. That seals it for me.*

"Oh, my God, what've we found?" Gina put her hand up covering her mouth. "People will kill for this."

"Antonio probably tried to translate it, but the centuries-old dialect must have stumped him. He put it here for safekeeping."

"The last place anyone would look."

A sudden chill came over Joe. "Let's get out of here." His hands trembled as he slid the plastic cover underneath his sport jacket. "We can read the other pages later. I don't wanna make it easy for someone to stop us."

They climbed back up the dim stairway to the Cathedral's main level, stepping out onto the Sanctuary's carved white marble floor. Warm light from the Cathedral's tall beautiful stained-glass windows washed over them in a spectrum of vivid blues, reds, yellows and greens.

Joe squinted, holding one hand against his forehead while his eyes adjusted. *Had the heavens opened and given their blessing? We might make it out of here in one piece.*

At the Sanctuary's opposite end, two men in dark suits squatted down inside the elevated tea-cup shaped white pulpit. One of them peered over the pulpit's lip, watching Joe and Gina's activity near the High Altar. He nudged his partner. "It's them," he whispered. The two men snuck out of the teacup pulpit, creeping down the twelve-step marble staircase wrapped around a tall white marble column.

CHAPTER 52

T he two men reached the staircase's bottom step, and the Sanctuary's gray marble floor. They skulked to the middle of the Sanctuary, twenty feet behind Joe and Gina who gazed at the stained-glass windows' vibrant colors flooding the altar. The taller man pulled a gun from his pocket. He pointed it at Joe's back. "You have a secret that doesn't belong to you. We want it."

Joe and Gina swung around, finding themselves staring into Tomas' cold dark eyes. His mouth curved into a cruel smile as he held them at gunpoint. Next to him stood a man in his late sixties, pasty-faced and scowling.

Joe stared at the unfamiliar older man. *Had he finally met his true nemesis? Was this the man?* The idea caused a strange and unexpected sense of calm to wash over Joe. For reasons he didn't fully understand, he had no fear. *Maybe it's because Dominic explained so much about what makes men like this tick.* Joe arched a sly eyebrow at the pasty-faced man, surprising himself with his boldness. "I've met Tomas already. But you and I haven't had the pleasure."

"I'm Lucian Drake." The man puffed out his chest. "No one meets me unless I allow it."

Drake... the name rang a bell. Oscar White's list include someone named Drake. "One of the *Business Plot* conspirators had the same name,"

Joe said. "You wouldn't be related, would you?"

"Your memory serves you well. That would be Oliver Drake."

"Let me guess. You're his son. Tomas and Hans work for you."

"You catch on quickly."

Joe's mind raced to put the pieces together. There was a "D" on the jumbo jet that flew in front of us, putting our plane in a tailspin. "It's your plane that tried to bring us down, wasn't it?"

"Rather creative idea, don't you think? If you'd crashed, we'd have claimed you accidentally veered into our wash."

Keep Lucian talking. We need an edge to stall him. His need to be the smartest man in the room might be the ticket. "I'll give you the secret. But first you have to tell me what you'll do with it?"

"Very well," Lucian cocked his head with pride. "You won't be around much longer to tell anyone. Two years ago, I learned Machiavelli discovered a powerful secret about wealth. I searched for it, hoping it could multiply my wealth exponentially… faster than any other way. But, instead, it appears the discovery strengthens the public and democracy, reducing my control. So, I had to find it before anyone else, and destroy it."

"That's why you killed the Ambassador and my two co-workers." Joe put his hands on his hips, staring a hole right through Lucian. *Only a monster could murder so many innocent victims. And in less than twenty-four hours.*

"I wasn't able to find it on my own, even after searching for years. But I caught a lucky break. The Ambassador stumbled onto the secret, mentioning it to Claude at the celebration. Claude told me what the Ambassador said. I put two and two together, figuring out he had the secret I'd been hunting for. I had to act quickly to bury it."

"When you found out I talked to the Ambassador, you sent your goons to my office to kill me."

"Unfortunately, the Ambassador died before he could tell us his discovery's location." Lucian grimaced and looked down at the marble floor. "You were the best lead we had. We didn't plan on you being called away from your office at the last minute."

A light bulb went off in Joe's head. *Hans demanded the Archives files from Oscar White, and Hans worked for Lucian. Lucian wanted them.* "You were after *The Business Plot* files, too, weren't you?"

"But, of course."

"You killed Oscar White," Gina said

"I found it necessary." Lucian gave her a blank stare "A small price to pay."

Joe's mind swirled like a rolling fog. *Murders, the Business Plot, greed and centuries old secrets.* He glanced up at the cross on the altar, remembering what Dominic had said –the money changers wanted Christ out of the way. The Business Plotters wanted Roosevelt out of the way. Then it hit Joe as recognition dawned on his face. *Lucian wants the current president out of the way, and he's got a plan to do it.*

"This is about a new *Business Plot* conspiracy, isn't it?"

"You're very clever," Lucian said. "If those files became public, citizens would never go along with my coup. They'd oppose anything enriching me, realizing my trickle-down crap was all a lie. My plan to become the richest man in the world would be over."

Gina gasped. "You traitor."

"What about the secret," Joe asked. "What are you gonna to do with it?"

"It's been hidden for a few hundred years. I'm going to make sure it stays secret a few hundred more."

"You'll never get away with this," Gina said

"But I will. Now, no more stalling. You've tried my patience long enough." Lucian held out his open hand palm up toward Joe. "Give it to me."

Joe looked past Lucian in the distance behind him. Fifteen new cathedral visitors and their tour guide strolled up the steps to the Sanctuary from the Nave's pews. Tomas had his back to the group. They couldn't see his gun.

I need the tourists' help. I've got to get their attention. Joe dropped to one knee. He exhaled sharply, giving the clear-plastic cover a hard shove, shooting it across the marble floor.

Lucian leaned over to one side, reaching out to grab the cover as it approached. But Joe had aimed to one side of Lucian. So, the transparent cover slid past Lucian with a hiss about three feet to his right. His top-heavy rotund torso toppled over as the prize scooted by just beyond his grasp. His outstretched hand hit the marble floor with a smack trying to break his fall, the impact to his wrist triggering the forearm mounted spring-loaded stiletto knife mounted under his sleeve. The five-inch shiny steel blade sprung from its holster past his palm. Lucian's chest fell on the razor-sharp edge, slicing into him like butter. He gasped his last breath and his body lay still, face down on the floor.

Joe's eyes grew large. *Holy crap. Lucian fell on his own hidden knife.*

The tour group stood cow-eyed at the sanctuary floor's edge fifteen behind Lucian's body. Two of them screamed at the sight of him falling on his dagger. The plastic cover continued sliding across the floor. It reached the visitors, stopping between the feet of two hooded monks, one slender and one stout. Hood openings hid their faces in an oval of blackness and shadows. The slender monk reached down, snatching up the cover before the others could react.

Joe gulped at the sight of a stranger holding the secret. *I had to take a chance. At least Lucian doesn't have it.*

Tomas ignored Lucian's dead body on the floor. He whipped around, aiming his gun at the slender monk now holding the plastic file. Tomas closed one eye and took aim. But, as he prepared to pull the trigger, the huge Saint Patrick's bell rang out the hour with a deafening "BON-G-G-G." The Sanctuary vibrated as the sound pounded his ears, distracting his aim. Tomas's arm jerked, causing the gun to miss his target and fire into the air mere inches above the tour. The bullet ricocheted with a "ping" off the marble pillar above the tea-cup shaped pulpit.

Joe and Gina stood temporarily frozen a few yards away. Members of the tour scattered, half-a-dozen diving behind the pews, screaming in terror.

The heavier monk pulled a pistol from his robe with lightning speed, dropping down on one knee in a single smooth-as-silk motion. He aimed the gun at Tomas with the two-handed grip of a trained marksman. "Put your hands in the air and keep 'em there."

The voice sounds familiar. Where have I heard it before?

Tomas swung his gun toward the voice, aiming through the barrel's sights. The heavier monk squeezed the pistol's trigger, firing it with a loud "pop." His aim was true. Tomas fell backward, crumpling into a heap on the floor. The heavier monk stood up from his crouched position, pulling back the cowl to reveal his face.

It's Claude Zorak. I'll be damned, What the hell is he doing here?

Claude strode over to where Tomas' body lay sprawled on the floor, his mouth open and eyes staring blankly at the Cathedral's tall arched ceiling. Blood oozed down his shirt from the chest pocket, collecting in a small pool of red on the sanctuary's marble floor. Tomas' gun lay two feet from his motionless hand. Claude kicked the weapon away. It slid across the floor toward the slender monk who reached down with a white cotton handkerchief to grab it. The slender monk straightened up, pulling back his cowl and revealing his face.

It was Father Dominic. Why's he with Claude?

Dominic clutched the transparent plastic file as he strolled over to Joe. A wry smile crossed Dominic's face as he extended his hand, offering the documents to Joe. "I think this belongs to you."

Joe 's hand trembled, reaching out to accept the precious, fragile pages. When he slid them across the floor earlier, he wasn't sure he'd ever get them back.

"You're aim's good." Dominic put his other hand on Joe's shoulder. "The folder skipped right past Lucian. He never knew what hit him."

"My hands shook so much, I'm lucky it didn't slide right to him."

Gina came over and hugged both monks, breathing a sigh of relief. "That was fancy shooting. You saved us."

Claude looked over at Tomas' motionless body on the floor. "My years of target practice paid off."

"That, plus a little help from Saint Patrick's bell," Dominic said.

"Claude, you surprised the hell out of us." Joe said, pumping Claude's hand. "What brought you around?" He knew it must have been something big for Claude to have changed so much from their first meeting at the Embassy's Machiavelli celebration.

"Lucian confessed to me he ordered the murders and he'd planned a coup to take over the White House. He admitted our think tank research was a lie. After I left his mansion, I became more and more upset. I did some soul searching. I even called my old news show sparring partner, Dominic for advice."

"I didn't know you two knew each other," Joe said. "But I'm sure glad you did." He listened spellbound as Claude described the details of Lucian's conspiracy. The threat of losing the nation to a greedy despot was horrifying. And two tyrants carving up the World was even worse.

"Dominic was next door at the Cathedral's rectory when I called," Claude said. "So, we met there. On the way over, I spotted Lucian's limo driver parked next to the Cathedral. I put two and two together, figured he was in here."

Dominic nodded his agreement. "When Claude got here, he told me about Lucian's scheme. To stop him, we needed the element of surprise, so I loaned Claude this cowl and told him to put the hood on."

"It came in handy." Claude tugged on his sleeve to pull off the monk's habit. We hurried next door to the Cathedral to search for Lucian. You know, do what we could to mess up his plans. Set things right."

"We thought he might lead us to you, too," Dominic said.

"You got here in the nick of time," Gina said.

Claude was still describing the details of Lucian's conspiracy, when FBI Special Agent Davis marched through the Cathedral's front doorway with other agents in tow. He flashed his brass badge to the group and introduced himself.

Gina's forehead wrinkled. "The shooting happened a few minutes ago. How'd you get here so fast?"

Davis leaned over Lucian's body, speaking as he examined the wounds. "Lucian's General plotted treason with a Russian agent at Arlington House. The old caretaker overheard them and called us. We tailed the General who led us to Tomas. Tomas led us to Lucian, and Lucian to the Cathedral and you. We were outside giving final instructions to our agents, when we heard the gunshots. Then we came running."

Claude handed Davis the shiny DVD he had pulled out of the video player in Lucian's study. "You'll need this."

"What is it?" Davis eyed it with suspicion as the studied both sides of the disk.

"It contains Lucian's plot and his co-conspirators names." Davis' eyes grew large as Claude described Lucian's takeover plans and his admissions about his pathological greed. "The recent D.C. murders were part of his scheme."

Davis slid the disc into his coat pocket. "Lucian's six billionaires, the General and the Russian spy, they're a formidable group of traitors. We're lucky you guys stopped Lucian in time. I'll issue arrest warrants on his accomplices right away. We'll round 'em up before they know what hit 'em."

Four FBI special agents hurried to secure the crime scene while ambulances took Lucian's and Tomas' bodies away. Davis thanked Joe and Gina, apologizing for having considered them suspects. He also told Claude he was free to go. Claude hadn't been aware of the takeover plans nor the murders until that day. And, he had supplied crucial help in stopping Lucian. Davis headed for his squad car.

Dominic wiped his brow with a white handkerchief as he glanced at Joe, Gina and Claude. "I don't know about you folks, but I'm exhausted. Let's go next door to the Cathedral's Rectory where we can relax. It'll give us a chance to sort this through in private." They nodded agreement and sauntered out the Cathedral's double front doors.

CHAPTER 53

J oe, Gina, Dominic and Claude stepped inside the front door of the four-story light stone Rectory building, next door to the Cathedral. The four gathered around a conference table in an office with stained wood bookshelves lining the walls. The room had a pleasant coffee smell. One shelf held a framed biblical print which read:

Whoever oppresses the poor for his own increase and
whoever gives to the rich, both come to poverty.

Gina closed the door behind them. "Let's see the secret that's cost so many lives and put us through so much danger."

Joe's fingers trembled as he spread the plastic cover's first delicate yellowed page on the table. It was the moment of truth. His three companions peered over his shoulder, their intent expressions reflecting the documents' importance. He read aloud, translating sentences on the fly from Renaissance Florentine dialect to English.

"It's Machiavelli's handwriting. He refers to da Vinci's work on the Arno river diversion crane during the war against Pisa, and says Florence's shortage of funds stopped the crane's construction."

"Sounds like today's budget shortfalls," Claude said.

Joe leaned forward to get a better look as the others stood next to him, wide-eyed. "He says da Vinci was determined to build it, anyway."

"Keep reading, don't stop" Gina said.

"Da Vinci and Machiavelli reviewed Florence's financial records going back centuries. They used da Vinci's scientific method to furiously sift through thousands of treasury ledgers for twenty-four straight hours. In the process, they made an amazing discovery... the key to a golden age of prosperity."

"Like the Holy Grail," Gina said. Her words referenced the cup from which Christ's disciples drank wine representing his blood. According to legend, the elusive treasure possessed miraculous power to provide unlimited abundance.

He looked back down at the page and continued. "The key was a seventy-two percent income tax rate on men of colossal-wealth. The tax would transfer their stagnant money to the Republic, who would then circulate it by hiring workers at good wages to build roads, bridges and water systems."

Joe paused, looking up at the others who exhibited gapped mouth stares. *This was the answer the world had been waiting for. So many destructive financial crashes and wars avoided. So many lives improved, so much misery relieved. Saving loved ones from loss in war, the young men who don't come home, the widows, and the children who grow up without a parent. Helping the hungry, the homeless. Saving those living paycheck-to-paycheck, those depressed at the lack of options, the sick, those lacking medical care, in debt from getting care, or denied coverage by their insurance.*

Dominic nodded, "Go on."

Joe peered back down at the page. "Those workers, in turn, spend that money on goods whose makers hire yet more workers to meet the increased consumer demand. The flowing money creates incredible growth. It also stops the frenzied speculative bubbles that cause crashes and depressions."

"Wash, rinse and repeat." Gina said. "The growth increases with each cycle."

"When a system's in balance with nature, and not top-heavy, living organisms thrive," Dominic said.

"*Mona Lisa's* 72 is the key," Gina said. "Antonio was desperate to save it."

Joe nodded. *Water covers more than 70 percent of Earth's surface as it circulates around the globe. Life evolved from the oceans. The rest is stationary land. If money is a reflection of our world... a measurement of the things around us, then it makes sense that money must circulate in the same proportions as circulating water, making it a law of nature.*

"Remember the painting in Villa Firenze's secret room?" Gina asked. "The one where wealthy ancient-Roman Cornelia wore a simple dress and no jewelry, because her sons, who were champions of justice, were adornment enough?"

"Yeah," Joe said. "The same sons who proposed the Agrarian Laws, ordering those with unthinkable-wealth to return stolen lands to the impoverished soldiers."

"Da Vinci must have got his idea for the *Mona Lisa* from reading about Cornelia," Gina said. "*Mona Lisa* was also a prosperous woman wearing a simple dress and no jewelry. Da Vinci wanted people to question *Mona Lisa's* lack of adornment. He wanted them to ask why she wore no jewelry... so they'd discover the 72 was her jewel. The same 72 that instructs men as rich-as-a-rajah not to hoard, to return their stagnant unproductive income to working people."

"You're onto something." Joe said. "Da Vinci counted on us knowing how to see his message. Saper Vedere."

Gina moved to the office's laptop computer, tapping its keys until The *Mona Lisa* appeared on the monitor. She pointed her index finger at the image. "Her tight-lipped smile confirms it. She has a secret -- the 72. That's why da Vinci never parted with her during his life."

Joe stared at the painting's excavated bare red dirt. *That's the Arno River diversion channel. It's the reason they needed da Vinci's giant crane and had to raise money. It's how they had discovered the key.*

"Hoarding, by a few men with astonishing-riches, has ruined societies since time began," said Dominic. "But they did their best to stop people from figuring that out."

Claude squirmed in his chair. "Lucian never wanted a golden age of prosperity for the public. He craved control and power. A shrinking pie suited him fine, as long as he still commanded the biggest piece."

"He liked fearful people living paycheck to paycheck." Dominic said. "Prosperous and informed citizens might challenge him."

Claude's eyes narrowed. "Lucian's crowd won't take this lying down.

They'll smear *Mona Lisa's* message by claiming it's socialist."

"It's not socialist at all, her discovery is the only thing that'll save capitalism," Dominic said. "If Lucian's group impairs circulation enough, we'll suffer a crash … leading to impoverished workers laboring in dangerous filthy sweatshops like Dickensian England. The public will revolt against poverty and servitude."

Joe looked back down at the vintage page. "The world's wisest men saw the dangers of income-inequality and wealth-concentration over two thousand years ago. Greek historian Plutarch warned about its evils." *He was right. Sixth-century B.C. Athens suffered from it so severely that the people considered armed revolution. The ultra-rich refused to budge and prepared to use force against the poor. But Athens' new leader, Solon, one of the Seven Wise Men of Greece, found a solution. He created a new progressive tax system where men with an-ocean-of-gold paid taxes twelve times the rate that the poor paid. His plan also forgave substantial portions of individual debt. Because of his wisdom, Athens avoided revolution and prospered greatly.*

"Lucian's rich-as-lords group opposed paying taxes, wanting control," Claude said. "I know all about that from my job." He decided to use his media savvy to spread the secret's good news to the press.

Joe was relieved to hear about Claude's change of heart. *That's a helluva lot better than spreading Lucian's propaganda.*

Claude shook Joe and Gina's hands. "Thanks for finding the key. For the first time, my politics and my spiritual life aren't based on blaming the poor. It feels good."

Dominic reached over and hugged them. "Lucian's love of money, his pathological addiction to money, was the root of his evil conspiracy."

"I can't thank you enough, Dominic," Joe said. "I'll never forget your description of demographic necrosis, where the prior generation learned that greed was evil, but after they died off, their descendants forgot the lesson.

"And I'll never forget your explanation of blood and money," Gina said.

Gina and Joe strolled out the Rectory's front door, down the pedestrian-filled sidewalk to the street. The sound of blaring horns and automobile engines filled the air. Joe raised one hand to hail a yellow taxi which pulled over to the curb, lurching to a stop. Gina climbed into the sedan's large back seat with Joe right behind. The grizzled driver swung around to face them, pausing for instructions on their destination. "Take us to Columbus Circle," Joe said.

Gina's eyebrows raised as she faced Joe. "Why on Earth are we going there?"

Joe had one more important stop in mind. He arched a sly brow. "You'll see."

CHAPTER 54

The taxi whirled around Columbus Circle on Central Park's South side, rolling to a stop near the park's horse carriage ride ticket booth. A white carriage with large wooden spoke wheels, plush cushioned seats and a canopy, stood next to the square kiosk. Harnessed to the carriage stood a coal black horse. A colorful blue plume sat atop its sleepy head. A rigid red uniformed driver sat in his elevated seat or box, in front, wearing a red overcoat and top hat.

"Is this the surprise?" Gina's eyes sparkled. "I'm impressed. Let's do it." She eagerly opened the taxi door and they traipsed to the booth.

Joe handed a pair of green cash bills to the attendant. "Two tickets please." The attendant slid two thumb-size yellow stubs across the booth's window shelf, before shutting the sliding window to keep out the cold. The horse's whinny plus the stamp of his hoof told them he was impatient to start. Joe walked over to him, patting his shoulder. The steed's large muscles twitched underneath his soft warm fur.

Gina smiled, watching them from beside the carriage. "When you're done making friends, I'm ready to go anytime."

Joe walked back to where she stood. He held her hand while she lifted one foot up into the carriage. Once she was inside, he grabbed the carriage side panel, hoisting himself up in one pull. They plopped down into the tufted upholstered red leather seat close together against the cold. The thin chill of winter air smelled crisp and clean and pure.

The driver clucked his mouth as he flipped the long thin black reins. The horse started at a slow walk, pulling the carriage along the blue-gray pavement into the park, the clip-clop of hooves on the pavement sounding a calming cadence. The carriage passed groves of trees with leafless tentacle-like limbs of charcoal gray framed by an orange-pink sunset.

Gina pulled her coat tight against her body.

Joe buttoned his coat's top buttons against the chill. He breathed a sigh, sitting back in the seat and closing his eyes. *It's been a long day.* Lucian had come remarkably close to pulling-off his money scheme. Joe shuddered as Gina laid her head against his shoulder. *If Lucian had won, we might have lost democracy forever.*

They rode in silence for five minutes before pulling up to the Angel of the Waters Fountain, better known as the Bethesda Fountain, where the carriage stopped. Joe opened his eyes. The 26 feet tall bronze sculpture had three tiers over which water fell. An eight-foot tall winged angel, dressed in a flowing robe, sat at the very top. Four cherubs stood in the middle tier above a grand pond at the base.

Joe and Gina climbed down from the carriage and walked to the fountain where she described it's history. "The original Bethesda pool was in Jerusalem. The blind, lame and sick would wait for the angel to stir the water so they could step in to it and be healed. The four cherubs represent temperance, purity, health, and peace."

Joe leaned over the fountain's base to get a closer look at the first cherub. "Temperance, that's what Lucian lacked. He couldn't stop his pathological addiction to money."

"Dominic said it… the love of money is a root of all kinds of evil."

Joe gazed off in the grass field to the side of the trail. The words reminded him of something he'd heard once, years ago. "Christ believed that you have to be willing to lose your life to save it."

"That sounds like a contradiction."

"Not really. People are happiest when they're generous, giving of themselves. Their sacrifice of time and talents gives their life meaning. It saves them."

Gina pulled her coat collar a little higher to fend off the cold. "Lucian never learned that. He had it all backwards."

They re-boarded the horse-drawn carriage, continuing down the trail through the park. Their ride meandered past The Pond, a reflective body of water surrounded by dormant plants. A small deserted island sat in its middle, populated by birds and turtles in warmer weather. The Pond's two V-shaped necks sandwiched a lush nature sanctuary, browned by winter's icy grip. A picturesque arched limestone bridge sat above the Pond's headwater, reflecting in the pool.

Gina stared at the bridge, her brow wrinkled. "It reminds me of the *Mona Lisa's* Buriano Bridge."

"Yeah, it does, only smaller."

Gina put her hand to her forehead like a visor, squinting to get a better view in the bright, gray light. "Look at the open space under the bridge's arch, and the arch's reflection in the water. It's shaped like an eye?"

Joe blinked, staring at the bridge. He hadn't noticed the reflection before, but it did indeed create an eye-shaped gap between the arched bridge and its upside-down mirror-image in the water. "It sure is."

"Remember da Vinci's favorite saying Saper Vedere, knowing how to see? Looking at nature in diverse ways from different perspectives to make new discoveries. He counted on us knowing how to see his message in the *Mona Lisa*."

"And his friend Machiavelli believed there are those who see, those who are shown, and those who don't see," Joe said. "Christ wanted his followers to use their eyes to see and their ears to hear."

"Maybe da Vinci painted the 72 in the river not only to emphasize circulation. Maybe he placed the 72 in an eye-shaped arch to remind us to see."

Joe fixed his gaze on her. She'd made an extraordinary insight he'd missed. Now that she'd pointed it out, he could see it as plain as the nose on her face. "That's brilliant. It's pure da Vinci. He loved using reflection, like his mirrored-writing."

Gina beamed in response to the praise, reaching over to squeeze Joe's hand. They rode in silence for several moments before she looked over to him. "What happens now? Will people use *Mona Lisa's* secret to make the world a better place?"

You asked the one question I wish I knew the answer to, but I don't. Joe shrugged both shoulders. "It's up to them. They can ignore it, and suffer depressions, money wars and dictators. And endure all the misery, wasted lives and untapped human potential. Or they can reject the trickle-down scam, finally trying what works. Only time will tell."

A worried look crossed Gina's face. "The media might not run the story. They may fear the loss of corporate advertisers. If the secret gets buried again it could be the last time anyone ever sees it."

Joe clasped his arms behind his head. "Maybe not. *Mona Lisa's* message has existed in one form or another for centuries. It's in art, literature, history, science, nature. It's only up to us to look."

They sat quietly for the next few minutes as the carriage rolled along, until they arrived back at the ticket booth where the ride had started. Joe stepped off the running board to the sidewalk and helped Gina down. They stood next to each other near the street while he waived one gloved hand to hail a taxi. A yellow cab pulled up to the curb, they piled into the back seat and she took off her gloves.

"Let's go back to Washington. It's time to help people see."

Thank you for reading my book

I hope you enjoyed it as much as I enjoyed writing it.
Won't you please consider leaving a review on Amazon.com?
Even just a few words would
help others decide if the book is right for them.
Best regards and thank you in advance.

ABOUT THE AUTHOR

Gary Rappard is an author and practicing attorney selected by the world's premier lawyer rating services for the highest attorney accolades many years in a row. In his private practice he represents individuals wronged by powerful institutions. His experience in this environment provides him a unique perspective to analyze the pieces of civilization's puzzle and interpret the world in ways that provide provocative and entertaining reading.

Made in United States
North Haven, CT
15 April 2024